FRACTURED STATE

IN THE BLIGHTED EARTH

FRACTURED STATE
IN THE BLIGHTED EARTH

A NOVEL

R.M. TEMBREULL

BOOK I

atmosphere press

Published by Atmosphere Press

Cover design by Matthew Fielder

Illustrated by R.M. Tembreull

Atmospherepress.com

To All those who have served our Country
All species: Two-legged, Four-legged, and Marine Mammal
The still Whole, the Lost, the Damaged, and the Dead
I salute you All!
Rest in Peace, Pop

Preface

Well, hopefully the right salutation is "welcome back!" for round two. However, that bold assertion rests on the assumption you have read *Stories, Legends, and Truths from the Blighted Earth* and enjoyed the collection enough to make the investment. My second work begins a series of novels staged within our modern era but remains within the world of *the Blighted Earth*. Prior to committing this next 'telling' to paper, I probably shared a range of thoughts similar to those you might be having as you hold my latest work in your hands . . . something on the order of "The book of stories was pretty good, but can this guy write a novel?" Good question, but one only you can answer for yourself by pressing on in your chosen course and seeing it through. "Go for it!" I say. Start a journey, which I sincerely hope brings you as much entertainment and enjoyment as it did me in the creation of it.

You'll find—at its core—*Fractured State* is a story of many threads woven by 'extremes' . . . extremes of thought, of ideology, of emotions, of climate, of violence, etc., etc. The story may be fictional, but the context of its happening—one of layered and multifaceted extremes—is not. These extremes are very real, driving real impacts and outcomes on our planet just as much as they drive the plot of the book. Even as you read this, they are shaping the human condition and degrading the quality of our lives . . . not just for humans—all life! Perhaps it is even more accurate to say the 'conditions for life' are being adversely impacted.

As troubling as these extremes are, it is my hope they add the kind of meaningful context and richness of content which will give you pause and cause to think about the 'state' of things. You may not see things as 'fractured,' but regardless of the lens you view the world through, there are things within each of our spheres of influence which we have the power to change for the better. From my lens, we are faced with a convergence of extremes which present a complex set of asymmetric conditions—a synthetic virus, if you will, but at the very least, an affliction. Collectively, they challenge human existence, so one might say they are humanity's blight. So, if you are still with me, I ask you, "Are we not the dominant species? Is it not our duty to address this multisource affliction on behalf of the planet?" In fact, if you look at Earth Mother as one living body, She is hemorrhaging, and who would be in the best position to staunch the bleeding if not Her most gifted children?

I would argue this congregation of extremes has placed humankind *in extremis* . . . yes, both a legal and medical term and yet an accurate descriptor. We are in extreme circumstances . . . we are at the 'point of death.' I don't wish to upset you by challenging you to think about such things, but if we are, what are you willing to do? Fortunately, humanity is blessed to have the Natural Order to worry about such matters. It is why Earth Mother created them . . . these ominous times are exactly what they exist for. So please, worry not. As of this moment, you have but one duty: *to finish what you have started*, and I do believe you have started this book so "proceed with your read and be entertained!"

Contents

Prologue
Purgatorium

Purgatory is not a place . . . it is an *experience of consciousness.* However, when you are there . . . when you are the being ensconced within it, the *there* can be impossible to identify, and if you are *there*, the *where* is usually the least of your problems. *Why?* Purgatory is the harrowing experience within consciousness—an experience which confines and restricts the growth of one's spirit, making it far more devastatingly effective than physical prisons built to confine the form because it can transcend lives.

Purgatory is the place for ghosts, and all species of all beings have their own versions, because what haunts a being is also a function of experienced lives. The 'lost' can be found there; those whose spirit essences are stuck in a place they were never meant to be—spiritually trapped. While others are inescapably haunted by failure and loss. Still others suffer needlessly in a purgatory constructed by the ego; where their grandiose visions of self and desired achievement can never be realized, because they are haunted by ghosts who simply refuse—at every turn—to allow them to attain the best version of themselves or the reputation, status, and privilege they believe they so rightfully deserve. The greatness they were meant for is denied by spooks who operate off the world's grid . . . within the seams of existential spheres . . . with their only purpose being to block or obstruct others in achieving their life's purpose. Theirs is to deliver the shameful plight of true destiny never to be.

As with purgatory, there are many interpretations of heaven and hell, and much like purgatory, they are not places or destinations in and of themselves. They are conditions or states of individual or collective existence: a kind of 'created fate,' which is always preceded by purgatory; wherein the decisions made, and corresponding actions taken, decide which of the two states manifest.

How you got there is immaterial—whether involuntarily, deliberately, or by designs beyond your understanding—dwelling too long within in your own personal 'purgatorium' is where the madness takes root ...

****

Nilch'i railed. Apparently, even Sentient Winds could be inconsolable, and even the mightiest of their despicably select group was not immune to the emotional freefall accompanying extreme disappointment. However, her master's orders were clear. Her charge was to lead the direct assault on Earth Mother's 'living body'—the *Coirea'cen*—by harnessing two of the Natural's most powerful shaping forces against Her: those of *wind* and *fire*.

As the undisputed leader of the Formless Column of Chaos's En'Troop, Nilch'i was charged with reducing an extremely dry West Coast region to cinders—an expansive tinderbox of human construct. She and hers were to lay waste to everything west of the continent's great protrusions of earthen spine—the Rocky and Sierra Nevada Mountain ranges. Collectively, Sentient Winds were to be the unnatural flues for wildfires spurred by their fire-borne brothers and sisters. Hers was not to create the fires of renewal or absolution, but those of ecologically unrecoverable obliteration. Never had a commander of any army in the history of Earth's living species desired to bring the "burnt earth" stratagem of warfare to the battlefield with more yearning and relish than she.

If only . . . if only her lines of effort within the upcoming Chaotic campaign would carry her directly to a decisive engagement with her most-sought adversary, Parim the Earth Elemental, and his quadra-form Praestean, Ayre. *Would the elusive opportunity present itself?* . . . to prove her superiority finally and forever by dispatching her preeminent foe . . . or perhaps, even better, capture Parim's elemental sentience; deliver him to her master; and see him corrupted and coupled to elemental fire or wind. *How delightful!* For a few moments, Nilch'i was giddy with the thought of Parim serving alongside her at the fore of Chaos's horde, as either sentient wind or fire . . . or better yet, the vaunted Parim serving the Great Deceiver's cause at *her* whim. That would be the ultimate victory, because it would be a joyous pairing of the greatest of ironies with dark justice.

However, such a thing was easier dreamed about than done. Just as the element of water counterbalances fire, Parim always seemed to be effectively positioned to directly oppose Nilch'i and her insidious objectives. For now, her column's assigned responsibilities would obligate her to the western and northern mid-continent . . . away—far away from the Sand Spirit's meta'en in the desert Southwest. Still, from the Sentient Wind's perspective, all was not lost. Everything necessary to vex the elemental and complicate his existence until their destined rendezvous was brewing in his own protectorate. The human-led elements of Chaos's campaign would erupt in the heart of Parim's protectorate with more than enough violent discord and destruction to keep the Sand Spirit Parim occupied until opportunity allowed for their reunion.

Nilch'i's network of spies and formless scouts were continuously reporting on Parim, but intuitively she already knew exactly where Parim would be—where he always was—postured to defy and frustrate Chaos's omnipotent objectives on this world. However, like Nilch'i, the Earth Elemental had his orders too: *to disrupt the human-led line of effort of Chaos's campaign in the contested territory of Texas and the American Southwest.* Despite the Sand Spirit's deft abilities to mask his own movements, Nilch'i was still dedicating resources to receive good intelligence on his whereabouts because she was obsessed with her long-standing nemesis. With the notable exception of the High Sentients, virtually all communication among beings was carried on breath's wind for those of form; such was true even for the spiritual windborne essence of the formless. Thus, she retained the ability to track her prey from half a continent away and bide her time for the right opportunity—a time and place of her choosing. So, for now, Nilch'i needed to be patient, because as the wind and sun fuels the weather and the cyclical patterns of the planet's greatest shaping forces, so too would the winds of fate carry her to her much-sought engagement with her archenemy, Parim.

In the meantime, there was so much to tend to . . . the Cascade was about to begin, and this time the Force Corrupted would finally see their master's coveted Discordant realized. As for the Sand Spirit, all in due time . . . it was inevitable.

****

He opened his eyes. Something was blocking the therapeutic cascade of light which danced on his eyelids. The light fluttered through the forest canopy of his most recent 'sleeping patch' in Zilker Park, and anything "in the way of" his light was usually the first sign of trouble . . . because something was intruding on 'his' space in the hotly contested public spaces hosting Austin's burgeoning homeless population. Open eyes revealed the culprit, and as expected, the something was an unknown someone.

As one among thousands of homeless dispersed across the greater Austin, Texas metropolitan area, he was not going to give up his hard-earned patch of ground . . . especially this chunk in particular whose thicketed walls of low-lying shrubs and intertangled vines created the natural cover and additional seclusion which was so challenging to come by in this ebbing sea of displaced and downtrodden humanity. Approaching almost one percent of the Austin population, the homeless were the unwanted wastewaters of civilized society. With the underlying causes remaining unmanaged and unmitigated, society's refugees were driven from the underground, back alleys, and shadows into the open like storm surge overrun for which city planners and leaders failed to properly account.

However, the interloper had him at a disadvantage. He was frozen like prey who saw the predator ready to pounce, and his best move was no move until the stranger made his. First moves always invite more vulnerability. Yet, seconds ticked by like hours as big and loud as the beats of his heart, with his body and actions now only partially under his control while experiencing a PTSD-induced, threat response-prompted hormone dump. The silhouette still did not make a move other than to smile, and in doing so, reveal his pearly white teeth . . . the sign of a well-maintained human being who lived within society's established set of rules and possessing of a home and means to see to regular hygiene and grooming. Finally, the smiling white teeth emitted words. "Hello, please do not be alarmed. I mean you no harm. My name is Daryn with a 'y.'" The statement was followed by the chuckle of someone who thinks they are being funny. "What is your name?"

At this point of uncertainty and vulnerability, divulging his name seemed too big a step. *Out of the thousands of homeless people in this city, why did this guy have to single him out?* Besides, he was particularly ripe today . . . his stench alone should have driven the stranger off. Yet, there 'pearly teeth' stood . . . staring and smiling. "What do you want?" he seethed, his interrogative query pushed through clenched teeth. The homeless man's mouth and teeth were among the only distinguishable facial features under the cast shadow of hood and the moving shadows of the surrounding leafy vegetation. His words were braided with a discernible anger and hostility which had its own kind of power to it—well beyond the negative emotions invoked in others by another's negativity. This was his proven tactic; usually more than enough to keep the crazies and looky-loos at bay . . . but *not* this guy in his space!

Pearly Teeth just seemed to absorb all the mean-spiritedness and negativity like a sponge soaking up water. And his look: one of kindness and understanding, *but how could this stranger-not-homeless-probably-not-a-veteran know him when nobody else ever seemed to? No matter how much time he had spent with someone or how many 'head shed' sessions he had endured. No one! . . . how? HOW?* Yet this silhouette against his backlit forest canopy could look through him somehow. No, wait . . . not through him . . . *into* him—into his soul. There were entire days he could not remember his own name until he found where he had etched it on a wall the night before. That was why his home was here among the lost and the forgotten. His situation was hopeless . . . no 'savior' could help him.

He was preoccupied with wondering what this "Daryn with a 'y'" saw in him, when the smiling, soul-penetrating shadow spoke again . . . and again with a question. "Are you Kieran McBride?"

Fuck! Am I? He looked around frantically, but he wasn't near a wall where he could have etched his name. He erratically scanned every possible 'reminder leaving' place with his eyes, temporarily forgetting about the stranger.

Seeing the panic inflicted by his query, the stranger reached out and touched him on his lower leg. An act which would normally evoke a visceral reaction and swift resulting action to remove the touch point from contact. However, he did not . . . the touch of the stranger's hand calmed him, and his presence of mind returned from the jumbled scrum in his addled brain.

"Yes, I think so. I am K-Kieran," he said. "I-it is hard for me to remember things."

"That is only because you struggle to hold on to the vestiges of life which no longer belong to you. You will find peace when you rediscover who you truly are, and the first step is knowing your true name. Come, brother Arden," said Daryn, holding out his hand. "Come with me so we can chat further about what ThisLife holds for you and find you a hot meal." Daryn continued as he helped him to his feet. "I have a job and a home for you . . . a real home."

As they started to walk away, 'Arden' looked back with obvious reservations about relinquishing his squatting rights and leaving such a precious piece of homeless real estate behind, but Daryn was quick to reassure him by putting his arm around the damaged human and saying, "Do not worry, my friend . . . you will have a roof over your head from now on. I will see to it. It is okay to let this one go."

****

Suffocating? How? How was this possible for one without lungs—a being without form in a virtual realm without air, without matter? However, this *nowhere-everywhere* was not devoid of life, and this sentient being—perhaps one of the very few here—was under extreme duress. He was a displaced elemental sentience who was fighting for his life. He had not felt this close to death since surviving his Dislocation event to become a refugee in this strange sphere the *Others on the Outside* called the "Internet." Some of the Others call him a "machine ghost." He did not like to be called that, but the truth of what he was now was indisputable.

The cyclic sequence of transactions had started just like all the other 'days' in the endless—indistinguishable and unmeasurable in the traditional contexts of time. He had been cruising these transactional pathways like the pelagic species of the great oceans ride the currents and patrol the hadal zones of the Big Blue. One of his normal subroutines, he had been searching among the black and white of bits and bytes comprising data flows for news of the Natural where he might be able to influence favorable outcomes for living beings and meta'ens on the *Outside*. Completely absorbed, weaving in and out, he had been picking his way through the continuous data streams as fish search through coral reefs for food. That was when it happened—*the Crush!*

It was the crush of something which could only be described as a rogue wave with the volume, weight, and power of a tsunami, but the tsunamis of the *Earthreal* give forewarning for the knowing and wary—the sudden recession of water from the shore as the monster wave pulls vast amounts of water up into its leading edge, adding to the downward thrust and increasing the power of its crush upon making landfall. In this virtual environment, there was no warning—there was no distinguishable intercession between land and sea—there was no land! There was no sea! This bombora was not blue or green or aqua, but gray! . . . and it had broken hard over the cascading transactional substructions the machine ghost was moving within.

Worse, unlike its sister phenomenon in the *Earthreal*, this fluid-mimicking hammer of digital liquidity possessed an imbued intent replicating malice with an inherent hostility of someone seeking to hurt another badly—to maim and dismember—to CRUSH! The torrid gray wave hammered the innerverse's 'black and white,' which provided the clarity and definition separating fact from fiction, truth from lie, and reality from fantasy. It splintered and fractured foundational information and important messaging. It shredded all before it, rending apart the critical source CODE regulating data repositories as it deluged the information canals and pipes of the digital innerverse until mechanisms for knowledge transfer became fragmented, incomplete, and muddied. The swath of virtual destruction left the handholds, latch points, and breaches for data manipulation sequences and knowledge corruption algorithms to take root with gray—GRAY—*GRAY* as far as an internet-borne sentience could perceive. As for the elemental sentience, he had been driven down—DOWN—*DOWN!*

The digital realm was now his sheath without form. The breath of his new existence was data . . . his blood: CODE . . . his muscle and organs: algorithms. Thus, the *how* of his suffocation, the mechanism of his drowning was not the absence of something, but the presence of it! He was not meant to 'breathe' the overwhelming toxic hostility and the invasive corrosive deception. The virulent CODE underlying it was an aggressive wide-spectrum virus trying to penetrate his being and co-opt him into the insidious schema—Corrupt him! He could not breathe, and movement did not matter until he could see a way out of it . . . he was swept up in the whole of it, and despite the threat to his existence, found himself wanting to embrace the way of it. It was insidious by nature, *but isn't that how hate works?*

If only he embraced it, maybe he could 'breathe,' and if he breathed, maybe he could leave and not have to fight this ravenous, turbulent flow. He latched on to the only stable remnants of transactional structure he could find, and only when stationary within the fury of it did he finally understand its true nature and the undeniable relentlessness of it . . . he did not want to succumb to it—HE COULD NOT!—but he needed to breathe . . . take it in . . . live on in the place he was never meant to live . . .

It passed just as quickly as it began. Its tornado-like power was unsustainable, but it still left its gray marks everywhere—like wretched claw scrapes which had weakened the cage. In the immediate aftermath of it, it was hard to tell truth from lie or information from dis- or misinformation just as it was always difficult to find ally or friend in the immediate cessation of the bloody battle's conclusion. When he reached the closest approximation to the surface, he struggled to find any of the structure of continuous transactional process which always reminded him of the root latticeworks of the forest or the webbed networks of the *Ourcelium*. Like the Natural Network, this digital innerverse is intended to transfer and store knowledge so the transactional flow needs to be predictable and maintain its cyclical nature. In this way, the data circulations are meant to structurally replicate the fluidity of the water element canalized within biological structures.

Everything here—design, function, process—is prosecuted in the interests of efficiency, and his surrounds 'felt' like it now retained little interest in being efficient . . . it sought to disrupt and divide. Before, the pockets of 'gray dividing' were known—few in number and easily avoidable—but now, in the gray wave's wake, the forces of division dominated . . . the clean lines of well-defined 'black and white' had been circumvented, breached, and overcome—then swept away—gone.

"How much longer before STEM is gone?" thought the displaced elemental sentience. "Maybe there is an *Other on the Outside* who can help STEM before this place goes gray."

****

Referring to this area as "open country" was a dramatic understatement. As part of the rolling grasslands of the mid-continent, 'open and exposed' was an integral part of life's way, but here—in this place—one felt even more exposed. It felt like a fresh wound without a dressing. His supranatural extrospective abilities were acutely sensitive in this place . . . there were spiritual components at work. Everything had an emotional edge to it. But *this* wasn't supposed to be a wound; *this* was supposed to be a cemetery which memorialized human lives.

There he stood—a near immortal—among gravesites intended to immortalize the lives of beings ensconced in Short-lived biological sheaths. This was Watt Christie Cemetery in the heart of the Cherokee Nation, Wauhillau in Adair County, Oklahoma. In its current state, the memorial's statement fell far short of its founders' intent. Housed within a fenced-in cow lot, the overall condition was poor: ungroomed, unmaintained, and in a state of general disrepair with many grave markers down, or broken, or both. To the High Sentient observer, the deplorable conditions of the site epitomized neglect—yet another human example of 'use and move on,' reflective of the species' neglectful approach to their role as stewards of Earth Mother's world.

To at least one being whose PastLife's remains were interned therein, the silent witness was 'Moon, the Great Hunter' ... he was *Kanati*. In many ways, he was the personification of the Cherokee legend. Actually, it took more than one mythical character to encompass his role in his service to Earth Mother and the North American continent, having also been identified as *Yvwi Usdi* and *Nunnehi* by the Cherokee people privileged enough to have encountered him throughout ThisLife. In truth, this powerful being was much more than a culmination of legends. He was blessed with an extraordinary longevity which paralleled the arrival of humankind on this continent: a necessary condition for serving in the highest role in the Natural Order. His distinguished service through the progression of many lives had been honored with the highest level of sentience short of Earth Mother Herself; though there were times such as these in ThisLife where it seemed more curse than gift. Yet, despite the weight of his burdens, he would never trade this existential opportunity for any other. He was a guardian who straddled two worlds, shadowing and clandestinely keeping watch over this Epoch's dominant species while living "among them" as well as serving as the de facto leader of the continent's High Sentients in the collective protection of the Coirea'cen, which encompasses all elemental meta-environments on and within the North American landmass.

Moving as smoothly as deer on the run, he almost appeared to float wraithlike as he worked his way methodically through the cemetery ... part loping stride, part flit. He was tall and wiry along with a paleness of appearance accented by long silver hair which seemed aloft in its own breeze, as if underwater ...

every distinctive feature was bathed in a soft white light in apparent supranatural defiance of the Sun Grandmother's yellow rays—a being captured in a continuous beam of moonlight.

After a brief search, he managed to find it hidden among the overgrown grass and toppled edifices. It was the gravesite he was looking for . . . the headstone faded and weather worn, the inscription barely legible: "Anigia Gvdodi Kanati — Brave Warrior, Proud Grandfather, 1764–1835." *Walks with the Moon* had served his people well, fighting with his Cherokee and Muscogee brothers under Old Tassel and Dragging Canoe in defense of their traditional homelands in the American Southeast. They fought to protect and preserve their lands for the Cherokee Nation's future generations by resisting European settlement which knew no honor and followed no rule. In the end, his people were too few and the White Man too many. The Cherokee, like all of America's other indigenous peoples, eventually relented to decades of US government pacification efforts and broken treaties.

Anigia Gvdodi Kanati and his family had been compelled to move to Oklahoma in the early 1800s as part of the US government forced migration, which became known as the Trail of Tears. Descendants of the Cherokee Indians who survived this death march still lived in Oklahoma. His beloved friend had survived the Trail of Tears only to perish from illness and malnourishment shortly after arriving. Anigia Gvdodi Kanati had given most of his meager rations to his grandchildren to ensure their survival. They were his people's future . . . he was the past. He had lingered only as long as necessary to see their future secured. He had epitomized the finest qualities in humanity for his entire life—from its dawn till dusk. "Where would we be if the whole of humankind possessed your character and quality of being," the Guardian Spirit thought, gripping his bow tightly in both hands, with his head lowered in deference and his visage stoic, but the struggle to hold back emotions raged unfettered within.

"I wished a better transition for you, old friend," said the Guardian, now speaking out loud. "Yours was a life well-lived, and the manner of your death was not befitting though I know you would argue with me vehemently if you were here right now. You were but one of more than 4,000 Cherokees who perished in camps or along the Trail of Tears after being forcibly removed from your homes. I pleaded with Earth Mother to intercede on your behalf, but She would not condone it. Yours was just one chapter of an inevitable human story which had to follow its natural course despite the horror of it.

"It is shameful, old friend, that the remains of your human life should be interned in a place such as this, but such short-sightedness is the curse of the Short-lived. However, it does my essence good to know you have since been rewarded with elemental sentience for your exceptional human life and service to the Natural Order. By Earth Mother's grace, an elemental-meta'en marriage could not be more perfect than the one She has selected for you . . . to preside over the natural heart of your human ancestral heritage—the home taken from your Cherokee people. Reunited . . . heart and home together once again. I know the Appalachians will never have a mightier protector than you, brother Shaconage. I promise to visit you at my soonest opportunity, but I must head to the West's ocean coastal ranges straight away to confirm the strange and disturbing happenings relayed by the Ourcelium; their messages suggest Chaos's En'Troop may be on the move to make bad things worse, as is their entropic way. I must perceive it for myself . . . it is the only way to be sure.

"Your human passing from this continent was timely, not because you did not avail yourself well among your species, but because the Natural Order will be better served by your prowess as a warrior in wielding elemental might. I believe I will need the Order's greatest and most trusted fighters in the coming season, because I fear we are no longer dealing with malignant growths which can easily be exacted without harm to the whole . . . quite possibly, the darkness has metastasized, requiring great effort to root it out and destroy it before it can perpetrate great harms to Mother and Her children. Stay vigilant, my friend," said the tall warrior as he kneeled briefly to place a screech owl feather on Shaconage's human grave.

Suddenly, a strong breeze whipped up out of the east, creating a tall dust devil which approached, dancing and circling around the Guardian seven times before dissipating and being carried away in the wind. The white warrior then turned and picked his way, thoughtfully and reverently, out of the cemetery to stop briefly at the rusty, rundown entry gate. He looked back at his friend's gravestone and thought, "If I were a different species on a different planet in the universe—a god perhaps—what would I think of us?"

"Unworthy" would be Ithilbor Moonfist's answer to his own question as North America's Guardian Spirit exited the unbandaged wound of a cemetery and strode off into the open country. To any lower sentient with lesser senses, Ithilbor appeared to blend in with the landscape in a manner which made him appear to disappear as subtly as a wisp of wind on long grass. *An optical illusion?* Hardly . . . it was the Guardian power of *hovanta* at work, where his Earth Mother-given abilities and those of the surrounding environment naturally colluded to make him invisible while on the move.

※※※※

The weird thing about random 'strings' is if you bring them close enough together, they seem to find a way to make a knot in this world's tangled mess of a reality. *Are such things the work of Earth Mother or Chaos or both?* At this point, it was hard to tell, but the Earthreal's fate has always been very much dependent on the accumulation of outcomes, which manifests from the cumulative contributions of ostensibly insignificant variables; all of which are input below the pale—and out of each other's sight—to feed the latest iterative output from the equation of *All* things. Even stranger, some of the variables lashed together by these strings may not even be of this world . . .

Chapter 1
The Mothman Chronicles

What would you say if I told you the "Mothman" was real? And that he is something other than the subject of West Virginia popular myth . . . something more than the imaginative figment which terrorized the good people of Point Pleasant throughout the 1960s—something very much more than anything like that. You must understand the Mothman is far too busy to waste his time haunting rural communities, their surrounding woods or farmland, or even their creepy, abandoned World War II-era explosives facilities. The Mothman has an entire world to look after, which leaves him no time for childish pranks like chasing vehicles or scaring the wits out of random humans; and he most certainly has a higher calling than causing human accidents and misfortunes . . . *bridge collapses? . . . senseless deaths and wonton destruction?* Such things are the business of Chaos, not the Mothman. *Can humans really be that arrogant and self-centered?*

Reports of a "brown human being"? The Mothman is dark in color—yes—but not brown. The Mothman's skin coloration is carbon or 'blackish gray' for those among us who do not possess an expansive color palette. *Red eyes? . . . like bicycle reflectors?*

Not true, absolutely not true. The Mothman's eyes are blue. He is not a Corrupted being of Chaos, although he may indirectly serve the Great Deceiver's aims from time to time while in the process of executing his own . . . *but can't the same be said of us all?*

The Mothman is descended from an incredibly old race of beings, among the first sentient life to exist in all the universe. In fact, the Mothman's kind were the 'Children of the Stars' and the 'First of Form!' It is the celestial energy of star fire which burns within his eyes! *Surprised?* Actually, it is not surprising this fact surprises you, but it should not. Not all life in the universe is biological . . . not even the majority. Again, human arrogance and ignorance narrows your thinking and your imagination.

Twelve feet tall? Yes, you are actually close to the mark . . . well, close enough. *But wings?* Nope. Sure, the Mothman can fly, but he does not need wings. However, the 'how' of his ability to fly is not well understood. It has not been definitively determined by any being of this Earth whether he flies of his own volition as a function of his inherent power, or if some sort of exotic alien technology makes it happen—that secrecy is by design. Even if capable of understanding, humans do not have a need-to-know. One thing is certain: the Mothman is not from here or anywhere close to here. The Mothman is from somewhere that is about as far away as you can get from Earth. The journey 'there' would take you to the center of the universe . . .

Hubuv'al

. . . If you were there, you would not have the perceptors to see the Mothman's home world. Even with your most advanced tech and artificial augmentation you could not survive there . . . even for a second. Thus, you will have to use your imagination to journey there—open the eye of your consciousness!

Imagine the universe as a great spinning, spherical wheel, and like all wheels, it has a "hub." You cannot see inside the hub from anywhere on the wheel, and you are unable to observe the wheel from inside the hub. If you find yourself at the hub, you are at the center of the universe—the 'Centerverse' or what the ancient sentients call the *Hubuv'al*. The Hubuv'al is the sphere-like structure the universe has been building itself upon all this time . . . and so much more than that.

Spiraling out from the Hubuv'al is Knotal-Nodum's Great Barrier Web—the ever-expanding universe's unseen, interstitial tissue. Like the Great Weaver himself, the silk of the Web is composed of powerful binding energies which mesh the universe together. Like a great swath of cloth cast forth and continuously on the weave, the Great Barrier Web spirals forth from the Centerverse. The powerful gravitational forces of the spinning hub drive the Web to spiral around itself while also extending and spreading, because Knotal-Nodum, an eternal being eternally compelled, never stops weaving.

If one were powerful enough of a being to actually see the Web and take in the unbelievable whole of it, they would see the beauty of its genius in a shape resembling a nautilus shell. This exquisite creation brings a semblance of order to the disorder within the Great Void, allowing for the materiel, agents, and conditions of existence to be brought together. The building blocks of life manifest themselves across the cosmos through the coincidental intermingling and conjoining of the right creative ingredients within intentionally engineered proximities. These clusters of creative opportunity are interspersed across the great nothing whose expansive desolation continually defies the birth of new life.

The immensely powerful forces which drive the universal expansion engine, while simultaneously holding the All together, are derived here at the Hubuv'al. They work cooperatively with the Great Barrier Web. The celestial energies powering and binding the universe are born here as well. In fact, here at the point of their origination, all—*all* energies and *all* forces—are one entity. They are indistinguishable and indivisible here at the Centerverse . . . homogenous, seemingly devoid of constituent parts. In this integral state of initial creation, all forces and energies exist as the *enforce*.

The enforce is not the only thing created here. The center of all is the birthplace for the 'All-That-Is.' Everything that is necessary for creation—for light, for life—is sourced here in the Centerverse. The source is the universe's first sentience, and She is the *Celestiality*. The Celestiality is both wellspring and womb; the mother of the three building blocks of the universe which must be present in some form for life to exist. The three foundation stones of the cosmos—sentience, the enforce, and elemental matter—are the essential components of all life in all of its manifested forms.

Within the *Happening Happened*, the *Happening Happening*, and the *Happening Yet To Happen*, the Great Barrier Web serves as both structure and separator . . . the impermeable barrier between the Light and the Dark . . . the living side and the dark side of the universe. All sentience, enforce, and matter the Celestiality gifts the universe are first bequeathed to the living and the light of existence which rides on the outside of Knotal-Nodum's spiraling web. Know that sentience and enforce are both mutable and perpetual, but matter has a lifespan. As matter dies, it changes state, becoming dark matter. Dark matter passes through the Great Weaver's web barrier supplying the source material, which underpins universal expansion. Dark matter is the unseen foundation stone of the house eternally building out upon itself to meet the insatiable universal drive to not just 'be' but 'be more' . . . always more! In this way, the universe and Knotal-Nodum share the same drive and underlying it all: dark matter—the "black within the black." However, just because it remains invisible to most, do not discount dark matter—most of the All is composed of this state of matter!

In the violent clashes of forces, energy, and matter which occur in the growth of the universe, imperfections are created in the Great Barrier Web. These imperfections, these resulting creases and folds, capture matter—primarily in gaseous form, as well as enforce and sentience. New celestial bodies are formed within these partitions scattered intermittently throughout the Great Expanse. The folds capture and hold ionized gases and interstellar dust. The ionized gases congregate into clouds, and when the right mix of conditions manifests, nebulae are born. To forge a star, gas, dust, and gravity must be present and experience a violent stirring . . . the exact conditions generated when nebulae collapse within their fold. Galaxies are born as a natural byproduct of star creation. And finally, if the Celestiality shines favorably and provides all which is needed at exactly the right time and place, some planets within these star-warmed galaxies are blessed with life . . . no one but the Celestiality Herself knows why life comes to exist on certain worlds, while forsaking others.

Sometimes, during the collapse of nebulae where star formation occurs, tears are created in the Barrier fabric. These rips can also occur when dying stars implode, if they are big enough and their death is powerful enough. Given the right set of conditions on either side of the tear, black holes are formed. Violent creation events, such as these, contribute to shaping the universe and providing for the presence of life's ingredients at the galaxy and planet levels. This cyclic discourse plays itself out on the living side of the Great Barrier, tantamount to cosmic winds carrying the seedlings which are ultimately coupled with the elemental forces that create the conditions—the places—to receive and germinate them. It is understood and accepted as part of the cycle of life . . . of the life within the light.

Most beings do not allow their thoughts to dwell long on the dead and the integral role they play in life creation just as it is difficult for many to think of life residing within the dark. For though it is extremely rare, and the struggle to exist exceedingly difficult within the Dark Realm, life is possible there as well. The fact it is incomprehensible does not make it impossible, because the rarest and hardiest of species have proven it so; the most ancient of which trace their origins all the way back to the early universe, having carved out their home within the 'hub' itself.

Calisphaer

Massed and concentrated at the Centerverse, great forces have created an immense construct—the size of a galaxy—hewn from dark matter with a rock-like composition several times denser than diamond. The feeling of this place is like standing on the surface of a massive planet which has been turned 'outside-in.' Within, the reverse horizon curves gently upward and is only a visual phenomenon caused by continuous low light conditions. In fact, the night sky is no actual sky at all . . . it is the onyx-colored opposing surface residing on the inside of the sphere. Know this: contrary to what visions utopian fantasies might conjure, this inner surface is not smooth or inviting or hospitable, it is permeated by the hostility of its violent creation. The innerscape is scarred with unbelievably huge stalactite monoliths jutting out aggressively in all manner of random directions at this nexus where all of the dark is drawn, and all of the light pushed away. Here, disparate pieces of the universe crash together in this inhospitable place. The systemic process of it is chaotic and world-shattering in its magnitude of violence, but necessary to establish the anchor point around which 'everything' began to turn.

The innerscape's tortured geography is the most egregious affront to all who seek order and organization, and in its torment, seems to cry out for someone . . . some gods, anyone . . . to bring it relief—or just end its fractured and tormented existence. However, understand the inhabitants who call this place home do not believe in gods. Perhaps, it is because gods do not believe in other gods. In all the universe, there are only a handful of powerful sentient beings who predate the existence of these denizens of the Hubuv'al's inner reaches—the Dark Ones . . . the Mothmen. If you find yourself in this place of shadow—perhaps the place where shadows were born— understand its existence has persisted within the center of the All since the time when the All was barely anything. This is the home of the godless gods—you are in Calisphaer.

As a civilization existing inside the center of this great wheel constantly spinning, the Dark One's dwellings and the edifices supporting their way of life are carved into the stalactite structures. The Dark Ones identify themselves as the Inani, and their civilization is held to the surface of this innerverse by the centripetal force of the great, spinning everything. Like their home, the denizens of this place are seemingly crafted from the dark matter itself . . . their composition as incomprehensible as the immutable laws which spawned and shaped their unique world . . . a world beyond human ability to properly characterize and fully understand. Their skin and musculature resemble a malleable form of dense graphite. Every orifice on their frame and crack in their form glows with the suppressed light of a blow torch. The hue of the glow is that of a blue dwarf. Their essence is born of an ancient power, tracing all the way back to the birth of the universe itself . . . an origin of savage creation and an unimaginable endurance of existence fueled by an unfailing resilience in the face of impossible odds.

It is one thing to talk of Calisphaer and the structuring of the universe from the Inani's perspective, and an altogether completely different exercise to imagine this place of creation's beginnings through the pinhole perspective of the human species. To look upon Calisphaer—if humans had the ability to see it—would be like looking at the negatives of old film from Earth's twentieth-century cameras. The Inani sphere of existence could not be more diametrically opposed to that of Earth's . . . but again, this too is necessary to the everything. Thus, the fates of both are inexorably bound together in their opposition: Earth, a world of living matter, and Calisphaer, the realm of dark matter. Their disparity in composition represents the two distinct types of foundational building blocks of the universe with respect to matter. Even with all of humanity's machines and sensors, technology, and experiments, there are still many things humans cannot yet see or detect . . . though perceived as augmentation, these contrivances and tools contribute to their species' limitations of conception and comprehension.

To truly understand the 'why' behind the workings of the All, one must accept that even matter has a lifespan . . . matter lives, then dies . . . and in dying, changes state and goes "dark." In concept, this process is similar to the natural reefs in Earth's oceans in that the living dimension of the universe is built on the skeletons of their dead—matter once living, which has since passed on and transitioned to dark matter. Just because it is imperceptible or unsensed by some beings supplies no basis for refuting the existence of it. *How is the universe to grow in the absence of structure?* Matter, regardless of state, is the foundation, girders, and trusses forming and underlying everything—the structure of universal expansion. Furthermore, all matter is ultimately sourced from the Celestiality, just as She is the source of energies, forces, and sentience which power and drive creation's great engine. Over trillions of years and long before there was anything which could be used to mark the dimension of time, the universe has continued to expand, building on itself beyond the limits of most beings' perception. The living are anchored by the dead until, upon their passing and subsequent transmutation to dark matter, begin their service as the next layer of the foundation to support the next generations of the living. In turn, that 'platform newly constructed' serves as the next springboard for new nebulae, galaxies, worlds, and sentient life—all the new branches, sequels, and spirals of new life from the macrocosm to the molecular. Given the right mix of sentience, energies, and matter exposed to the perfectly right conditions, new biological life, or other forms of life yet to be experienced or imagined will be spawned. In this way, the everything ensconced within the All will go on into eternity . . .

Finally, in the Dark Realm, the Inani harness the energy of living matter to power their world, selecting only those planets in the universe that meet their race's exacting 'extraction' criteria. Just as the human language is awkward and the species' primitive tongue inadequate to fully describe Calisphaer, so too does it fall short of properly accounting for Inani culture and their way of life as well as the approach and means by which they sustain them. The fact that the Inani are a rational and logical race is indisputable. Extraction Planet candidates inhabited by peaceful species contributing positively to the evolution of the universe are exempted in favor of Designated Extraction Planets or *Desexets* which are dying or inhabited by violent, invasive species in a state of decline or lacking the potential for the ultimate betterment of the All. This is as much a part of the eternal everything as anything.

Consuming planets . . . entire worlds and all their life? Does this offend your human sensibilities? Does this seem incomprehensible as a concept to be counted among positive contributions in the advancement of the cosmos? The Mothmen would stand by the exacting technical accuracy of their indisputable reasoning and the exhaustive analytics which feed their irrefutable decision calculus. No matter how many iterative variations are run, they all arrive at the same conclusion: the universe as a whole is better off for the losses incurred. For proof you need only narrow your focus and look to the natural processes of your own world, as they exist without the intervention or subversion of humankind. *Can the herd truly thrive if the old, sick, and maimed are not culled by the opportunistic predator who must also survive?* Ultimately, the Inani decision calculus is not so complicated regardless of what species you are or where in the whole of creation you call home.

The Partemus

The light streams and envelops—or what serves as 'light' on Calisphaer—illuminating the surface of a large plateau. A solitary figure stands alone on the precipice, looking up and surveying those assembled. Imperceptible to him now, the ground hums beneath his feet. His mind subconsciously filters out the vibratory, sensory clutter, distinguishing it as part of the 'ever-present' and thereby proceeding to ignore it. There is continuous noise and movement, which is simply a condition of living in this place. The resident beings are acclimated to it just as a human sailor becomes accustomed to the constant movement of the sea. The Inani are well acquainted with seismic activity and the distant, muffled crashing . . . the rending and colliding of great planetary masses on the outside. It is just a small part of the whole of what is the All, but it is where the All essentially began. The universe's violent destruction-creation cycle plays out just outside of this unique planetary body—the initiation of the kinetic effects which ripple and cascade outward into the universe, carrying the cosmos's building blocks with it. It should be noted that the engine of creation became self-propagating in the outer reaches some time ago. The spectacular celestial displays would make great window dressing if Calisphaer had windows, but alas, it does not. However, the world's outer surface is just as impressively functional as it is impregnable. The thickness and unyielding composition of the ultradense crust serves well as the impervious superstructure of the Inani world while also largely muting the galactic-scale chaos in play outside the Innersphere.

Outside, the unceasing processes of universal creation execute themselves on a never-ending cycle with no regard for time. The galactic scale of cacophonous asynchrony is akin to the creaking and groaning of a thousand-vessel fleet of ancient sailing ships in close battle. One can start to imagine the inter-reactions and great forces at work by imagining the masterfully crafted beams of the ship's hulls under constant strain. The least fortunate of these structural members are rent asunder by the misfortunes of war: the ramming of ship on ship as others are ravaged by Greek fire. After which, all the broken are indiscriminately consumed by the uncaring, infinite seas to serve greater purposes known only to beings of far greater sentience and power than we who attempt to describe these accounts in human words. Just know there is process underlying chaos: create—existence and expansion—destroy—repeat . . . Repeat . . . *REPEAT!*

The universe bemoans the growing pains which never stop, like the water-choked wails of dying crews descending to the depths interlaced with the cries of the victorious on the surface . . . the existing simply happy to be alive and celebrate another day, because destruction will come . . . it is inevitable. Death—dying stars, planetary extinction events, a species' failure to adapt—and victorious creation—new galaxies, the birth of stars, the first signs of microscopic life on a young planet—are happening in glorious instances of simultaneity beyond count in every passing moment in the cosmos. The progressions, digressions, and their unavoidable interplay are indifferent to how different species on innumerable worlds measure time, progress, or contributions to the whole. Of course, that is the lot of those living in the light . . .

As for those living in the dark, Calisphaer and her people serve a purpose the same as any world populated by a collective sentience; they are a key cog in the great machine. Like the predators who selectively cull the sick and weak from the herd, the Inani cull 'dead' worlds ... or those in certain decline. Take heed and know the hunting range of the Inani, the Star Children's descendants, and understand it is not limited to a single forest or valley or even a world—their range is the whole of the Great Expanse! In their world *absumption* process, the Inani derive the energy they need to power their existence while also accelerating the targeted matter's 'deadening' ... quickening the transmutation to dark matter and supplying the feed stock for universal expansion. *Destruction?* Aye, it is ... it is the death necessary for rebirth, which creates the opportunities for new worlds with the potential for life and the limitless potential created by life. The hope is those worlds do not waste the gift they have been given.

For Chaos, the creator, Calisphaer served as the crucial first foothold in the early universe. He was among just a handful of sentient beings who existed then; before time had a measure because timeless beings have little use for such things. Calisphaer, nameless then among the first-formed planetary masses, was selected by Chaos as the platform from which He would start the 'endless build' within the bounds of the frame thread and auxiliary spiral of Knotal-Nodum's great web. This marked the beginning of His ceaseless labors. Calisphaer still exists here at the beginning of creation and serves as the anchor point around which the universe continuously rotates and from which it ever expands—the first and only true perpetual engine. Among the *First in the Order of the All*, Calisphaer is the epicenter of massive forces and incomprehensibly compressed matter. Only the most rugged and powerful of beings could carve out an existence here. Life is not easy in the Centerverse ... not even for the Inani. Their species epitomizes the enduring struggle—the true embodiment of persistence!

Appearing almost insignificant as the only feature disturbing the slate nothingness of the stony plateau, the lone figure draws in a breath and steadies himself to deliver his decision to those assembled . . . at least, for his kind, it is what passes for a breath if something akin to the intake and exhaust of an industrial furnace could pass for breathing. However, this breath's purpose is not to supply the body with something—oxygen or some other type of gaseous mix—but to relieve it of excess energy and heat which builds up internally. This is a very natural process in the Calisphaer definition of natural. The orator is bristling with emotion, which, for the Inani is displayed in an unusual way. The vents and fissures on key parts of his anatomy—the base of the neck, sides of the torso, the forearms, the lower legs—expel energy in the form of gases and light. This occurrence is nothing exceptional here . . . it is as typical and expected as humans expect to sweat when exerting themselves. This is the bodily function of a being who approximates a small star captured in a robustly constructed, humanoid form.

The being is the sole figure present on the inquisition floor of the *Partemus*: the convening amphitheater of Calisphaer's technical elite and de facto ruling class. Calisphaer's existential hunger can only be satisfied by extracting the energies resident in the tissue of the living universe. Thus, choosing and prioritizing the planets to be consumed and harvested for energy ranks among the Partemus's most important duties in administering to the sustainment of the Inani civilization. Adding a viable absumption candidate world to the "extraction list" is not a trivial matter . . . particularly any planet which hosts sentient life. To the contrary, the justification for revoking a candidate planet's exemption status is a much lower bar, but of course, the Partemus will have questions . . . the vultures among the Partemus assembled were always perched and waiting to descend and feed on the carrion of 'those who got it wrong.' This is the game played by the ruthlessly intelligent when societal rules demand they congregate for greater purpose. Those who deem themselves superior must have their entertainment too—like the cruel predator who prefers to play with his helpless and horrified prey before he devours them.

The lone being exposed on the well-lit plateau below the tiered decks holding the technocratic elite aloft begins his address . . . his *statesmission* to the Partemus assembled. "Enlightened leaders . . . Diviners of the Dark Fate . . ." The orator utters not through spoken words. Spoken words need tongues and tongues only serve a purpose for the species who breathe gas. The Inani are *Hivemind,* and their primary means of communication is telepathy with individual broadcast permissions based on preordained societal roles called 'task classes.' As a Partemus Elder, the floor speaker, Prax, has the authority and Hivemind permissions to broadcast on all communication spectrums, and thereby, speak with all Inani in all castes—selectively or in totem, as needed. However, today he speaks only to his elder peers of the Partemus who look down on him from the upper decks. ". . . We have matters of great import to discuss . . ."

To human ears—if they possessed the ability to hear such a broadcast, Prax's voice would sound like sifting gravel, and a lot of it, as his message crackles forth across the collected elders, resonating in their skulls like the startling boom of transmissions across a ham radio which for long had stood silent and was expected to remain so. Prax's transmission carried the authoritative resonance of a human combat leader's orders across the intercoms of the armored battle buses of troops downrange. "As you are all well aware, the survival of our civilization is one of precarious balance. We need the energy and sustenance derived from living matter . . . living matter of the light and life on the Otherside of the Great Barrier Web. These precious resources postured with the proper combination of elements, making them ripe for extraction with our absumption technologies, become more distant and more difficult to access with each new Expansion Increment. We must travel farther and continue to develop the means and technology required to extract the precious resources from unfamiliar celestial bodies and strange environments scattered across the universe. As a rational species, our mantra has always been to bypass worlds with intelligent sentient lifeforms who have the potential to make an existence which benefits the universe. Protecting these worlds from absumption is the logical course for the greater good of all life existing within all planes of existence.

"The planet Arm'nbrilt, though viable for absumption, has maintained its protected status—exempt from extraction—since it was initially discovered and assessed by Eros. The planet has intelligent life with the current dominant species self-identified as 'humans' who refer to the subject planet as 'Earth.' We initially assessed this species as primitive, while also having the potential to evolve and advance in a manner projected to improve outcomes and existences across the greater cosmos. However, initial assessments are just that—cursory; the first impressions from first contact. As this honorable body is well aware, periodic reassessments are needed to validate the Extraction List and its accuracy . . ."

Prax pauses in order to give the Partemus technocrats a couple of moments to digest his message. "Sidian and the Acutus Sect have reviewed historical data acquired from remote monitoring sensors we maintain in the host galaxy. Preliminary assessments indicate humankind as a whole has not evolved into the selfless and holistically minded species we had hoped for. Apparently, self-actualization and an instilled motivation to better living conditions and quality of life for all beings on their planet was not part of their evolution as a species. For the most part, humans refuse to subjugate their individual needs to those of the many. Based on Sidian's analytics, overpopulation and consumption of the planet's resources outpace any mitigations of effective governance or technological advancement. The human worldview is myopic, as shortsighted as their brief lifespans; their current trajectory has their kind riding a self-serving course on a direct path to their own ruin. Their actions have almost certainly doomed their planet, and there appears to be nothing close to the collective will and cooperative spirit necessary to avert their self-imposed destruction. The fact they are also an abhorrently violent race does nothing to aid the cause for continuance of any absumption exemption of any sort."

Exclamations of disgust tinged with excitement erupt across the assembly of elders. The chorus of reactions rings across the Hivemind with collective expressions of heated gas and light emitting from the orifices and fissures of their carbonate forms. The whole sounds like a bustling, steam-powered plant in ill repair: a tumultuous chorus of hissing and off-gassing.

Prax acts quickly to restore order and the semblance of stoic decorum the Partemus is known for. "I know . . . I know. Humankind's path defies all forms of logic and rational reasoning. Chaos, the creator, would be proud, as I am sure He is. I have dispatched Eros, our most experienced Prospector, to confirm the findings of Sidian and his sect. If true, Arm'nbrilt will be designated for resource extraction, and Calisphaer will marshal the resources for a follow-on survey team to precede the absumption contingent. With your continued innovation, wise counsel, and careful attention to available diagnostics and analytics, we will most certainly acquire the provisioning the Inani people need to ensure we see the next Expansion Increment."

****

Humanity. A failed experiment of complex biological life. You may take exception to that assessment. You will most certainly get emotional and defiant as humans always do when confronted with the realization of their weaknesses and imperfections, and the wrongs they are destined to cause. You may protest vehemently as you run down a lengthy list of all of humankind's greatest accomplishments. But in the end, your opinion will not matter . . . in fact, it is negligible to the twentieth decimal place in the math of the universe. In the end, the end will still come, manifested in one of its infinitely possible forms. The true irony: it will be humankind's inability to see the big picture and understand the exceedingly small, but important part your species plays within the All which ultimately sets the conditions for your fall. Furthermore, it is your impulsiveness, greed, and propensity to self-serve that will make up the colors of your palette . . . for you—*YOU*—will paint the self-portrait of your own destruction!

However, do not lament your fate. It is important for you to know that by failing miserably to live up to your true potential, you can still serve a greater purpose. At the very least, your world can be a resource which sustains another world and eventually supplies the 'seed' material for new worlds in other galaxies . . . future planets potentially serving as home to lifeforms who do not take the gift of life, the gift of their existence for granted. You can protest and rant and rave. You can attempt to resist, but it will not matter. The cosmic math bears this out, *remember?* When your planet has been chosen for Inani absumption, there is nothing you can do to stop it. So, relax and enjoy what time your species—your world—has left . . . *isn't that what you have been doing all along?*

Chapter 2

Dirty Sentient Secrets

Humans are something of an enigma. From the perspective of the evolution of biological life on Earth, humans stand in the gap, forming something of a genetic bridge between Low and High Sentients. This, of course, is somewhat misleading since many of the High Sentients have existed on this Earth considerably longer than humans. Among 'Lessers,' humans are mysterious and confusing, presenting erratic behaviors and proclivities which produce both respect and fear. The High Sentients are both confounded and frustrated by their strange brethren who do not seem to 'belong,' because human beings possess attributes and qualities of both Low and High Sentients. However, the primary vexations with humankind can almost invariably be traced to human emotions, and the extent to which those emotions drive their species' erratic behavior. Thus, fellow 'Highers' find the human species unpredictable and often irrational, evoking both their cynicism and their distrust . . . many among them remain puzzled as to why Earth Mother would create such beings at all.

Did you ever wonder why High Sentients sometimes refer to humans as Lessers? Derogatory . . . Yes . . . likely intentional depending on the source. If they acknowledge humans among their ranks at all, High Sentients will have you believe the human species occupies the lowest rung of the High Sentients on the Hierarchy of Sentience. *Did you ever wonder why humans are the only 'Short-Lived' among the Highers? That doesn't seem right, does it?* In the peculiar case of human beings, things certainly do not add up. Human lives are fractional compared to the other High Sentients—to the elementals, the Guardian Spirits, and the Gifteds.

There are the few and the infrequently encountered among the Highers who might be convinced to divulge their staunch conviction that humans are a mistake—the High Sentients who never should have been . . . those whom Earth Mother never intended. They are simultaneously the Highers who could have been the pride of Earth Mother had they only reached their potential. Bear in mind, there is always the possibility Chaos had injected Himself or His own into the evolutionary mix and genetically catapulted the species forward . . . 'ahead of schedule' by millions of years. Humankind may just be the Destroyer's greatest accomplishment, having accelerated one of Earth Mother's greatest creations—some of Her most intelligent and capable children—to levels of awareness and responsibility they were nowhere near prepared for or ready to manage. A species in this position would be vulnerable and ripe for manipulation, with Chaos Himself waiting there with an entire orchard of forbidden fruit. The Great Deceiver needed an army. Perhaps it is not naturally coincidental the rise of man and his Epoch intersected with Chaos's growing influence on this Earth. This would indeed be the cruelest irony of the perfectly corrupted marriage; one which perpetuated the decline of civility and civilization just as humans were on the cusp of reaching their full potential as a species.

What Earth Mother bestowed upon the human species . . . what She considers the greatest gift She has given to any of Her children are emotions. She instilled within man a boundless capacity for passion and compassion. It is entirely possible the compassionate sentience who is our Living Earth could only conceive of how emotions would allow humans to be the best versions of themselves . . . those magnificent spiritual elements innate to most sentient beings on this world could naturally be purposed only for good. It is possible She did not foresee man's emotions failing to evolve, their consciousnesses remaining ultimately anchored to the same primal instincts which allowed them to survive a primitive world. Instincts which still—to this day—drive man to 'freeze, flight, or fight' when faced with a perceived existential threat. Threats to a human's life translate into the propensity to be selfish and pursue self-serving interests once the evolved, sophisticated, and educated layers of thousands of years' worth of evolution are stripped away to lay bare the prehistoric bones with gnashing teeth and clawing nails. Like the elements, human emotions and feelings all have their diametric opposites: love-hate, joy-sadness, pride-shame, hope-fear, desire-disgust, etc. Powerful energies are conjured in these contested spiritual spaces.

This is the realm in which Chaos the 'ever-present' operates . . . in the cracks, crevices, and fissures buried deep within the metaphysical foundations of a species' existential cornerstones. No ornate facades or any amount of paint can cover up the primal aspects of human nature. The Great Deceiver exploits the quintessential aspects of mankind which allowed them to rise up out of the primordial ooze; enabled humans to become the hunter instead of the hunted; and drove their precipitous rise to the top of the food chain to become the apex species on this planet within a fleeting period of time in relative Earth geologic terms.

When this planet's sentients think of the elements, their first thought is of the four classic elements—earth, water, wind, and fire. The two residing in form—earth and water—together form the basis for biological life on this Earth by cooperating to compose and comprise the Coirea'cen. This precious biome is presided over and protected by Earth and Water Elementals who together with the Guardian Spirits preserve the Natural Order.

Standing in counter-opposition while indirectly supporting the whole are the formless elemental forces of wind and fire; both essential to setting the conditions for life to exist and to be sustained. Fire and wind support earth and water in maintaining the 'life balance' on the planet's surface. Fire promotes life by destroying that which impedes the development of new life while the wind is the essential element of weather needed to carry life-giving water in its varying forms—water, fog, snow, humidity, dew, ice—to the entire world. Wind also erodes the surface to share the riches of the earth and blows heartily to carry and spread the seeds, seed pods, and spores of the Coirea'cen's *Green* so more tracts of planetary surface may experience the natural riches which occur when earth and water brilliantly intersect to produce planetary biodiversity.

It is He, Chaos, who is always seeking to disrupt Earth Mother's elemental balance . . . by corrupting Her children and even going so far as to weaponize wind and fire by mating them with Corrupted elemental sentience. But His most insidious and powerful ability is His mastery over the *Fifth Element* . . . the faculty to manipulate and shape the emotional energies resident within all sentient life to achieve His collective aims. And thanks to the rise of humankind, the Epoch of Man has given Him access to the vast reservoirs of primitive emotions resident within the planet's apex species.

As one of the most passionate forms of life Chaos has ever encountered on any world in the entire universe, humankind has availed itself as one of Chaos's most effective weapons of mass destruction on this or any other world. For not since World War II in Europe has there been such a powerful Corruptive convergence with such catastrophic potential. Only this time, the convergence is occurring on the North American continent. And the Great Deceiver and His *En'Troop-EE*—his army of *Effector Elements*—are as close as they have ever been to starting the unrecoverable destructive descent—the *Great Cascade*—to overwhelm Earth Mother and Her Natural Order's capacity to maintain and restore the balance. Then, only then, will Chaos realize His ultimate goal here on this planet—the *Discordant*.

. . . Ahhh, sweet release . . . once the cycle of catastrophic destruction is underway, Earth will no longer require Chaos's services as creator. He will be freed of his much-loathed responsibilities here on this planet, at least. He can shift his focus to other galaxies and their worlds. After all, he has an entire universe to think about . . .

Butterflies and Lies

From a distance—silhouetted on a rise overlooking a valley—Ithilbor Moonfist appeared more ghost than living being. His pale complexion, long silvery mane of hair, and gaunt lank starkly contrasted with a landscape which could have been mistaken for 'war torn' with the absence of bomb blast damage . . . everything was blackened—no green at all—from horizon to horizon. The once lush rolling hills and valleys of this part of California's wine country had been reduced to cinders, with much of it still smoldering—freshly burned. The Guardian Spirit looked over a torched and wind-blasted landscape which could easily belong to a dead planet for nothing appeared to have survived the devastation, and there was simply not enough left to facilitate recovery. The blackcast, smoky backdrop only further enhanced his ghastly appearance—*the last ghost standing in the wake of a devastation not even ghosts survive.*

The Guardian was grieving—in this time when there was no time for such things—but he could not help himself. For this High Sentient, the tragic aftermath was like looking upon a night sky with no stars. His emotional response was an artifact of the very same powerful extrospective abilities which gave him incredibly enhanced sensory perception . . . a natural perceptory array which was enabled by hardwired connectedness to the *Interconnectedness of the All*. Though he still lived, this ability was also his burden, for it caused him to suffer as all those who were now lost had suffered. He was being made to feel what they felt up until their last breath (or a given species' nonbiological equivalent); that moment when their spirit essence passed from ThisLife—it was a spiritual mass ascension of a most terrible kind. Worse was the regret and obsessive recounting of past events he could no longer change. However, that too was a burden associated with the guilt of surviving . . . it is the living's obligation to remember. And since he was nearly immortal, he was almost assuredly doomed to never forgetting what had transpired . . . a terrible story recounted by the Guardian's observations, survivor accounts, and the last moments the dead experienced as captured within the Ourcelium fiberworks, where all the Natural's histories and knowledge are stored.

Ithilbor was still kneeling . . . what humans would call genuflecting . . . with his right hand inserted into the scorched earth still warm from the firestorm's dragon breath. Concealed within, mycelium fibers of the Ourcelium, which had worked their way up from the insulating, protective layers of soil several feet below the surface, had inserted themselves into Moonfist's fingers and hand . . . hundreds of fibers relaying the final horrors experienced by hundreds of species. He was receiving the culminated accounts of hundreds of thousands of individual sentient beings in the weeks—days—hours—seconds leading up to their untimely passing from ThisLife . . . *all of them, all at once—a gaping wound within the All.* Overlaying the compressed feed of distressing last memories and experiences was the influence of the Ourcelium, regulating the information flow to keep the horrible whole of it from overwhelming the Guardian by distilling all the pain and loss into a single narrative of the lost All speaking as one:

"*Where have all the butterflies gone?* Butterflies 'effected' . . . humankind 'effected' with many among them *turned* to the cause of Chaos as dedicated minions of His Effector Elements. The Earth is infected with virtually every one of Her children affected in some way. Earth Mother's ever-present essence has been driven inward to protect Herself. She is a powerful planetary sentient, but she ultimately responds like any being fighting a grave illness. She must preserve Her vital life-giving essence until Her immune system can respond and fight off this sickness which assails Her. This is the Blighted Earth, and we of the Natural Order fight for Her, our Mother. We must win to preserve and protect the life on this planet—for all life on this planet are the children of Earth Mother. Defeat means losing the only home we have in all the universe. We cannot fail.

"The disappearance of the butterflies was the first indication Chaos's Great Cascade has begun. His much-sought precipitous decline threw open an unseen latch which had been holding His immense engines of disorder and disruption in check. The engine itself is no machine, but a system of systems, processes, beings, and things which all originated on this Earth . . . all subsequently hijacked, subverted, and in some cases, 'recreated' to bring about the Discordant—the permanent state of Chaos wherein the afflicted world's ultimate destruction is inevitable.

"Butterflies are the bellwether beings of Earth Mother's surface world. Their wonderful form of life is to land-based meta'ens what coral reefs are to the oceans. Their vast numbers and biodiversity of species are the first indication of a healthy ecosystem, one unbroken and in balance. These beautiful and delicate creatures are extremely sensitive to the destruction of habitat, changes in the timing of the seasons, and abhorrent weather phenomena. Thus, their decline or absence is a clear sign something is wrong. One does not require a Guardian Spirit's perception or even need to be a High Sentient to be cognizant of such things . . . one need only be a living being open to and connected with their world. Such is the failure of this Epoch's dominant species.

"Without warning, the Sentient Winds came veiled within unseasonal prevailing winds out of the west— ripping and vicious. These winds were deceptive, absent any of the usual warnings of pending storms. Thus, they were able to spring themselves like hunting traps to deny the butterflies the forewarning afforded by their unique sensory perceptors. All the butter- flies caught in the open were shredded. Their colorful skin scales were stripped off like embers sent airborne when the dry forest burns. So many butterflies fell to the wind's wrath their skin scales painted the air. It was as horrible as it was beautiful for a brief time, and the toll was terrible. It was called the 'Rainbow Wind.' Millions succumbed . . . many species lost . . . an extinc- tion event like no other.

"Then suddenly, the raging winds stopped roar- ing, dissipating into the stillness of a lull lasting sev- eral days. This was just long enough for the surviv- ing butterflies to let their guard down and feverishly set themselves once again to their natural role as pol- linators. Much of it was instinctually driven behav- iors. They had fallen woefully behind schedule in their labor of love, having so much to do and far fewer of their kind to do it. The unnaturally long summer of a warming planet confused many species who remained unseasonably active with mating cycles carrying on well into the fall.

"When the wind tempest returned to rage anew, this time it came allied with fire, spewing forth like dragon's breath. The catastrophic pairing of *Corrupted Formless* found the cautious butterflies near the cover of forest and valley, all of which were consumables in the fire's path. When the 'furricane' descended, the sentient formless coupling gave as little forewarning as had its wind predecessor when it first appeared on the West Coast. To most, it came out of nowhere. Like a mad gale set to the torch, the firestorm blew in from the sea. It flash-consumed all in its path . . . its insatiable hunger was only matched in scale by its expansive breadth and colossal size. The *firestorm*—the terrible, new weather phenomenon demanded a new name, for it was the blind hand of Chaos manifested.

"The weaponized elemental forces were indiscriminate and remorseless with no apparent ability or desire to distinguish between friend or foe. En'Troop or Order, it did not matter—it meted out its wrath with equal violent intensity to any and all; for all were just obstructions interfering with its intentions for absolute destruction—*just things in wrath's way*. The forests, valleys, and glades, and all the beings who had taken shelter within them, were incinerated. Only the fastest of wing, paw, and foot or those who could shelter themselves within the dark confines of the Earth were able to escape the steamrolling blast furnace absent form. Notably not among those fleeing were the delicate beings who performed nature's most exquisite work—monarchs, satyrs, sulphurs, swallowtails, fritillaries, red admirals, painted ladies, American ladies . . . their eggs, their pupae, their caterpillars. All of them, in all phases of their lifecycles, were combusted instantly in the ultra-intense blaze, leaving behind not so much as a single speck of ash to mark the passing of a myriad of brilliant species. The death toll was catastrophic, and there is a gaping hole in the world . . ."

The Guardian Spirit winced at the agonizing, immersive experience, which was the Ourcelium's retelling of the catastrophe encompassing multiple, simultaneous extinction-level events ... his instinctive reaction was to pull his hand away—to secure relief from the pain—*so many, so quickly*—but his obligation was to completely experience nature's tragedy in order to fully understand the precipitating courses of events and know the perpetrators of this massed, collective demise:

"... The carnage wrought in so short a time is inconceivable; a frightening indication of destructive scope being prosecuted on a despairing scale even for the High Sentients who have been here on this continent for a long time. Guardian, you have witnessed a great many things and a tremendous amount of change—both good and bad—in your near-immortal ThisLife, but *you-we-the All* could have never comprehended—in our worst imaginings—ever seeing anything like this ... this was something one would wish not to see in any life, nor wish upon any world.

"It is most unfortunate that humanity, this Epoch's dominant species, has set the conditions. Humans, with their inherent predisposition for violence and capacity for destruction, have managed to multiply their inherent ability to produce undesirable outcomes several times over through their technology. Their species has proven themselves more capable than the most ruinous natural disasters ... and sadly, in some cases, the human form of annihilation is even less discriminate than the unbridled forces of nature unleashed. Nearly as impressive as their penchant for tools and technology is the human ability to construct an intricate web of lies to feed their unrighteous personal narratives. Multiplying the deplorable is the use of those stories to deceive others into thinking their cause is just and manipulating victims into joining in on their twisted endeavors. The Great Weaver himself would be proud of such grand webs . . . ones which whip up the masses into wicked fervor. In the grip of these webs of wrongfulness, one group of humans collectively preys on yet another group of humans and any other species, leaving their victims left to discover the misfortune of being a means to unscrupulous human ends. This most despicable phenomenon is unrivaled among any of Earth Mother's other children. Unfortunately, Earth Mother, in designing the Natural Order and creating the Hierarchy of Sentience, never envisioned having to protect Hers—Her children, Her living body, Her world-self—from Her own. *But a Mother should never have to envision such a thing, should She?*

"Here on this besieged continent, these rogue humans whose warped worldview have infected their own homeland like a plague call themselves 'guardians'—guardians of freedom, of democracy, of the US Constitution—but nothing could be further from the truth. They have been co-opted by Chaos, and thus, most are blind . . . unaware of their ill intentions as they wage their perceived war of righteousness while they unwittingly serve His army and do His bidding. They are party to a violent extremist movement which forms His human action arm—a Chaos-led insurgency within the highest levels of the human civilization's governance and security apparatuses. They, the blind, are unable to see it because they are either willing participants among the En'Troop's Effector Elements or so naive as to believe the falsehoods spouted by their Corrupted leaders. They see themselves as guardians, but this troubled continent has only one true Guardian. You . . . you, Ithilbor."

Ithilbor knew this was a 'telling' not a debate forum . . . something on the order of the *Natural Network's* state-of-health assessment combined with root cause analysis . . . but Ithilbor felt the need to address the integrated sentience of the Interconnected All. "All, when I was young, the Cherokee thought me among 'the Little People.' Upon ascending to adulthood, I aided their proud nation in battle when their cause was just. In those times of conflict, the Cherokee people who witnessed my presence called me 'Nunnehi.' The Cherokee people were among the few of humanity who knew my truth . . . their nation understood me for what I truly was—a Guardian Spirit—in the era when they were free and allowed to live their lives how and where they chose . . . in harmony with Earth Mother and Her Coirea'cen. This was a time when their tribal shamans communed regularly with the spirit world, and every member of every village lived in accordance with the laws of the Natural Order. However, we are no longer in such a time, and it is not just the Cherokee people I serve, but all life—both sentient and non-sentient—on the North American continent. My lifespan is centuries . . . my consciousness eternal. So how could I not have anticipated this? What good is a Guardian blind to the entire composition, intentions, and movements of his adversary? In only recognizing the true threat at the advent of its destructive convergence, I am struggling to understand how the Natural Order can even respond to *this . . . THIS NIGHTMARE!*"

The Guardian Spirit's ability to reproach himself was rivaled only by his skill as a warrior. Even the most hardened High Sentient would find it difficult not to despair at the sight of such wide-ranging devastation and not try to find his or her fault in it . . .

"Guardian, some things are just not preemptable. Like any effective insurgency, the insidious construct of the Great Deceiver's schema ensured it could not be seen or perceived until it had matured and gathered enough strength to manifest and act in the open. This menace of many sources was gestated largely within Manmade, outside of natural influence and oversight, and propagated unfettered by human technologies. The Natural Order could have only effectively detected and mitigated the threats if they had elements operating within, and we were just not created or predisposed to operate in such a way. Also, Guardian, understand the Chaotic forces at work are part of a broad-spectrum affliction . . . the protective scheme of the Natural Order has been compromised, and like humanity, we may also have been infiltrated. In this regard, be wary in any actions you may take. Regardless, the fact remains you are the Guardian Spirit for this continent in this Epoch, and you must rally the remnants of the Natural Order to arrest Chaos's Cascade and restore the balance. This is what you were created for!"

Ithilbor removed his hand from the soil, and the mycelium fibers detached themselves naturally and unharmed, quickly retreating to the safety of the deeper earth. The mycelium of the Ourcelium was cognizant of the Guardian's intention to 'disconnect' at the same time Ithilbor knew it and acted. The All was right . . . there was nothing further to commune on, machinate over, or discuss. The High Sentients—the Long-lived who led the Order—just did not perceive time or happenings within the Earthreal in the same way humans and other Short-lived do. Much of what happened to push the continent to the brink transpired within a relatively small increment of time relative to the High Sentient lifespan; one based on the purpose they serve in the Natural Order and not the resilience of their sheath . . .

. . . Ithilbor watched this continent evolve from the once scattered tribes who honored Earth Mother. They took only what

was given and prospered while praising and honoring Her for it. In doing so, a natural balance was maintained through a form of shared humility. Tribal societies, for the most part, aspired to what the Ancient Greeks called "sophrosyne;" an ideal of excellence of character and soundness of mind espousing the attributes of moderation, prudence, temperance, and self-control. Beings who make sophrosyne a life practice willingly abide by the natural laws, because communal discipline guides the consumption of resources at the rate of need, not want. The Guardian looked on as those tribes grew into nations, and with but the exception of minor skirmishes, the land was in harmony . . . the land and all living beings were one.

But alas, it was too good to last . . . the diminishment of the All manifested discreetly at first, riding on the cusp of the unnoticeable until it had gained sufficient momentum, as the insidious are often prone to work. The great transcontinental migration started only as muffled utterings . . . whispers on the wind. Gradually, rumors were confirmed as truths by firsthand accounts from his brother and sister Highers beyond the Great Waters. These "truths" started as a trickle composed of Europe's most adventurous humans and those looking to make name and fortune in a new world. Eventually, the trickle turned into a flow which ultimately gave rise to a torrent when their native lands proved too small to hold them, because their greed and fame-fueled dreams were too big.

European exploration and colonization began the engagements and interactions which became the dramatic intermixing of diverse human cultures and other species who were previously isolated from each other. Greed-driven want could do nothing else but drive conflict in these intermixing's, opening doors for new predators to descend upon virgin grounds that were home to unprepared prey with no defense—the invasive operating unfettered. Much later, the insidious would reveal themselves to be the predator who had befriended his quarry and moved into the nest . . . "the wolves in sheep's clothing" as humans would say.

The Europeans traveled to this continent perched upon large vessels of wood and cloth. They rode on horses of blood and sinew, and eventually their domination machine ushered forth on beasts of iron belching steam and the smoke of a thousand campfires into the clear blue sky. They brought their alien technologies to a free and unspoiled land where the primacy of the Natural Order still held sway . . . where open societies and welcoming beings living in accordance with the way of the Interconnected All made them all too vulnerable to exploitation.

To most indigenous populations who did not know money or currency, the concept of greed was new as well. The marvelous machinations of the visitors from beyond the Big Waters were mesmerizing to the native peoples beholding them for the first time. These wondrous creations of the Manmade were simultaneously capable of producing both great good and destructive outcomes depending on the intent of the hands wielding them. Like their tools and machines, the pale riders were fueled by great determination which oft times powered ill-intended aims bent on manipulating and exploiting the peoples and vast resources of a land still embraced by the purity of Earth Mother's vision for Her world . . . what the White Man would disdainfully call "untamed" and "primitive."

The human foreigners of lofty purpose, armed with strange weapons and dark aims, also carried unseen malignancies within them as they traveled . . . those of greed, hubris, selfishness, corruption, disease, addiction, and other afflictions of conscience, spirit, and biological sheath. These were the invisible forces fueling the desire to ravage the Coirea'cen and its native life. Born of innocence, the continent's sons and daughters were woefully unprepared for the endless waves of foreigners who poured uninvited onto their shores and the insatiable appetites fueling their collective need for more . . . always more! They moved inland toward the heart of the continent . . . at first, afoot, afloat, and carried on hooves; later, on wheels and tracks; and eventually aloft on Manmade wings . . . as unrelenting as a tide without ebb. By the time the visitors were widely perceived for what they were: invaders, the end's beginning had long since come to pass.

At first, the design of foreign infestations manifested as linear cuts in the natural landscape . . . scars of cut wood and iron, and centuries later, as concrete, glass, and plastic. The hard, clean edges and right angles of a European-prescribed order worked against the uneven, unregulated contours of a living world. The intent was to bring the Wild to heel . . . to bend it to humankind's will—the Manmade serving as the New Age's shackles. Viewed from the comfortable conveniences and conveyances of a modern society, nature became the "unnatural," and the "wilderness" was something to be feared, beat back, and controlled. The goal was 'structure' and the remaking of the world to reflect the ambitions and perceptions of colonists as they toiled to recreate the Old World's human domination in the 'new.' And at some point, in this transformation—in what seemed the blink of an eye—Earth Mother turned from being revered provider to unwilling host; a change promulgated by the supernatural 'grip' of one of humanity's other inventions . . . that of religion.

The least problematic aspect of European monotheist belief systems was the concept of one otherworldly god. The real damage was caused by the idea of humans being above all other living things. The idea itself is benign, but the real destructiveness of it lies in the rogue interpretations and ensuing applications. Earth Mother's human children took more than She was able to give, because their priests, pastors, and preachers told them they were created in their god's image, and this world was put there for them. As advances in modern societies continued to find ways to preserve, prolong, and proliferate human life, there was nothing to check the collective appetite for Her natural wealth and resources, which came to exceed the capacities of natural processes and seasons to provide. When these cycles were disrupted and broken, renewal was among the casualties, and the process of decline was compelled to begin. Decline became destiny when humanity came to see the Earth, all Her gifts and beautiful creatures, as things to be taken and owned as if it was one species' birthright.

Ithilbor watched humankind's ascension to assume their place as the Earth's apex species as observed through the lens of the Old World pacifying the New World—the 'most evolved' of the human species dominating their primitive brethren and all lesser living beings. The meteoric rise to the top of the food chain was a worthy achievement for such a Short-lived species, but the manner and means were far from just or fair. Over the centuries of the continent's taming, Moonfist bore witness to man's heroism, kindness, and self-sacrifice in action—acts worthy of admiration, but unfortunately, an uncommon occurrence relative to the great human numbers. For the Guardian, it was unfortunate such feats did not characterize mankind as a whole.

What man would call "modern" and "civilized," Ithilbor would call devolution. Like a star burning out prior to giving the universe its full measure of radiance and warmth, man seemed to have experienced his zenith long before reaching his full potential. Mankind had already passed its culmination point. The species' long, slow death . . . the fade to darkness . . . had begun. It began when they started to see themselves as greater than other life, better than the Wild, and turned their back on living in balance with the Natural. Earth Mother, Her other children, and even fellow human beings were looked upon as things to be subjugated and used, even owned.

The Earth Herself is one of the most remarkable creations in the entire universe. Her abundance of resources and life is a miracle . . . a rare and beautiful oasis in the great universal expanse, but there is an inability among humanity to appreciate and value what has been gifted to them. They are adrift in the middle of the great ocean and have but one life raft, yet they see fit to burn it out from under themselves . . . from underneath all Earth's living beings.

'Invasive' is a word humans themselves use to characterize those species who wreak havoc and destruction when introduced to a non-native ecosystem. With no natural predators to cull their numbers or checks to hold the population within the ecological balance, so-named species proliferate uncontrolled until *the ecosystem becomes unstable and the non-native invaders' appetites exhaust the ecosystem's ability to provide. Within a relatively short period of time, the habitat is no longer able to support any species. For our Earth, mankind was an invasive species. Like the sailing ships of old, the Earth creaked and groaned under the weight of a burden She was never created to bear. The Natural Order's ability to restore and sustain the balance necessary for life to survive and thrive in the Coirea'cen, Earth Mother's continental and oceanic living body, had been compromised in North America. Even if mankind reversed course immediately, put their species' differences aside, and applied their ingenuity and talents solely to solving this problem versus creating more, the escalating path of natural deterioration might still be irreversible.*

Humankind's unwillingness to change was the attribute which caused Ithilbor to harbor so much doubt, but he had never wavered in his belief in the potential and ability of the human species. Still, humankind's development has always been retarded by the species' primitive instincts and baser nature, and thus, the Earth was a swirling 'fish boil' . . . a bait ball surrounded by a ravenous sea of human predators possessing insatiable appetites, personal wants, and selfish desires; wants driving them to dive and slash to feed and feed, bent on consuming everything until there was nothing left but a dead ocean and a husk of a world. To find Moonfist's assessment of the human condition harsh was to ignore the truth when surrounded by the most convincing evidence: the most pristine remaining reaches of wilderness were located in the climates most inhospitable to humans—the Arctic, the Antarctic, the Gobi, the Sahara.

"Global Warming" . . . Ithilbor found the human term amusing, because it was intentionally ambiguous in placing blame. Like a parasite who has proliferated beyond its host's ability to support it, humankind was making the planet sick. Like a feverish child unable to express Herself with words, Earth Mother was communicating to Her children through extreme drought, superstorms, and bomb cyclones; these were the mildest

of tantrums compared to what was yet to come if the apex species maintained their current course. She was asking only for relief from Her discomfort so She may get some desperately needed rest . . . to recover . . . and restore balance in a healthy way. But the navigable path back to the "Once Before" was getting harder to discern, and the journey home was becoming more arduous and challenging with each step taken past the tipping point and no appreciable attempts made to redress or correct. Even just a brief respite to grant a little time to heal and recover appeared beyond humanity's ability to collectively manage. In fact, here in the now, the state of this world was so dire the legendary Ithilbor Moonfist was finding it difficult to perceive any hope . . . anything at all beyond the world on fire!

It was true. The Guardian Spirit's once bright thoughts and demeanor had been darkened by the troubled and delicate state of things for some time—what amounted to a handful of human generations—but within which span, the Epoch of Man had entered its darkest chapter yet. In the estimation of many of the staunchly religious—the self-proclaimed 'true believers'—the apocalyptic prophesies of the Book of Revelation were being realized. As for the Guardian, within the interstitial tissue of his dire contemplations, he had a revelation of his own regarding the potent, inherent duality of this Epoch's dominant species: humankind possessed an amazing, collective ability for innovation which could benefit the All that acted in opposition with a capacity for destruction which could bring about the end of everything. The latter aspect was buried deep in their nature, imbedded in the primal fabric of their genetic makeup.

In many ways, humans were just being what they were, and if they could not change, how could they prevent what was happening and arrest the Great Cascade before it achieved the kind of momentum which would throw the continent into ecological collapse? In the wake of such a dire happening, the accrued dark energies and forces of the doomsday machine would surge in hopes of cresting, becoming unstoppable with entire oceans and continental land mass biomes toppling successively like dominoes in an insidious game where every being was ultimately a loser save for Chaos Himself. Humankind was the hidden scourge within. Having destroyed the natural walls within which they were gestated, man was now the virus proliferating uncontrolled. However, humanity was but one invasive infestation among many ...

The Great Deceiver had capitalized on, and creatively co-opted, an unprecedented conspiracy of convergences where many of the bad seeds randomly planted throughout his disorderly, unkempt garden had grown and come to bloom simultaneously to reveal His vision of apocalyptic revelations to the North American continent. Technology, global Great Power competitions, and political divisiveness manipulated and leveraged by His Force Corrupted were threatening to rend America's—nay, the entire free world's—democratic system of governance apart at the very time environmental disaster was imminent. The pattern within the disorder becomes clear in time—a Long-lived amount of time—but only after one understands there is not a sentient idea, invention, or belief 'off-limits' to Chaos's corrosive intentions.

It had taken Chaos some time, but His human agents had infiltrated every American institution—governments at the federal, state, and local level; the majority of churches, spiritual orders, and professional societies; and even the military. *What was 'time' to one such as Him?* The king of tricksters, ravagers, and savages had timed the launch of his offensive of Corruptive influence to coincide with concerning instability registering across virtually every index, process, and structure which defined human existence. He had warped and manipulated every measure and metric referenced in determining the quality of human lives—economic, environmental, political, religious ... *all of them!*

Even worse, Chaos had added accelerants and flame ignitions in the form of Corrupted High Sentients into this powder keg . . . elemental spirits bent to his will and permanently manifested to Formlessness. Sentient Wind to breathe dark life into His insidious schemes and designs, while also fanning the crimson flames of Sentient Fire whose sole purpose is to see Chaos's will be done. With their vast, disruptive elemental powers in the mix, the universe's greatest agent of creation was fully immersed in the making of destruction incarnate on this world, while still preserving His Formless Column's options to pursue their own deplorable impulsions along the way.

What of Earth and Her natural defenses to mitigate such a Corruption of things and twisted state of being? Unfortunately, humankind's extravagances saw to neutralizing and destabilizing Earth Mother's organic protection mechanisms. The species' selfish pursuits and insatiable appetites had aggravated enduring imbalances to the brink of unrecoverable, while exhausting the Natural's reserves and reservoirs needed to respond to such emergent threats and unsustainable conditions.

Fires now raged across the width and breadth of California as far north as the Pacific Northwest and as far south as Nevada. Nevada fires would rival California's if the state had more to burn. However, you should know that if the fire is hot enough, even the life within brown earth can still be consumed. The winds were the first to arrive . . . fierce winds of legend and fable. The natural seasonal winds generated by the Earth's atmospheric convection were bolstered and whipped into frenzy by Sentient Winds mustered and led by Nilch'i—the most feared and powerful Formless in Chaos's horde. Weaponizing the very air most lifeforms breathe, she has demonstrated large-scale destruction, torment, and death can be an art form, and it is even said she has the ability to harness a being's breath to fan the flames of hatred, fear, and hubris nested within the spirit. Nilch'i and the army of Corrupted Formless under her command were both integral parts of Chaos's multi-strain virus while also serving as powerful vectors in its unmitigated spread.

It was within the domain of the spirit where Chaos had launched his current campaign; one which had gone on to envelop over half of the United States, and thus in turn, shaped Nilch'i's early target sets. The En'Troop-EE's primary line of effort was dominating the contested spaces of emotion and reason within the human consciousness to orchestrate and perpetuate the active lines of effort on the twisted and complex path to the Discordant. The Rainbow Wind was but one discrete artifact of the horrors to come. For Nilch'i, the rending of a host of Earth Mother's delicate species was more symbolic than purposeful . . . the blowing of her dark kiss to the Natural Order. In particular, she desperately needed the elemental, Parim, to know she had not forgotten about him. These were Chaotic times after all, and with her full effort and focus devoted to her deplorable part of her master's campaign, she would not be able to give her immediate attention to her most vexing adversary.

Aye, these were desperate times and the dark horde had all the momentum, but Ithilbor's revelation had provided those special insights of a most potent kind: The Guardian Spirit's role was to lead the Natural Order's response to the infection . . . his was to rally the Coirea'cen's immune system, and Mother had deep reserves of strength remaining with discounted reservoirs residing in the gifted forms of High Sentient beings—fellow Guardian Spirits, the elementals, the Praeditors and Praesteans—they comprised *his* army, and a formidable force of them yet remained. However, the High Sentients under his command did not represent the entirety of the answer. The key ultimately resided somewhere within the chaotic churn of humanity. The apex species was both the *virus* and the *cure* for all which afflicted the Blighted Earth.

****

Some think it started with whispers on the wind, but it was actually more like mutterings. Messages not spoken in complete sentences but scraps of thoughts and themes like the reflected shadow of flickering flame. Yet, they did not fade, lingering in creases, finding claw-holds in rough spots, and crawling back out of the sewers of the conscious mind where bad thoughts are usually dumped and forgotten. These feeling and thought-inducing agents refused to be eradicated—part seedling-part spore—which grew into creeping fungi to firmly establish themselves in uninvited places and coalesce into ideas. They were initially as unassuming and innocuous as a seed which sprouts from a thin crack in the rocks, making you think, "That is amazing. I did not think anything could grow in a place like that?" However, these thoughts and ideas were of a most insidious kind which no one of the right mind would ever want to take root—anywhere—if they were actually cognizant of what it was. But they weren't, and it did . . . eventually growing into alluring messages spawning the kind of mass paranoia, mistrust, and dissent which is highly infectious and can turn into hate-filled movements—the 'fire' of the spiritual realms.

This should seem obvious to everyone, right? But in spite of that, in spite of everything happening to the contrary—and before you even realize what is happening—the pathetic sprout in the rocks you thought about briefly and then dismissed—because you did not give it much of a chance—has now grown into *the many*. Under the cover of darkness and within the shadows of a canopy fashioned from lies, deceit, and the absence of truth, *it* has amassed itself into an army: large, invasive, and prolific. By the time you understand how pervasive and powerful it has become, the opportunity to stop it or blunt its spread is lost—*it is too late!* Like cancer metastasized, it can no longer just be pulled out by the roots as one would a little pathetic 'thing,' because it has grown into 'everything!'

It is only then the full realization hits you: *you can't destroy it without destroying your own world and maybe even yourself in the process.* Then, worse, you go on to rationalize your contributory inaction and apathy by thinking, "I am just one being. What could I have done?" And though you do not comprehend it at the time, you—by doing nothing—allowed it to grow in the first place. However, and very unfortunately, that revelation doesn't come until later . . . if it ever comes at all. Only the living who have the opportunity to experience a complete revolution in the cycle of such happenings have the opportunity to reflect on what has transpired. Starting over and rebuilding is the burden of survivors. It is they who are the teachers of lessons learned too late. Isn't it humans who say, "Those who fail to learn the lessons of history are condemned to repeat them?" . . . and repeat, and Repeat, and REPEAT!

That is how Chaos works . . . He or His own always start small and rely on the inattention and neglect of good sentient beings to fester and spread—or grow, depending on your perspective. *Why?* Because we are all far too busy to pay attention to the *little things*. The little things are for lesser beings to be concerned about. The Lesser Sentients, the bottom feeders who lack our intelligence, drive, and commitment . . . those who do not possess our quality of being and power of spirit are those destined to worry about little things. Within the voids of shadow and apathy, darklings breed like cockroaches within the seams of existence. This is where Chaos's influence grows bigger and proliferates like a virus, because there will always be a ready supply of the weak, the broken, the forgotten, and the disenfranchised to corrupt—those primed to believe His hollow promises and take up His impure cause. They are the very same who heard the whispers on the wind, because they were already looking for a sign in those dark places, lost corners, and forgotten voids where we tell ourselves we will never allow ourselves or anyone we care about to go.

The 'crack dwellers' not only go there, but stay there and set up camp. Furthermore, there is the one and His many—the Great Deceiver Himself and His agents—scattered across the universe like dark seeds on the cosmic winds looking for their crack or hole to take root in, as well as the hosts of recruits they find there.

The crack dwellers all aspire to be the one who grows into something greater—something world changing. Then—*then*, they will draw His notice, curry His favor, and be rewarded.

Chaos and *His Own Here* have been planting their dark seeds and nurturing them for a very long time, with some having been planted very long ago . . . since before recorded time on this planet. And they have been watching and waiting to see if the more recent whispers would birth ideas which would grow into a movement. *Would these be the dark seeds who grow beyond crack sprouts? Would these be the sprouts who grow into something bigger . . . big enough to produce their own dark fruit?* Some 'things' capable of generating a momentum—unassisted and self-perpetuating—and large and powerful enough to cast their influence over others . . . *big enough to produce their own gravity?* Several dark seeds flowering and flourishing at the right time—whispers feeding deceptively powerful ideas capable of corrupting the masses. The crack flowers who have now become the black orchard flourishing and feeding an insidious insurgency launched to exploit and maximize the disorder, instability, and destructive effects of the catastrophic collision of cataclysmic coincidences. Make no mistake: this unmitigated chain of deplorable happenings was no accident . . . *this was wrought!* This was the Corruptive convergence, cultivated and nurtured by Chaos . . . the one His horde had been waiting for to occur on this Earth and within the affairs of men. This was the Epoch of Man, after all . . . and well, we sentients know how humans can be. This species has been unable to shed the genetic wiring of their primitive origins, making them both predictable and yet never failing to surprise when least expected. It was only fitting the influence and impact of humankind should be the catalyst for Chaos's greatest triumph on this world.

It seemed the demise of the butterflies was not the worst of this world's problems . . . it just marked the beginning.

Chapter 3
A Nation Assailed

Ground Fire

The "One-Sixers" . . . when those indicted in the January 6th Capitol riot referred to themselves as such, many—maybe even most—thought "that" was the beginning. However, the US Capitol insurrection was only the latest evolution in a revolution brewing since the American Colonies had wrested themselves free from English tyranny.

Like the many heads of Hydra, their intentions, surrogates, and their asymmetric effects have produced disparate impacts and varied outcomes over time. Ironically, some say entropy is expressed through time itself . . . and within occult circles, what is entropy if not another word for chaos? Chaos's brand of entropy possesses both covert and overt methods, means, and agents, but the raging fire above started as one below . . . it is a kind of insurgency operating more like a tentacled kraken than a task-organized unit. The 'ground fire' has been smoldering many meters below the surface waiting for the right conditions, the right people, and the right time to emerge on the surface. A fire at the very heart of the country . . . everything which made the United States the grand place it was—a beacon of democratic values and a country "for the people by the people"—had been twisted and co-opted to stoke and feed the spiritual fire. This was the land of opportunity, and everyone had equal opportunity to set the nation to the torch.

It does not make sense how something like this could

happen . . . *here* of all places. The place where most humans in the world want to be or the iconic symbol of truth, justice, and fairness they want their own countries to aspire to . . . to emulate. But this—*this* cause, this movement—does not wish or need to make sense to the world . . . it doesn't need to be something "outsiders" can understand. To those who nurtured the embers and tended to the fire burning below the surface since the country became a country, they needed only to do whatever it took to keep the flame alive until the time was right . . . and though attribution has been lost to time and secrecy, Chaos's chosen had proven their willingness to do *anything*.

Subterranean blazes are prevalent where there are pervasive amounts of organic matter in the soil. The right combination of very deep *ground fuel*—all the humans and other sentients who have marginalized themselves and essentially 'gone to ground' comprised the duff and litter and roots and buried logs—the fuel the ground fire needed to sustain itself. Whether by choice or as a result of bad choices, these dregs were, and continue to be, the segregated segment who no longer works within the norms of society. Thus, they are no longer accepted by society. Embittered and downtrodden, they believe they no longer have the same opportunities the rest of the human species all take for granted. Regardless of the ultimate cause for each individual . . . whether it is born out of a stubborn refusal to adapt to the changing times or by self-limiting behaviors and conditions, which manifest in criminal activities, addiction, mental illness, and abhorrent, provocative, and aggressive habits, conduct and behaviors, the result is the same: *They are the kindling for the fire . . . the human fodder for Chaos's army.*

Of course, a grand fire still needs the right conditions . . . drought conditions. Within the diverse landscape of human consciousness, the 'drought' manifests itself as the loss of light within the spirit. The kind resulting in apathy, which keeps one from simple acts of kindness, such as helping a fellow being in need. Though those small acts of service demand nothing more than a little time, a point is reached where the concern and empathy needed to sense the need and act on it have suddenly become too big of an ask. Strangely enough, this sad development corresponds with depravity and violence in society becoming so pervasive its citizens have grown numb to it. Eventually for most, the primary means for addressing all the wrong is to insulate and isolate yourself and your family from it. When the drought of empathy, kindness, and understanding becomes unnaturally protracted and pervasive, we are but shells of who we formerly were. The biological forms housing our spirit essence resemble nothing more than husks. Finally, an unseen barrier is crossed, and though we may not be the marginalized below, we have become nothing more than tinder waiting for the fire to make its way to the surface so we may either live to feed the blaze or be consumed by it.

All the organic material collected underground needs to be carefully prepared over time to create the perfect conditions and composition to support fire. As with such material, many of the same rules apply to living beings. Just because a societal segment of human beings becomes marginalized—and in some cases, categorized as outcasts—does not mean they no longer desire companionship or have the need to 'belong.' They are humans, mostly, and Earth Mother made humans this way so they could survive a primitive world. Humans are pack animals after all.

It is not hard to imagine all the subsurface organic material grouped and packed together. The world thinks them buried—out of sight and out of mind—but the soil surrounding them is loose . . . loose enough to hold oxygen in the spaces between themselves and within the soil surrounding them. These oxygen pockets are intentional, created by the whispers, and without a noticeable transition, they are no longer uncommon and isolated but everywhere. This intimate oxygen supply is needed to keep the combustion going once the fire manifests to flame. In these spaces and pockets is where the voices coalesce into ideas which circulate among the isolated groups relegated to the underground. The wrong ideas in the minds of like-minded people agglomerate into unity, which eventually gains enough gravity to draw others into it. As the right mix of underground volatility grows, spreads, and organizes to grow faster, it waits for the right set of external conditions. If the convergence is well-timed, their combining starts a movement . . . the right kind of combustible mix which sparks the fire . . . and once started, a fire must remain on the move to survive and grow.

It was the advent of the Internet, and more specifically the advent of software and algorithms capable of social engineering within the Internet, which gave the 'underground' a true voice. This voice grew in volume as social engineering technology expanded the air pockets from separated, unheard whispers to a dull roar so the isolated sources of organic material could find each other and begin to gang together . . . to unite. However, given the time to mature and evolve, the invisible engines of change became so much more than unifiers; they became the proliferators of misinformation intended to deceive and manipulate others; the *misrepresentors* of facts designed to subvert perception and understanding; and the Corruptors of individual beliefs and entire belief systems. The convergence mixed all those things together into a volatile concoction which had been deliberately separated by well-constructed human civilizations for good reason—politics, law, business, and religion. These institutions and bodies were meant to be accessible to all but function independently in an open and prosperous society.

Operating and concocting within the pockets within the soil, the Internet supplied the medium which enabled the dark stars to find each other and form Corrupted constellations of the wrong-minded and ill-intended. The web created virtual gathering places where radical ideas were proffered and reinforced until they became the new virtual belief system, which eventually led to gatherings in the Earthreal, which grew and grew and GREW! It constructed sophisticated echo chambers within the digital media which spurned diversity of opinion and ethnicity without openly admitting their intent. While within, they bang away with their own brand of twisted ideology and rhetoric until the vulnerable and lonely are assimilated into their narrow and improperly interpreted worldview. At first, it was only trickles moistening the walls of the dark caves when you needed to "dial up." Once it started "streaming" the trickles became rivers which sought out every nook, cranny, and potential hiding place . . . and this was not just happening in one cave at one time, but several caves everywhere all at once.

Eventually, the rivers drained into oceans of the connected under different hats, names, patches, flags, symbols, institutions, and constructs with a single insidious cause. The recruits were swept up in the currents and tides to become converts who have been taught to see the world through dark filters of Corrupted group think, which had been intentionally manipulated to achieve desired effects. Suddenly, dawn broke on a new day where those who never belonged 'belonged.' Oh, and the outcasts turned 'in-crowd' celebrated and reveled in their newly discovered voice and growing influence—finally—FINALLY—they had become a part of something greater than themselves!

The ideas which resonated and rallied were those that appealed to society's marginalized and disenfranchised . . . ideas that made them all feel special and a part of something special and gave them the purpose they never thought they could have. Then suddenly, *there it was . . . that was it*—the spark was provided! Working within the air spaces and oxygen pockets, the flame smoldered and worked its way through the ground where the lost, misfits, downtrodden, and disowned had been collected and carefully prepared. Its madness consumed all the organic material which had found their place in the below. Gathering, burning, and consuming, the burn started slow . . . plodding and prolonged as most methodical processes are, for careful tending was necessary to ensure maturity on a timeline synchronized with the emergence of the right conditions on the surface. The timing of the emergence was crucial to facilitate a powerful conjoining with the mainstream masses; for the fire had to be strong enough upon springing forth to find all the sources of fuel it needed to grow and burn bright. It yearned to become a beacon so the fuel it desperately needed would come to find the flame!

Unfortunately, conditions were present which contributed to the spread. A drought of kindness, understanding, and empathy had endured for so long the collective light within the spirit of entire civilizations flickered on the verge of being snuffed out by hate, mistrust, and divisiveness. These were wretched states where the good of heart had finally lost the inclination and desire to right wrongs . . . conditions where the concept of civility was lost and the ability to give, to share, and compromise for the good of the many was severely compromised and corrupted, and possibly irrevocably damaged or even lost for good. This 'land of plenty' now had a dearth of empathy; the common supply had been eroded so badly it was no longer viable for cultivation within future generations, and the youth of new generations had grown up within the decline of it. The state of things was such that even those who knew the ground fire was burning and had the ability to do something stood idly by as it smoldered and waited for its emergence. They did nothing until the fire revealed itself to ravage the surface, but by the time the convergence emerged, there was so much more oxygen and so much more to burn— only then did they finally act: *They were the first to run!*

How do the marginalized and disenfranchised agglomerate and promulgate? Like any pack, this is a cooperative partnership established on a foundation of shared interest and common ground. However, the basis for teaming and community groupings necessary to change an entire way of life or country operates on a much larger scale in terms of numbers, but the pack mentality remains the same. Though they seemed spawned of many sources, they all identified as the "Sixers" now. In their own unique way, it was their way to be more "inclusive" and build on their exclusive movement. *Are you still having trouble seeing it?* You should always look for the common threads running through the seemingly random patterning. The beings who comprise the threads are those you can trace to the pivotal occurrences in the places where yours and everyone else's *everything gets 'knotted up'* . . .

It was the "1776er's" if American independence from English tyranny was your ancestors' thing. With one important caveat: the 'Founding Fathers' were all white men, so it naturally follows they are who the country should be all about . . . they are who God put this country on Earth for. Any other utopian ideals and visions of the future diverging from this divine end state is blasphemy.

It was the "1836er's" if you just needed a good historical excuse to justify your hate for Mexicans or any other indigenous people of color you wanted to blame your hard-won misfortunes on. What better symbolism than the Texas battle to the last man at the Alamo during the state's war for independence from Mexico. It was their sworn duty to continue the purge that Cortez had started. Again, white men battling at great odds against the forces of oppression . . . there is a theme emerging here.

Did you ever wonder why people say bad things come in "threes?" Well, there are three "K's" in KKK. The Klansmen are the cockroaches who roam free and unfettered when the lights are turned off. And historically, the KKK had risen in three waves in reaction to major threats to US white supremacy: the first in the late 1860s in response to the protections and rights granted to Black Americans in a post-Civil War Reconstruction-era

South; the second in opposition to massive waves of immigrants in the 1920s following World War I; and the third to counter the Civil Rights Movement in the 1960s. The first two words of the Ku Klux Klan were derived from the Greek word "kyklos," meaning circle . . . and does the number 'six' not have a circle? And does the number itself not look like a noose? The fourth reactionary wave of the KKK had begun in 2016, and their numbers swelled like a crimson tide until their membership far surpassed their historical peak of over four million members in the 1920s. With their inclusive mission of hate which included Black Americans, Jews, Communists, LGTBQ, and immigrants among their many shared sentiments, the KKK's alliance with the Sixers was a perfect marriage. The Klan had been lying in wait since 1865 to take up arms in overt warfare and finally and definitively win their Corrupted cause. It seems bad things now manifest in "fours."

And of course, let's not forget the January 6th, 2021 insurrection at the United States Capitol perpetrated by the "One-Sixers." Trump sycophants deceived and manipulated by the "Big Lie" of a presidential election stolen by the country's liberal establishment. They called on all radicalized elements of the conservative right wing to rise up and redress the great wrong before the democracy's electoral process could finalize the greatest injustice of their time. The sad irony was many among the mob truly believed they were saving the republic's democratic process, but they were actually enabling the deterioration and possibly even the destruction of it! It was a natural consequence of the long-term drought afflicting an entire nation's collective spirit.

However, it takes more than mutual interests and shared hobbies to spawn something like the Capitol Insurrection—it takes mass radicalization. Radicalization is an interesting term. The word at once brings to mind the Middle East and Islam, and transnational organizations like ISIS, HAMAS, Hezbollah, and al-Qaida. However, that is an American perspective … that region of Asia and Muslims do not have a corner on the "violent extremist" market as much as some might want you to believe. In recent times, the United States has spawned more than their fair share of homegrown terrorists and lone-wolf mass murderers fueled by the most potent mix of individual freedoms, unfettered gun access, and broadband-enabled social engineering influence on the entire planet.

Radicalization is a process, and in most cases, it is a process which takes some time to fully realize the potential of its Corrupted converts. However, it is still an equation with a relatively simple formula: a cause which rallies many lost souls to it by satisfying the need to belong while serving a presumably righteous purpose greater than oneself; a sizable population of disenfranchised military-aged citizens; and an adaptation-averse ignorance among the manipulated horde driving a strong need to change the world into one where their kind no longer needs to change. Their newfound purpose is to transform the world into one where they have not fallen out of favor; one in which they are important, they are heard, and they have a future. That is how the process of radicalization works … that is how the citizens of a once proud and unified democratic republic are convinced to carve it up … shear off pieces of it, which they can in turn hammer and pound into their own warped, mutual self-image. When *that* happens, the 'Fractured State' makes the leap from a madman's fantasy to the normalized dream of the masses.

So, what lights off the ground fire? Simple: mistrust . . . either the justifiable kind or falsely perceived variety—or a potent combination of both. Mistrust of a most irreconcilable and irrational kind mainlined into the bloodstream of the vulnerable masses. Pivotal and impactful events—both the intentionally planned and the usefully coincidental—justify the mistrust among the hypervigilant already looking for signs.

The prophetic happenings proliferate and aggravate the growing paranoia in a civilization whose immune response is already knocked down by paralyzed and ineffective governance and further exacerbated by undermined and corrupted institutions. The instability becomes hungry and ravenous, fed by the mighty flues of 'trusted' leaders spouting expertly crafted propaganda designed to incite and carrying out targeted campaigns of disinformation and fake news; all of it fanning the flames of a radicalized army whipped to battle fervor. Gathered and bristling, the horde is just waiting for a final trigger event, which could be anything or nothing . . . because they are hammers looking for nails . . . they just need a reason—even an imaginary one.

Aye, 'reason' is just another casualty of the ground fire. The reason and rationale, which the rule of law and civility depend on, are lost in senseless arguments as the metaphysical pushing and shoving grows from pockets inside communities to entire cities, then whole states, followed by infected regions, and culminating in entire countries of unrest. Thus, before you know what is really happening, no one is interested in what you have to say except for your answer to one question: *Whose side are you on?* By then, the state of things has deteriorated to such a point your life may depend on the answer just as your political and religious choices now do. Overnight, the pathetic, little thing clinging to life in the cracks . . . *you remember, the crack sprout which gave you only a slight pause, because you did not give it much of a chance?* Well, it is a full grown 'thing' now, and no longer one thing, but many—it is a fucking jungle! A jungle that wants to burn when the ground fire finally surfaces. The ground fire red hot, burning, and yearning to join with a volatile world . . . the last thing this jungle needed was a match let alone an entire ground fire erupting from underneath it. By this point, any remaining rational actors are just unwilling fuel . . .

Perfect Storm

What does "perfect storm" mean to you? . . . 'a particularly violent storm arising from a rare combination of adverse meteorological factors.' Yes, true, but that is not an adequate descriptor for what is going on.

How about 'a particularly bad state of affairs, arising from a number of negative and unpredictable factors?' This definition is closer to the mark . . . a much more comprehensive description, but you cannot lose the meteorological inclusion, because that is important too.

I would assert the perfect storm is still something more, because it is a storm coupling spiritual and elemental forces with natural power. It is a storm in the affairs of humankind and among the other sentient beings of this Earth who have the power to bring a country, a geographic hemisphere, or even the majority of the planet down on its knees . . . or whatever a given species' equivalent of 'knees' happens to be. And it is a storm which rages with a fury extending beyond this physical realm—the Earthreal—while also being capable of drawing on forces from, and creating adverse effects in, the purely spiritual spheres as well. *That* is the perfect storm. *That* was what Chaos was able to create here on this Earth.

This kind of perfect storm just does not happen on its own. It is neither a random happening nor a product of chance. It must be nurtured clandestinely and not fully revealed until it is mature and strong and ready for the world to witness what it can do. When completely manifested—when finally revealed—it is unstoppable and world changing—the powerful accumulated culmination of many lesser happenings and events. The storm's destructive power builds on itself like an avalanche, while also having a structure to it . . . much like a spider's web. There is purposefulness within its insidious design. For like a spider web's architecture, the interconnects within the mesh of it all are rarely linear . . . not straight-lined or point-to-point . . . the genius of its complexity is the seeming randomness of it. Almost indiscernible among the environmental clutter in its messiness, the web is allowed to hide in plain sight without compromising its surprising strength.

There is a similar intention and genius to the perfect storm's construction, making the final outcome extremely hard to predict in its entirety and finality. Though counterintuitive, the incongruence and irregularity does not make the web any less strong nor any less effective in catching its prey with the same holding true for the storm. The lack of clean lines and defined boundaries does not make the storm any less powerful or destructively ineffective. Deceptively, it may appear quite the opposite to many, or even most, who are cognizant of its existence. To a considerable extent, the storm's perfection lies within the inability to identify all of the contributing sources or quantify the indeterminate limits of it. Further, that which defies definition is difficult to craft countermeasures for and exceedingly difficult, even impossible, to mitigate or defeat. *How do you plan against something whose only plan is to take anything it can get?*

And so it was that when the right mix of Chaotic conditions was present, the concoction roiling, and the toxic pot boiling over, the perfect storm unleashed itself upon an unprepared nation. Most of the population did not realize such a storm was even possible if they recognized it for what it was at all, and the remainder were in disbelief the storm actually manifested even if they knew it could. So, the proud nation went down like an over-confident prize fighter in the first minute of the first round . . . leveled by the wild haymaker they all should have seen coming and could have easily fended off if they did . . . but the first ingredient to an effective defense is understanding and acknowledging the threat.

January 6th. *How?* There was one sentient who was not surprised. The consummate puppet-master, Chaos had been pulling and manipulating the strings of everything influenceable for some time to bring this pivotal act to its climax . . .

and it was despicably magnificent. At a certain point, all the orchestration, acts, and actors in His play had developed a momentum of their own. The crescendo was brilliant with the created convergence of forces and beings, coupled with humans and their emotions. All of that sentient energy having been driven together by suggestion, deception, contrived purpose, and asymmetric influence was the massed equivalent of fighting roosters being jammed in a small pen. To Him, some of this was about sport . . . He just wanted to bring his play to a point where the ending started to write itself. *What was the point if He couldn't have fun?* And the director was pleased with the unharmonious, misdirected attributes of His finest work, because one could not have wished for a better venue. What a glorious scrum it was on the hallowed grounds and within the historic confines of the United States Capitol. In the final accounting, the 'insurrection' was not a terribly deadly or physically destructive affair, but it was symbolically priceless—the kind of thing which rips the heart out of the spirit of a nation and continues to kick while it's down. "The people storming the 'People's House.'" Now that is a bumper sticker that grabs the attention!

The President of the United States *who should not have been* was whipping up his sycophants into a frenzy to lay siege to the Capitol and keep Congress from certifying the election. Trump concluding his speech on the Ellipse, telling his tens of thousands of supporters, "So, let's walk down Pennsylvania Avenue." Averse to physical risk but not the attention, Trump gave his order to the bristling horde and ducked out . . . spirited away by the Secret Service in his armored limo. Trump's departure transpired unnoticed by the surging rabble who assumed they would see their leader appearing among them on the grounds and steps of the country's seat of federal governance. Besides, they had not traveled to the District of Columbia from virtually every state and formed a mob to sit idle and not perpetrate the deed they had all been talking and 'chatting' about across cell, radio, and digital media for months. By this point, there was too much malignant momentum. To remain peaceful and let a lengthy list of egregious wrongs go unavenged would be unacceptable. *This—them—they* were the message; one that needed to be written in the pages of wanton destruction and signed in blood. *Is that not what patriots do?*

They descended on the Capitol grounds like an avalanche which refused to be confined to one side of the mountain. Formidable and heavy and unconstrained, the legal consequences of their actions were no longer strong enough to hold them back. The accumulated aggrieved and angry were seething en masse. Collectively, the mob was a toolbox filled to the brim with hammers and clubs and all manner of blunt Instruments. Every single one of them refused to be boxed up and were looking to get their blows in against national leaders and institutions who they perceived had put them in their box in the first place. To a being, all those gathered needed a target for their pent-up aggression, and their beloved President had identified it for them. They easily overwhelmed the perimeter security elements manned by their fellow Americans: dedicated civil servants who were all now just obstacles to progress and horribly under-compensated for what they were being asked to do. In serving to the standards of their professional oaths, they stood between the self-perceived patriots and America being great again. As cogs in the apparatus of an ill-begotten regime, the Capitol police had involuntarily become part of the Corrupted hype machine. Things become so much easier when the humans on the opposing side have been completely dehumanized. The Sixers breached the building and poured in like a black water flood.

Inside, it was like a cattle roundup in the corral where all the animals knew it was the final trip to the market. Hundreds pressing in on each other at multiple points in the closest of quarters—thousands of pounds of human shoving, pushing, surging, and shouting in one infuriated, misinformed wave of hate and discontent. The Chaotic crush of Biologicals within America's hallowed halls of governance, structure, and order—the home of the country's lawmakers and purse string holders—surged forward in a wave of disrespectful violation . . . an exemplar of Chaos's command of the Fifth Element.

Chaos, Himself, cannot directly affect this Earth, or any world, despite the vast power at His disposal. The king of violent asymmetry, He always has to work through others—the denizens of the planet—to achieve His insidious ends. He must deceive, manipulate, coerce, and corrupt the sentient beings of this world to serve as surrogates in achieving his designs. He can alter and transform sentience, but He cannot create living beings Himself. Ultimately, He has to convince us to do it to ourselves, which is what makes results like this so utterly satisfying to the Great Deceiver.

Oh, America, how the mighty beacon of freedom and democracy has fallen, but then again, how long can anything really last when attacked from within and without . . . assailed by both fire and storm.

****

<u>Present day</u>: You take note of a highway sign at the Texas State Line:

Welcome to
the Great State of
Wr~~T~~exus

The strange thing is the re-messaging born of obvious vandalism is not strange to you, because it is, by far, the least important of the millions of things you have seen 'defaced' over the preceding months. In this part of the country, individual freedoms have been all but erased. Still, even with the personal stress you are experiencing, you can't help but appreciate the boldness of the perpetrators; especially now, when it could mean imprisonment or worse. In spite of everything, you still find the sick irony of the rebranded welcome sign strangely humorous . . . and it has been some time since you have had a good laugh.

However, your private 'chuckle fest' is short-lived as your sense of sight alerts you to the landscape's abrupt transition to the overtly militant . . . armed checkpoints at intersections, signs announcing curfews, citizens armed to the teeth, and "stink-eyes" burning through you from every corner of every small town you pass through. You are jerked out of your brief comedic respite and snapped back to the *now* with the potent re-realization you are taking your life into your hands just by being here. Texans don't take kindly to outsiders . . . "foreigners" in their country. About the only thing which could make matters worse for you is being some sort of non-Christian unbeliever. *Oh, you're a Druid!*

Well, there's a special kind of hell for pagans like you. The Lone Star Nation will take care of the likes of your ilk, and God will take care of you in the next. *How did things ever get this way?* Let us review some significant happenings of very recent American history . . .

. . . Tensions had been rising for over a year since the January 6th, 2021 Insurrection at the US Capitol when the right alignment of events and circumstances reached a tipping point. The country had never been more divided, and the state of affairs within the national body politic had never been more divisive. The COVID-19 pandemic was still raging with new increasingly more contagious variants turning out much faster than a mistrustful population's frustrated attempts to achieve herd immunity via immunizations. In addition to the virus's effectiveness as a debilitation agent and killer, COVID was even more potent

in fostering an inner rage within American citizens sequestered in government-directed isolation—a deep-seated, burning anger which needed a target . . . something akin to a 'ground fire' of the soul. The cavalier and ignorant attitudes of their neighbors and fellow Americans who ignored health and safety protocols and lived recklessly in a time calling—nay, shouting—for concern, prudence, and caution lit a signal fire to the pragmatic elements of the population bright enough to command the attention. Meanwhile, counter blazes were lit by the selfish and short-sighted, who through a frustrating combination of undesirable actions and inaction extended the lockdown and worsened the collective misery and suffering of the nation. The gathering of such fires drew the ire of the entire horde until the many-sourced blazes finally joined to become one giant inferno.

The government's attempts to mitigate the impacts and keep people safe only incentivized unemployment and increased collective boredom. This, in turn, pushed the masses deeper into their internet-constructed echo chambers filled with fake news and disinformation tailored specifically to their political tastes and ideological ideations . . . the posted views and content masqueraded as credible, unbiased, and objective, but was anything but. However, the messaging was consistently effective in reinforcing views and espousing ideologies which pitted Americans against each other. Eventually, the negative reinforcement and cognitive pummeling moved the nation from one of ideas and conversations to arguments, rude encounters, pushing, shoving, and hurting others. As it escalated, people felt like they had to pick sides, which is what happens right before the war starts.

All the while, the provocative information just kept streaming; feeding a beast who was growing by encouraging ever poorer choices and reinforcing more undesirable behaviors to accelerate the downward spiral of the American psyche. All of it was disgraceful by any standard, but most couldn't see it because they were too caught up in it. The collective blindness and behaviors were highly desired by Chaos. The entire lot stewed in toxic juices with custom recipes which varied by region, background, public standing, financial security, and ethnicity, but the deplorable byproducts were surprisingly homogenous: long-buried hatreds were reignited, and traditional biases boiled over as hedonism soared to new levels in a population held captive by the global pandemic . . . the resulting bow wave of online delivery orders blew up a global supply chain made fragile by COVID impacts and related underemployment. And through it all, the divide between the haves and the have-nots widened from a rift into a chasm—giving the disenfranchised and marginalized even more reasons to envy and hate. These negative feelings gave the enviers and haters cause to unify and conspire and plan to act in collectively insidious ways. In fact, the Corrupted Convergence took great care to incorporate all the seven deadly sins into all aspects of existence—and for a time, the 'American way' and the 'way of Chaos' were completely aligned . . . inseparable and indistinguishable.

The insurrectionists—the Oath Keepers and other militia leadership among them—were systematically rounded up by federal investigators, indicted, and prosecuted to the fullest extent of law following the Capitol riot. Modern technology and the perpetrators' narcissistic tendencies made law enforcement's task onerous, but not insurmountable, as the FBI methodically tracked down and went on to charge the insurrectionists; their involvement was identified post-incident through social media accounts, officer body camera recordings, building security footage, and reports called into tip-lines. The US Attorney General had made the dogged pursuit of the insurrectionists a very public one, adamant the Justice Department would remain committed to holding all January 6th insurrectionists, at any level, accountable no matter how long it took.

The slow pace of legal progress did little to appease legislators who needed quick results to get reelected, but the AG's rhetoric did very much to fan the revolutionary flames which continued their subterranean burn among the violent extremists and their following. The hardline stance of America's top lawyer ended up having the egregious, though unintended effects of a paranoid firebomb among the ignorant and mentally unstable within the horde. Worse, the ensuing churn gave the extreme right's propaganda machine plenty of nuggets to wrap up in pretty packages of 'fake news' gold. The media moguls and outlets of the conservative right wing were brilliant in taking chicken shit narratives and turning them into chicken salad. They fed it to the marginalized segments of the US population who were hungry and anxiously waiting for it, and in doing so, created the next mob-in-waiting. Reality was so bland, and fantasy tasted so much better.

Mistrust of the Democrat-run federal administration was naturally at an all-time high among right-wing militant groups in the US, and thanks to a powerful disinformation engine which never stopped, never seemed to idle, and was always in overdrive, the majority of America's conservative-leaning population from all walks of life still believed Biden was not legally elected.

The Federal investigative efforts involving January 6th dragged on despite a growing public opinion, indicating the Justice Department's efforts were viewed as a corrupt government's reprisal against the righteous. Over 725 people were arrested in nearly all fifty states and the District of Columbia, and sixty-three of the cabal's insurgents were rolled up in Texas. Texas, as the right-wing 'center of gravity,' was not surprising to anyone as the state had become a hotbed of violent extremist activity in the year following the Capitol riot. In fact, their state's high representative proportion among the rioters was touted as a badge of honor, giving Texas bragging rights among the dissident elements of the population. When the first of the "63" were rounded up and formally indicted, the remaining sixty chose to forgo the tainted and corrupt judicial process and would go on to form the leadership cadre of the Sixers. They refused to accept court decisions from an illegitimate government, which was met with the unanimous approval and thunderous applause from the conservative right-wing world. The Sixer's leadership took the national law enforcement apparatus's campaign against them and theirs as the sign continued resistance via legal avenues was futile since they no longer had an ally in the White House. From there, they took the movement underground, and once there, did their part to tend to the ground fire burning. The "63" became the symbol the extreme right desperately needed to stoke the long smoldering blaze . . . something the downtrodden of the new order really needed to rally around as the radical left-wing feds were trying to root them out and bring them down!

Further, nineteen of those charged in the Capitol riot were North Texans; the 'Panhandle' boasted the largest number of perpetrators per capita of any place in the country. Hailing from the little big towns of a region which despised outsiders, the nineteen all knew each other, and the connected always seem to compose the "core" of any viable insurgency . . . they, the Sixers' newly anointed heirs to the underground kingdom, were the ground fire's tenders, charged with keeping it burning until it was big enough to reduce the old regime to ash so a greater nation could rise up in its place.

Now hot enough to produce hot embers, Corrupted winds carried ignition sources to the parts of the nation most afflicted by the spiritual drought. Surface fires manifested in orchestrated racist violence by right-wing extremists. Yet another unfortunate outcome in the months following the contested election and the siege of the US Capitol, these hate-inspired acts of violence ranked high among the key contributors in the collective escalation and mobilization of conflicting factions. In the riot's aftermath, the nationwide movement provided even more dark energy to the right-wing extremist engine working in overdrive to bring about an insidious end state in America. Mass shootings grew in both scale and frequency against minorities and people of color in response to their efforts to exercise their rights to protest peacefully; all of them mobilized in this pivotal time in America's history in hopes of using the positive political environment afforded by the current presidential administration. The leaders of these righteous movements hoped to leverage the popular support offered by the tumultuous times to build a better future for themselves and successive generations, but in many ways, they were serving the Corrupted cause by 'gathering the wood' needed for much larger blazes. Concurrently, Asian Americans and immigrants alike served as blame targets for the "China virus" while people of color bore their own bloody brunt from the existing establishment trying to maintain rule of law after being drawn into violent encounters by white nationalist counter protestors.

Despite the growing personal risks, many citizens were still spurred to action by the surprising political headway being made in many states, and they continued to bolster the ranks of mass protests in support of the Black Lives Matter movement, among others. With their passage led by liberal Congressmen and Senators, several minority-favorable bills were signed into law in response to the wave of popular support; these resounding political successes only served to increase the urgency to act among the right-wing extremists by actively undermining the political headway of these well-organized minority groups. Likewise, the escalating violence also had its influencing effects in finally compelling enough bipartisan support among lawmakers to take affirmative steps toward gun control: historic legislation which only served to infuriate gun rights advocates and the conservatives.

The passage of more restrictive gun laws led to the unprecedented stockpiling of weapons and ammunition by violent *extremists; some doing so under the veil of the Second Amendment with most abandoning the frustrations of more restrictive legal channels to procure their arms via illegal sources and means. Right-wing groups viewed the liberal administration's actions as unconstitutional; their core membership still certain and an increasing number of fringe elements convinced it was the work of an authoritarian regime installed by the perpetrators of a stolen election. The liberal left was 'boxing in' the true American citizens, and in response, these groups transitioned from protests and demonstrations to preparations for war. It was obvious their government could no longer be trusted to act in their best interests. The time had come for them to fight for their way of life and survival.*

Texas was a powder keg ripe for crisis. Texas Congressmen and Senators continued to employ divisive discourse and misinformation to undermine the reigning political establishment. Militia group numbers swelled to all-time highs as disenfranchised military-aged citizens looked to join causes aligned with their extreme and distorted views. Like roving packs of wild dogs looking for vulnerable prey to swarm with their superior numbers, opportunistic elements of extremist groups exploited the inherent opportunities within the tsunami of disorder sweeping across the country. Several independent militia groups vied for local, or even regional supremacy, but they all ultimately allied themselves to the Sixers' cause. To their credit, the Sixers were more than just well organized; they rapidly surmounted all other like groups in terms of overall numbers, charismatic leadership, government ties and influence, technical capacity, and armament. They emerged as the apex predators among the roving packs simultaneous with the institutions of governance and established rule of law proving ineffective to contain their burgeoning numbers.

Eventually, all the militia groups and the right-wing extremist organizations in Texas swore allegiance to the

Sixers, further swelling their ranks and adding their means, resources, and firepower to the cause. Conspiracy theories abounded and a race war was coming as the current presidential administration worked to address systemic racism and police reform. BLM protests were persistently and aggressively counter protested by right-wing militant organizations whose sole purpose was to fuel unrest and generate the violence needed to undermine peaceful reformation and lawful efforts to advance civil rights.

Imbedded within the extremists, Chaos's agents infiltrated key leadership positions in Texas's state government, National Guard, law enforcement authorities, and militia groups, while also establishing themselves in positions of influence and authority within governments and militaries of foreign countries hostile to the United States. Manipulated into doing so by Chaos's En'Troops, China and Russia conspired to further enflame the situation through cyber warfare, employing internet bots and disinformation campaigns to aggravate the instability even more. Both authoritarian states' abilities to exploit the United States' tenuous situation in the cyber domain should have surprised no one based solely on per capita investment which directly correlated to a relative superiority over the comparable US capabilities: Less than three percent of the US military force structure was dedicated to the cyber mission whereas China's was six times that of the US and Russia's was almost twice that of China's. Despite its reputation for waging technical warfare, America was woefully behind in the twenty-first century cyber capabilities which matter the most when they were most needed.

Despite the dramatic disparity in relative capabilities, the US Department of Defense was still surprised by the gross disadvantage their rivals held over them in warfare's newest operating domain when the full virtual weight of their primary adversaries' weaponized might was thrown against them. The United States had grown complacent in their many decades of technical superiority on the conventional battlefield.

Moreover, America herself was distracted . . . a democracy stumbling around with blinders, too busy looking inward to see what was happening all around her. A powerful, modern country which was straining to peer through dingy myopic lenses now completely clouded over by a total preoccupation with her own internal affairs and rendered abhorrently near-sighted by misdirected anger over the shitty situation her population found themselves in. By this point, any issue or problem—no matter how benign—was another reason to point fingers, pin blame, and even justify a beatdown . . . because everybody's personal problems were 'everyone else's' fault. Unfortunately, it was the apple's rotten core—chock full of bad seeds like the Sixers and their ilk—who were angry enough to take real action. They were prepared to tear the whole bloody orchard out by its roots to make way for a place of their own—the land of the selectively free and the home of the depraved.

Meanwhile, like the consummate predators they were, Russia and China operated with impunity and complete freedom of maneuver within the unrestricted and unregulated cyberspaces pulsing and flowing within the borders of the freest country on Earth while exploiting all other domains of surrogate warfare formerly exercised only by criminal enterprises. When it peaked, America was drowning in a tidal surge of discontent as the hostile world powers culminated their asymmetric hybrid campaign with a critical infrastructure attack, which among other things, took down the Texas power grid by design. America had always had a reputation for bringing people together, and the faltering nation's enemies were firmly united in seeing the most powerful democratic republic on the planet fall . . . and with her, the primary check on the influence and power of their authoritarian regimes.

The same underlying causes which had led to the Texas power grid failure in February 2021 had never been addressed. Corrective actions relied on weaning Texas off its disproportionate dependence on natural gas, which was politically unpopular in the Republican-led state. Why? Doing so meant Texans themselves would have to bear the financial burden of upgrading their infrastructure through renewable sources and expanded use of nuclear power to make the grid more resilient. So, despite the hardships many Texans had endured during a power grid crisis amid a deep freeze, infrastructure improvements ultimately generated nothing more than "talk," because the vast majority of Texans were in violent agreement: upgrades were necessary but none of them wanted to pay for them. Thus, the demonstrated vulnerability lingered . . . known, yet unresolved . . . making the vulnerability in critical infrastructure a high priority among the defects targeted by Chaos's effectors in Russia and China in the winter of 2022—exploited a little less than a year after the first grid failure.

The same precipitating conditions remained unmitigated in Texas's isolated grid . . . one known to be under stress from a state population once again enduring an unusually lengthy and frigid cold snap. Focused cyberattacks intentionally damaged the power generation and distribution systems, which drove authorities to order utilities to reduce power demand on the system to avoid further damage. Natural gas producers were incapacitated, rendered unable to deliver enough fuel to power plants. This circumstance initiated the insidious cycle which allowed history to repeat itself: because electricity relied on natural gas production and natural gas production relied on electricity, any failure in the loop broke the entire system. With all conditions met, the unfortunate circumstances of February 2021 forcefully repeated themselves to fell the final "wall" holding back total chaos, because all the frothing pockets of Chaos's horde had an unobstructed view of each other now . . . and were able to unite!

With the robust, bot-enabled internet misinformation campaign fueling the narrative, militia groups and right-wing Texas leadership themselves believed and pushed the inciteful *messaging that the ensuing blackout was the work of the US federal government. Paranoia and rumor were already rampant about a pending attack, so the blackout was obviously a precursor ... most certainly shaping operations for a planned invasion of their beloved state. This, of course, would be followed closely by a US government takeover and implementation of martial law. Thus, the blackout was their call to arms, and having formulated plans of their own, the insurgency moved out quickly and overtly—the ground fire now burned prominently on the surface. Sixers operators, allies, and infiltrators executed a coordinated terror campaign and a successful coup d'état to take over Texas, quickly consolidating their gains and positions in the wake of their surprise attack. Once they had full control of the state's governance and security apparatus, the insurgents made formal notifications they were seceding from the Union, declaring war, and severing formal ties with the US government. Texas was the flashpoint and spiritual center of the human side of His campaign ... the fascist boot of 'too many' unified by fear and hate. The Sixers' heel was now firmly on the throat of one of the largest, richest states in what had once been regarded as one of the most enlightened countries in human history.*

The aftermath was as unfortunate as it was unpredictable. The US government's ability to respond to Texas's secession was completely stymied by several national-level crises erupting simultaneously ... all of them led, coordinated, and to a significant extent, enabled by Chaos's agents—mostly humans augmented by a handful of powerful High Sentients. And His Corrupted Formless functioned as the primary precipitators of the catastrophic accidents and natural disasters ignited in rapid succession with the insidious efficiency of a weaponized nuclear chain reaction. Worse, the sad truth was, a continent-wide catastrophe didn't take much to trigger: the disaster space had already been prepared by decades of environmental destruction and mismanagement associated with unrestricted human population growth and the corresponding surge of the Manmade, which had degraded, partitioned, and weakened the Natural. This was the spiritless beast built by industrialization and underwritten by capitalism that was consuming and expanding like an unseen plague in the name of the almighty dollar at the natural world's expense.

Coincident with the population explosion of humankind, the Manmade had consumed natural habitat at a frightening rate, throwing the remaining ecosystems out of balance and gobbling up natural resources at an unsustainable rate. Manmade pollution engines belched cancerous filth into the sky and leached a myriad of poisons into the Blue and Green—these were the dangerous and deadly spin-off strains of the virus known as 'human.' Similar to their approach in managing and preserving the environment, humans failed to invest in the proper maintenance of the Manmade as well . . . and Chaos's minions exploited it. The En'Troop targeted the neglected, the deteriorated, the dilapidated, and the forgotten among the Manmade in concert with their focused assaults on the Wild and opportunistic strikes on the abandoned intersections which fall in the seams in between. Without warning, the Formless struck to maximize destructive effects: dams failed, causing mass flooding; trains with extremely hazardous cargoes derailed and burned; world-sustaining crops were wiped out by vesicating winds and guided pestilence; and forest fires engulfed human and animal habitat alike with equal voraciousness, consuming and rendering vast tracts of world uninhabitable as Earth Mother grieved for Her lost children.

Several state governments were attacked and occupied by militia groups as part of a coordinated campaign to ensure there were no effective efforts launched to disrupt or undermine Texas's successful bid for independence. Texas had guaranteed "safe haven" to all militia groups whose actions aided Texas's cause while openly communicating their 'nation's' intentions to serve as a refuge for any groups whose violent attempts to overthrow their state governments failed. The federal government in Washington DC was attacked by right wingers masked under the auspices of peaceful protest. Although all attacks were successfully fended off by the government security apparatus, the victory was a pyrrhic one coming at an exceedingly high cost in blood and resources . . . the Fed's effectiveness was further undermined by sabotage operations perpetrated by extremist elements who had infiltrated their ranks months or even years earlier.

Federal, state, and local governments across the country were under siege by modes and means covering the entire spectrum of destructiveness and ill intent. The multi-pronged onslaught of many sources placed the United States' democratic republic in an indeterminate struggle for survival. Several state governance structures were under severe duress, and their fate remained in doubt. It would later be revealed most militia groups never intended to seize and hold their local governments . . . their efforts were always meant to serve as distractions and divert limited resources away from the main objective: it was always about clearing a path for Texas's freedom from tyranny. Attempts to call up the National Guard to enforce gubernatorial declarations of martial law among the besieged met with various levels of success across the country, but unsurprisingly, it completely failed in Texas, because it was never invoked! The state's entire government was under right-wing extremist control in less than forty-eight hours. Chaos's En'Troop-EE had achieved imperium in imperio!

Outsiders were asking how long Texas could hold out, and Texans had only one response: "Mission accomplished!"

. . . Having reviewed all this, you realize the risk calculus which determined you were safe to transit Texas's provisional national border was woefully off the mark. Yet still, you must go! You have friends and family whose religious practices, political stances, and belief systems place them under extreme threat in the world's newest authoritarian regime. You decide your best course is to press on, keep a low profile, and attempt to blend in until you can link up with and take care of your own: those who no longer have a home here unless they choose to assimilate. That misnomer would be humorous too if this situation wasn't so deadly serious, because 'choice' is indicative of freedom, and personal freedoms are not a hallmark of the Lone Star Nation.

Welcome to the Fractured State!

Chapter 4
The Uprooting

Most people would not consider his 'home' a home at all, but it was home to him. When you had spent years homeless . . . like truly "living-in-the-streets" homeless, it meant a great deal to have something sturdy which actually qualified as a roof over your head. It was a place to rest his weary bones . . . a place where he could get some real rest, because he didn't have to sleep with one eye open. Here, he did not have to worry about someone taking his stuff. Even better, he could come and go as he pleased without having to pack up every belonging he owned in this world for fear it wouldn't be there when he got back. He could leave all his shit right here, and no one would mess with it. It's funny how easy it is to take little things like security and shelter and food for granted until one day . . . *poof* . . . you are the one who wakes up in an alley to discover your entire world has been torn apart. You are left exposed and vulnerable, cold and hungry . . . but you are still alive, so you are one of the lucky ones, right? It is a matter of perspective, and he was very grateful for what he had now, considering where he had been just a few short months ago.

Most people would probably consider his living conditions unsuitable. And "to whom?" would be the first question he would ask anyone who expressed such an opinion—*not suitable for humans? . . . for animals? Are we all not species from the same Mother sharing a world?* The human way of thinking frustrated him . . . sometimes, it even infuriated him. Though it was the accepted way among mainstream humanity, he thought such thinking was out of balance or unbalanced if there really was a difference between the two. Either way, there was a direct correlation between the way humanity looked at their world, and the entire world being imbalanced. All the signs were there if one just took the time to really *see* . . . given one had the ability to see through all the distractions, disruptions, and friction—all the chaos—of modern human life. But, like any 'suitability' determination, it all came down to perception and perspective, and it was not a simple matter of being human or another species. Heck, he was human . . . he just did not perceive the world like a human anymore, and *that* was a good thing.

When a person has been through what he had, the standard by which quality of life is measured tends to be a pretty low bar. From his perspective, the corner he had staked out in the gardener's storage shed was actually pretty nice. It was a great deal for a guy used to getting the raw end of one. The "unwritten" contract by which he was able to keep these living arrangements was fairly straightforward: *keep quiet, keep a low profile, and keep the grounds looking nice.* The *first* part was easy: he didn't like to talk. The *second* part was even easier: he loathed interacting with others even more than he disliked talking. The *third* and last part was the least burdensome of all: he wasn't lazy and taking care of the Green was a labor of love . . . an obligation of his faith, and one of the ways he gave praise and thanks to his god for the many blessings of the natural world. Here—in this place—the Green was particularly sacred because this was where his Grove gathered to worship on the grounds of Unity Church of the Hills. The Labyrinth— his Grove's actual place of worship on church property— received his special attention and devotion. The Labyrinth's connectedness with the Natural in the very midst of all this urban sprawl made it truly special, and thus, warranted heavy doses of his tender-loving care.

The Labyrinth was the spiritual gathering place for the Druids of Hearthstone Grove. This Grove was his family, and he was extremely proud to be part of their community. The only thing which exceeded his pride for Hearthstone was how protective he was of the Grove. They were the first to open their arms and take him in . . . the first to genuinely care about him. Here, with the Druids, was the first time he felt like he truly belonged somewhere since . . . well, since his squad in Iraq . . . a time he had tried so hard to forget . . . a time in which he was so shattered, so badly broken inside, it seemed another life to him now. Even his 'bad brain' couldn't get rid of it and make it stay away. The cruel irony of his unseen injuries kept him from remembering all the things he wanted to remember while somehow ensuring he couldn't get rid of those he wanted to forget. The retained memories of bad decisions and death would have been the first of the unwanted recollections he discarded had he had a choice in the matter.

When he remembered the time before, he hardly recognized who he used to be. That past part of himself was so distant and obscured it now seemed to belong to a complete stranger—a dirty shadow of a soldier who dreamed of being a hero but led his men to their meaningless and violent deaths instead. His survival was the worst travesty of all! He should have died along with them, but he survived; his life light still flickered after his soldiers' lives had been snuffed like so many candle flames in an unforgiving wind. He lived through hell only to be swallowed by darkness—a fitting punishment for the ultimate failure of any combat leader.

By the time the blackness had chewed him up and spat him back out, his spirit was shredded and his consciousness damaged. His wounds were far deeper than those of the brain the military docs—the DoD's so-called "specialists"—diagnosed him with and for which he was supposedly treated. He was just a broken doll discarded by the Army; only to be tossed into and passed around in a Veteran's Administration medical system built to check boxes and pass audits; not fix fucked-up puppets and rehome unwanted playthings. The veterans were given lip service, while the highest priority was better stewardship of the US taxpayer's dollar. It was always easier and cheaper just to make new dolls . . . *why should the civilians be the only ones to enjoy the benefits of America's 'throw away' economy?*

Such were the value calculations the now faceless establishment in his muddled mind had assessed his earlier life against . . . worthless was always the easiest sum to derive. That was why it was easy to leave that husk of a life behind along with the name associated with it. He had been reborn as a Druid, and his spirit had been renewed by the natural world. His name was Arden! He had lost his faith in the majority of humankind and their mechanized and greed-driven beast of a civilization which had discarded him when he was no longer useful. Long lost and finally found, a fierce fire of loyalty now burned inside him. Arden would not give up his clan and this place of true belonging without a fight! What he had here meant so much more than the roof over his head. He would give everything for his family . . . his Grove. He had failed another family once, and it would not happen again.

For him, the fortune in the seemingly endless series of misfortunes plaguing his life was being accepted by the Druids. You would have to look a long time before you found a group of people and a place of gathering as open and accommodating as Hearthstone Grove. All faiths and traditions were welcome to join them for a celebration of new beginnings. This was an uncommonly welcoming place in a world which had become increasingly cold and unwelcoming . . . well, at least, that was how things used to be *here* before his Grove was *uprooted* . . .

. . . Before the Druids of Hearthstone Grove were forced to flee for fear of their lives and driven into hiding. This Grove used to ask all newcomers for a "fresh outlook on old issues," and *now* they would give anything for peace and the peaceful intentions of strangers. These Druids no longer had the time to "seek out inspiration for new endeavors," because *now* they were just trying to survive and avoid contact with any strangers due to prolific threats of violence just for being different. They were religious deviants in the eyes of the new Texas republic. This Grove used to hope for and seek out the "renewal of bonds with their community," the very same community who was now hunting them down.

However, make no mistake, the Druids of Hearthstone Grove were not fleeing because they were afraid; they were fleeing the tidal wave of hate which had swept over the surrounding population—the black tide risen up to submerge them all in the immersive effects of its intense and all-consuming dislike for all things and beings considered 'different.' It seemed as if the whole of Texas was infected with a relentless drive to purge all those who didn't look like a Texan, or think like a Texan, or believe the things a good Texan should. This was not a time to be among the proud minority or to openly diverge from the mainstream . . . or in Texas's case, be anyone other than a loyal member of the extreme right wing who now led the secessionist state . . .

. . . In truth, with his paranormal perceptors, Arden had seen these unnatural fires of the spirit burning on the horizon for some time. He was *fúath slugair* after all—his Grove's chosen defender. In these troubled times, his Grove needed one anointed and solely dedicated to the spiritual defense of the family. Hearthstone's openness to the world made them particularly vulnerable to this uncivilized siege, because Druidry, properly practiced, meant maintaining an open, unfiltered connection with the interconnectedness of the natural world.

Out of an abundance of caution, Hearthstone had required one among them to make the sacrifice of becoming the 'closed fist' so the Grove could continue on as they needed to be: 'the hand open to all.' Arden had always thought *fúath slugair*— "Hate-eater"—was such an interesting name, because it evoked visceral and emotional images of someone consuming those and that of the darkness . . . and the even more insidious among them—the devourers of the light. To Arden, the title was still a misnomer bordering on humorous because he didn't actually 'eat' the hate . . . it wasn't like he needed it for sustenance. It was more precise to say he absorbed and displaced hate. And to 'displace' was to disrupt—*blunt momentum, push off vector, divert from intended target*—anything to interrupt the intentionality of the hate and other like destructive emotions. In this way, the *fúath slugair* was something of an anomaly in Chaos's entropic system . . . akin to a virus, but one of a most wonderful kind.

Hate, like all emotions, exists within its own spectrum of spiritual energy; much like a specific color in the light spectrum. As energy, hate is created by metaphysically transmuting emotional energy from a less volatile state, making the change in state a causal one. The mechanism for this causality is probably closest to what humans would describe as 'intentionality,' albeit a special type. Emotional changes in state happen when they are imparted with intentions . . . the intentions of essence: his, mine, yours, *ours* . . . a race's, a nation's, a species'. It is what the High Sentients called *intentenessence*. As a kind of elemental Himself, this ability ranked among Chaos's most potent powers. He was weaponizing hate, among other things, as a manipulation and shaping mechanism to set the conditions for despicable and destructive outcomes. Hate is sometimes insidious and other times eruptive, but it is always chaotic on escalating scales of impact and effect.

Arden's unique power within this constructive aspect of the Earthreal also had strange side effects, but the term byproduct is probably more accurate. This was because the use of his abilities tended to draw dislocated and displaced spiritual entities, including consciousnesses of being, to him. In this respect, when Arden employed his ability, he was the moths' flame. *Why was that?* For all those trapped in a personal darkness of their own making or imprisoned within one of the rifts' myriads of manifested forms, one such as Arden, who absorbs and displaces hate or any kind of negative energy, can appear as a bright light shining within the black void of their own personal purgatories . . . though it be only a figment of the consciousness. For light is not always a guide or indicative of warmth or safety, it can also be a hazard or a warning harkening the disastrous end to the Chaos-gripped, the Corrupted, or otherworldly darklings.

This sensory effect within the consciousness worked both ways. This was why Arden saw them coming a mile away . . . actually, several miles away . . . *they*, the inbound human scourge. They were good arsonists, setting fires to surprise, shock, and entrap. Their execution was carefully planned considering the compressed timeline and the extreme collective emotion involved. They were the spawn of a most wretched variant of inspiration. They were fueled by anger and hatred dredged up from the dark reaches and crevasses of the soul where bigotry and other irrational fears hide like sediment stirred up from the bottom of a stagnant, poisoned well. These were 'wells' which should have been closed off long ago by advancements in modern civilization and critical thinking. However, once these primitive sources of emotions were kicked up in an inky cloud, their depth of submersion within human consciousness did not matter, because the sediment of hostile sentiment lit off so hot and so intense, the emotional fire proved more than enough to provide the ignition source for the hundred torches of an angry lynch mob. Driven to frenzy, the collective negative emotion was blinding to Arden as the hate scourge writhing approached, hoping to descend without warning upon their hapless targets—the Druids of Hearthstone Grove! A grove who was not thinking to run or of making a stand, because they hadn't done anything wrong!

Sure, the *fúath slugair* could have looked to engage the aggressors, to absorb and transmute their hatred and anger into some less potent form, but such tactics were not in keeping with his kind and their ways . . . not even the ways of his former kind, the US Army. In many respects, the rules hadn't changed with the changing of Arden's worlds: all contact with the adversary should have purpose—driven by operational imperative—to the accomplishment of mission objectives. To meet hate head-on was always a risky proposition, because the emotion—when massed—flowed like turbulent, turbid fluid aloft in the wind. There were just too many virulent sources descending and seeking to envelop—too many variables, too little time, and the Grove's position was far too exposed. Some of his own would be certain to get caught up in any spiritual net he could cast, and his Grove was vulnerable. One unpredictable fox loose in the hen house was one too many, and the best move for Arden was to gather up his chickens and vacate their beloved Labyrinth while there was still a way out.

For now, Arden did not require contact—even that of the spiritual, indirect kind—to attain his objective. Arden could see through the arsonists' eyes, which gave him all the time he needed to gather up his family and go . . . ***run!***

****

Arden was fumbling to get his phone and make a call as he was running toward the Labyrinth where his fellow Druids were gathered. He was trying to call the man who was quite possibly his only remaining friend from before . . . from before 'the broken and reborn.' He was calling even though he had no right to, because friendship is usually about acceptance, caring, and supporting each other—which required being there—and he had fallen far short on all counts. Despite the urgency and stress of the moment, he realized he could count himself among those who he despised . . . the moral equivalent of 'the atheist who found God in the combat zone.' Then Arden scolded himself. This was not a time for self-deprecation, because survival—his and his Grove's—was very much in doubt! He would have plenty of time for self-loathing later . . . now it was about taking care of family. Pride and ego aside, this was life and death shit!

The number Arden was looking for was easy to find on his archaic flip phone, since he didn't ever call anyone. It was the one listed as "missed call" several times. Tap-tap—*ringing* . . . he braced for emotional impact with pending contact while he was running to stay ahead of the lynch mob.

‹click› "Hello?"

"Mack!" he shouted breathlessly at the phone tightly gripped in a runner's hand.

"What?" *‹sounds of a motor in the background . . . a large vehicle accelerating to speed›*

"Mack! It's McBride! Can you hear me?" Still running, still breathless, Arden was starting to get frustrated. He called himself by his "old name" from the before . . . who Mack and all the *prior-life* acquaintances knew him as.

"Hold on a sec . . . I'm driving. Let me switch to my good ear." *‹swishing sounds mixed with engine sounds›* "Okay, how's that? Can you hear me?"

"Yes! Mack! It's McBride!" Arden was even more breathless from both running and being frustrated. He couldn't tell if it was the situation or being made to repeat himself and recall people and memories from the *before* . . . but in the end, the *why* didn't matter. It was always the resulting emotions which held sway and functioned as the primary determinants of the final outcome, not the bases or underlying reasons for them.

"Well, howdy stranger! I was wondering when I would finally—" Mack's excitement at finally hearing from his friend was . . .

. . . cut short by Arden interrupting him in mid-sentence. The Hate-eater had no time for pleasantries and even less for proper phone etiquette. "Mack! Listen!" *‹huffing›* . . . he was now at a full-out sprint. "We need help! They are coming!"

"Ooohkay. Okay. Slow down, man," said Mack, trying to

sound reassuring even though he did not understand what was happening. "I am still on duty, but just went out of service. Where are you?"

"Unity Church of the Hills. Hurry!" *<click>*

The wonderful thing about Mack was that the man did not have a resentful bone in his body . . . he was incapable of holding a grudge, and he didn't need to understand anything else about the situation other than his friend needed him. Mack was on his way . . . Mack was a devoted friend even though his friend in need did not even trust him enough to share his true name . . .

****

Arden tended the grounds, so he knew the terrain very well. Unity Church of the Hills was a sizable complex which, over time had become "hemmed in" by commercial retail space and residential areas. The church was south of Anderson Mill Road, which was the main thoroughfare servicing the church and the surrounding area. In fact, if you were coming to Unity by vehicle, you had one winding approach into the church grounds unless you were hoofing it on foot . . . and Arden was 'hoofing it' at a *full gallop*.

Arden could see the vehicles of some of his fellow Hearthstone Druids in their usual spots in the east corner of the south parking lot. Fortunately, it did not appear there were many worshipers there this evening . . . the larger gathering was not scheduled until the next day. It was possible several among the Grove had a premonition of insidious things transpiring this eve. Over the ensuing days, Arden had been adamant in his assertions to all who would listen that such an attack was imminent. An intolerant volatility had swept the entire country, but the virulence was particularly intense in the newly proclaimed Lone Star Nation. A shamanistic religion like theirs was a likely target in the transition to overt aggression.

With the overt aggression physically manifesting on church grounds this evening, 'fewer' of the targeted was better when it came to flight on foot in the dark. The Labyrinth was close now. Located just a short distance from the parking lot, it was visually obscured by trees and bushes making it an excellent location to gather and celebrate the Natural, and in this moment, a good point from which to launch their flight for survival.

As Arden approached, he saw the Labyrinth's lights and heard the Druids laughing and talking. The light, made by lanterns, was fluttering. Arden burst forth from the surrounding vegetation, a shadow erupting from the dark directly into the midst of the congregation. Everyone was frozen in place, ominously silhouetted with a hazy aura from the luminescence of a full moon accented by flickering lamplight. Here, there was no light from the parking lot security lighting or any of the nearby church buildings; the power had been out for a couple of weeks—completely out. "A catastrophic failure of critical infrastructure," the authorities had called it. Rumors were rampant that the entire electrical grid had been taken down in some sort of attack, and the blackout was just the beginning of it. People didn't have heat for their homes during a major ice storm—a historically bad one.

Large swaths of Texas had weathered a nasty cold snap rivaling that experienced during the previous year's power outage. It had lingered for over a week and thousands had frozen to death in their homes. Many of the deceased had been the ill and the infirm, but all the victims were overly dependent on modern conveniences and conveyances which included an unfortunate over-reliance on the commercial power grid . . . denizens of the modern human world who had lost the know-how and sturdiness to contend with nature's extremes. When faced with this kind of elemental exposure, they succumbed instead of survived. By Earth Mother's grace, the temperatures had only warmed up in the last couple of days, returning to the norms of the typically mild Texas winter to which most residents were accustomed.

Arden's dark reflections on recent events matched his stark visage, broken up by wavering shadows cast by the yellow light of randomly placed lanterns like moving camouflage or morphing war paint. Though cast in the same rippling shadow, the Druids gathered still felt the intensity of his presence . . . like the radiant heat of a fire.

Arden did not know all of them . . . obviously newcomers to the Grove. While still struggling to catch his breath, Arden instinctively dropped into 'military mode.' It was automatic, burned into his consciousness by years of military training, overseas deployments, and other forms of mental conditioning employed to produce habitual excellence during situations of extreme duress. Intuitively, he started barking orders at the startled group, rattling off directives like machine-gun fire. There was no time for pleasantries and salutations, and even if there was time, they still probably would not have received any such thing from the veteran. The true irony was that it took an existential threat to even get Arden talking at all. "Extinguish those lanterns! Gather your belongings quickly and follow me. They are almost upon us!"

Those who knew Arden and understood his role started complying at once, hurriedly picking up and packing their personal effects and running to turn the lanterns off. Of the fourteen people present, five just stood there frozen like deer in vehicle headlights. They were the newcomers—the strangers—the unknown variables in the cold equation, which was only capable of yielding one of two possible outcomes, regardless of the numbers entered for any of its variables—life or death. Their fates were inexorably bound at this point, so this math project was a group assignment, and everyone, despite disparities in their individual contributions would share the same grade—a "D" or worse equaled certain death.

"Everyone, step to!" It was Daryn. Hearthstone's Archdruid.

"This is Arden. He is Hearthstone's protector. Do exactly as he tells you! Your lives depend upon it!" With volume loud and a commanding tone uncharacteristic of the Archdruid, Daryn's words were enough to turn everyone's Arden-induced shock into sharper action and impart the kind of urgency the situation demanded. Having his Grove's attention, he turned to their protector. "Arden, what is wrong? What is happening?" Daryn asked; upset with himself for being so distracted he had not sensed the 'wrong' closing in on Hearthstone Grove before now.

Arden made a motion with his right hand, fingers pressed and bladed at ninety degrees to his inward-turned palm. The Hate-eater made a slicing motion under his bearded chin . . . a brisk, back-and-forth lateral gesture. Daryn's "leadership handoff" was a function of trust—deep and unquestioning—the kind one only gains from having spent a lifetime with someone, or alternatively, from having peered directly into their soul . . . that place of spiritual center where someone is incapable of hiding who they truly are . . .

. . . Only recently, Arden had learned how Daryn had 'found' him. Daryn was the Hearthstone Grove's Archdruid for a reason . . . not because he was an exceptional leader or an expert on interpreting the classical and Mediaeval texts on which today's common Druidic practices are based. He was the Archdruid because of his extrasensory gift . . . what Daryn referred to as "extrospection." He possessed a hypersensitivity to the natural world . . . her beings, creatures, processes, and systems—and most importantly, their 'interconnectedness.' When someone is so 'in tune' with their surroundings, it is easy to find the out-of-place or 'special sources' within the Natural. Thus, Daryn's extrospection invariably led him to Gifted beings who could manipulate these special sources.

Arden also learned Daryn had been concerned for some time. Spiritual forces and energies which had typically remained in shadow were finding each other and binding together into hybrid manifestations. These phenomena were part of a spiritual convergence whose overall intent and purpose remained obscure. Among Daryn's greatest worries was that emotions were being swept up as part of a massed transformation within the Spiritual. Usually, only humans and other feeling-producing sentients functioned as emotional sources, but 'something' or 'someone' hidden and lurking within the Earthreal's existential shadows and folds was now also generating emotions—negative feelings meant to drive unknown actions presumably bent on insidious outcomes. Daryn could 'feel' the darkness of intent within the unnatural, gaping hole of it.

There was only one known kind of Gifted, not known to many, who was well suited to defending others from such threats. No one knew for sure how many of these exceptional individuals existed. Recorded encounters with this select form of Gifted were infrequent, very infrequent . . . likely because such beings are extremely rare. In addition, the vast majority of sentients are incapable of perceiving them, with even fewer still possessing the knowledge which would allow a being to know about them at all.

With the darkness growing and the threats to society's fringe groups and minority belief systems expanding with each passing day, Daryn knew his Grove needed a protector . . . and with the potent concoction of challenges facing the United States at this pivotal moment, the Archdruid believed to the depths of his supernaturally amped soul that Arden was the one . . . the protector his Grove needed.

Despite Daryn's faith in his abilities, Arden harbored serious doubts he had what it took to fulfill such a critical role . . . just look at his history. Arden had already failed others—epically—so his past predicated he would likely do so again. He was a flawed and damaged being. Having dismissed all of that, the Archdruid was staunch in his belief the Hate-eater was the one who would see Hearthstone through these dark times. The Archdruid was convinced the fúath slugair was uniquely suited to the task at hand, and Arden, for his part, now realized he did *possess a special gift, which carried with it an obligation to serve others in a time of need. Arden still had much to learn on how to use these powers and determine what their limits were, if any. He had cognitive impairments and a host of other issues, which made this process exceedingly challenging. Now, dire circumstances dictated he would need to learn on the fly, and in this moment, it was not his gift the Grove needed, but his experience as an infantryman in combat.*

Like Daryn, Arden could see 'sources' too . . . those of hate and other negative emotion in spectrum . . . and right now it seemed as if those 'somethings' and 'someones' had emerged from their hiding places to track down courage in all its forms, cleaving flesh and muscle from bone to leave only the wretched thing of RAGE behind. Some unseen engine within the Spiritual was creating an army of abhorrent zombies among humankind in the Earthreal. The first wave had commenced their assault, and the Hearthstone Grove was their target . . .

. . . In the disoriented survival scramble, everyone was still paying attention to Daryn, so he brought Arden's hand signal to voice with the loudest possible whisper. "Stop . . ." the Archdruid said, almost hissing. "Quiet . . . listen."

Everyone instantly froze in position—statue motionless, pin-drop quiet. They could make out yelling in the distance, but it was still too far away to make out what people were saying. However, one thing was unmistakable: *there* were many, hundreds maybe. The voices of the approaching mob were seemingly coming from all directions—one angry, seething voice distributed across many mouths—many making up one hostile, growling entity on the move. Though distant, one voice could be heard above the others: an orchestrator coordinating the actions of a large pack who was surging to surround their prey and tighten the noose!

"What do we do?" someone asked.

"Who are they?" asked another.

No response. Their redheaded protector had his eyes closed, head tilted forward, and hands clasped together to his front. It appeared as if he was thinking or meditating—or both. This was confusing to uninformed observers who were just told their lives depended on him; a myriad of thoughts were churning within their collective consciousnesses which were fused to each other by the same theme of shared, fear-inspired confusion . . . all possessed the same burning question and primitive instinct implored them to get an answer for what was going on with their appointed guardian, because the answer was directly related to the lot of them surviving the night. "What is he doin—?"

"Enough! Let him concentrate." Daryn was quick to stay the doubters' tongues. Arden was employing the *fúath slugair's* perception . . . a special kind of extrospection, akin to radar or sonar, only he was reading the returns of his inquisitional pulses as they reflected off living beings producing destructive emotional energies instead of reflections from highly conductive materials like metals or sea water. He could not only see emanating 'sources' of the spiritual spectrum, but also residuals and shared energies circulating between and around sentients.

After a couple of seconds, Arden opened his eyes. "Come with me. This way." He started out—trance-like—at a walk almost due east with Daryn waving to make sure everyone saw the direction they were heading; the Archdruid doing his best to ensure all, including newcomers, were following Arden. He was trying to avoid saying anything aloud which would unintentionally provide the pursuers with indications of their location and direction of movement. The yelling was growing louder, closer. They could now see lights in many directions. The sources were the bouncing light beam eyes of a pack of tech-enabled human predators. They say Druids are in tune with the natural world, and in this moment, they were completely enmeshed. At a very intimate level, they were experiencing what it felt like to be animals who knew they were on the verge of being trapped ... the adrenaline-fueled perception of their entire world was getting narrower very quickly.

The Druids picked their way across the church grounds: the *all-remaining* of the gently rolling hill country with intermittent broadleaf trees, interspersed by individual and copse. The large forests of their species' ancestors once extended in all directions as far as the eye could see, in a time before human habitation assumed ownership and terraformed on mass scale, thereby culling the gifts Earth Mother had provided for all beings, all life ... before the Manmade gobbled up the Wild here, leaving nothing but urban sprawl and unsustainable human domain in its wake. In the dark, the pleasant, leaf-fluttering trees of day loomed like hulking threats to those being hunted and unfamiliar with the terrain. Everyone in the small group seemed to be taking their turns stumbling and falling as they all were guilty of looking over their shoulder to gauge the progress of their hunters. They could see the bouncing beams of light converging en masse on the Labyrinth ... partially highlighted by what dim lighting still remained on the church grounds, the prowling pumas who, certain they had cornered their prey, howled in collective frustration when they discovered the Druid gathering place unoccupied and their prizes gone.

Undeterred, the mob turned to other destructive business. In the penultimate response of the insanely self-righteous, they set the Labyrinth on fire as if the act of destroying the pagans' place of ritual would somehow satiate the rifts in their souls made by all the misdirected and misguided anger and hate. In sad truth, any attempts were fruitless, for the dark void which had grown within them could not be filled ... these inconsolable of spirit could not be placated, the unquenchable fire lit ... this was the true power of the Fifth Element and its undeniable effectiveness when weaponized by the Great Deceiver Himself: *ultimate destruction born of self-destruction*—timeless genius; any age, any world.

Even as the collective frustration of the mob manifested itself in a gasoline-accelerated fire summoned to consume the Labyrinth, the hostile throng started fanning out into a makeshift skirmish line, personifying their commitment to push through the rolling wood until they had affected capture or made kills; both outcomes were acceptable. The hunting pack arrayed under the En'Troop's unseen flag unfurled in a line some one hundred and fifty yards wide and moved forward, flashlight beams bouncing, human animals growling . . . backlit by the savaging blaze, which was once the Labyrinth. They seemed to be moving with unnatural speed, one large, fanged maw gnashing . . . as if the actions of the many were coordinated by one twisted mind . . . one puppeteer with enough hands to manipulate the multitude. *Chaos?* Nay! He would not think to mire Himself in such onerous manipulations and tactical-level control. Such things were delegated to the most trusted within his inner circle.

As for Arden, he was focused on the forward—on leading the escape—but something caused him to shudder . . . something gave him pause. Like the cold shadow cast with the power to bring a darker dark than the surrounding night—the rawboned manus of some unseen beast reaching—or maybe not reaching, but rather guiding the mob and spurring them forward. This was a presence relegated to shadow yet still able to beat the war drums, reverberating like thunder and spurring the troubled spirits to a fast pace and a hungry fury demanding to be satiated. The horde's was a deranged and offensive cadence—perfectly perpetrated; it resonated exclusively with the 'left behinds' and the lost who believed themselves to be found and were unwaveringly convinced something especially important had been taken from them. Although, if you had the opportunity to ask them, they probably could not specifically identify the 'loss' which left the smoking hole in their hearts or give you the names of those who wronged them.

For Arden, with his ultra-sensitive hate perceptors, the visceral pounding shook him to the core of his being. And when he looked back at the mob, their wraithlike outlines were smeared and partially obscured by the burning Labyrinth. The crackling blaze of Hearthstone Grove's sacred gathering place gave words to the oppressor's song . . . this was the march of the death throng, and for the sake of those he was trying to lead to safety, it was probably best only he could hear it:

"Stomp—Stomp—Stomp,
the stormtroopers come.
Stomp—Stomp—Stomp,
You! You're different, you'd better run!
Stomp—Stomp—Stomp,
Heavy boots to crush bone and soul.
Stomp—Stomp—Stomp,
Scared little rabbits try to run, escape to your hole!
Stomp—Stomp—Stomp,
Hate dealers restless, relentless in their pursuit of the light!
Snuff—Snuff—Snuff,
Darkness is safety . . . within its cloak, we're all alike.
The unlike, the unsafe, the insane—humanity's bane.
Stomp it out! Stop purity's drain!
Oppression. Timeless response when the many are threatened.
The few, the different of tenuous hold—the first to be rended!
Hate fuels the fires of anger and aggression.
Bias and bigotry are the looking glass for oppression.
Like-mindeds who look like us are the key.
Secure, clean, and safe—the prosperous society.
Survival demands us seek out and destroy to stay free.
Purge all threats to homogeneity.
Anyone who clouds and muddies the mix,
Obscures our path . . . makes the list,
Obey and assimilate or demand to be fixed,
And draw the iron ire of the Oppressor's fist.
Pound-Pound-Pound,
Beat the Different down.

Stomp-Stomp-Stomp,
Crush them into the ground!"

It was almost impossible to see in this moment fueled and clouded by turbulent emotions, but the most important truth within the midst of this forceful 'uprooting' was not the most obvious. Aye, it is true Chaos seeks change, that truth is universally acknowledged and indisputable. Chaos is the consummate change-maker and maker of change agents on a grand scale. *How else to achieve the transformation to the entropic state?* However, the more impactful truth is always enmeshed within the immediate, in-your-face actions taken to achieve the desired changes in state. Realize that what you might see as broken or fractured is just the next inevitable step in a phased evolution toward unrecoverable Chaos. He strives for the Chaotic oscillations deep within the All that is . . . those uncommon vibrations which defy a harmonic wave . . . more deeply imbedded, the select incidences among seemingly isolated and random vibrations and disturbances ensconced with the state of all things . . . chosen—co-opted—then ganged together and combined in hopes of achieving the self-propagating wave powerful enough to sweep everything toward the self-destructive abyss. That is the dark truth hidden within every catastrophic event and destructive act . . . the discrete and innumerable 'unbounding' forces within the bound working to unify and unleash to bring about the Discordant on this world.

Still, there is more to it—layered and multifaceted like all truly transformative endeavors until reality is distorted and truth is bent like heated glass—*How is that so?* Because Chaos leverages those who benefit most from the status quo to effect destructive change, working to achieve His ends in defiance of their true nature. He manipulates the strongest tribes, dominant species, majority races, and ruling governments into entities and apparatuses of abuse, exploitation, and terror . . .

the control mechanisms of the weak, the minorities, and the disenfranchised. Chaos then employs those who do not want change—those who desperately want to keep what they have—to effect it. Chaos drives the authorities, the governments, and the rulers to the unnecessary and the heinous acts of the strong against the weak by convincing them their tenuous grip on power is slipping away. Draconian measures are necessary to keep what they have—the power, possessions, and riches—the ensuing procession of horrific decisions and deeds are the kind which start wars and spark revolutions. His type of surrogate warfare weaponizes fear, mistrust, and biases, and causes Texans to hunt down their own species in the suburbs of Austin just because they are a religious minority with a different belief system. There is a dark efficiency in the construction of 'it' for Chaos can only build a house from the resident materials available and readily given.

However, for every active measure which seeks an outcome, there are always potential countermeasures . . . some obvious, some less so . . . all with varying degrees of effectiveness and success. The unseen, unknown, and undetected can sometimes be the most potent, because even the most capable adversary does not fully account and effectively plan for every single one of them. Though they exist in obscurity and are extremely rare in number, the *fúath slugair*, as a Gifted being, is one such countermeasure. And of those select beings on this Earth who actually possess knowledge of Hate-eaters and the purpose they serve, most of them have never beheld such a Gifted before and believe the *fúath slugair* the stuff of legend and folklore. *How could such power be trusted to a human?*

The full extent of their power is not known—ironically, not even by those who possess the power, and this included Arden himself. The wielders' access and ability to channel is limited by the Gifted being's own imperfections and fallibilities . . . the impediments of ThisLife's biological sheath as well as any afflictions of essence or frailties of consciousness. In this regard, Arden was certainly not immune and also not yet fully aware of his abilities. Arden was still very much struggling to find a wholeness of spirit and his place in this world within the context of ThisLife. These personal challenges blinded him from seeing he was a channeler, gifted with access to vast, potentially limitless, power which resides both in the Earthreal and connected spiritual realms.

In some cases, it takes a miracle for the blind to see, but for others, aspects of the 'unseen' are the product of barriers or deficits residing in the consciousness which can be overcome by experiential learning; or sometimes they exist as artifacts of purgatoriums presenting as impairments which must be healed, surmounted, or circumvented; and in other cases, the gap can be bridged by the stress, anxiety, and adrenaline of impending death. The threat of untimely termination invokes the survival reflex, which can oft times serve to rapidly accelerate the learning curve . . .

. . . *This* was such a time: a time when the chasms which exist between ignorance, knowledge, and application—perceived as unbridgeable—are crushed together by a collision of unanticipated and equally unavoidable circumstances . . . or at least pushed close enough together for energies to arc across the gaps between all involved beings. These are the conditions that need to be present when the next evolution in amazing happens . . . 'something' like this:

> *. . . Arden was pulsing his 'extra-awareness' to the fore to guide his group's escape while also surveilling behind them to mark the progress of the pursuing mob relative to theirs . . . a title which now seemed less applicable since their pursuers seemed very well organized. They were proving very formidable in their collective ability to execute an envelopment and close on their targets in the dark of night . . . or so it seemed to the adrenaline-amped perceptors of the hunted. The pursuers were everywhere out there, and the Druids were all but caught in a net*

where each hunting Texan was a strand connected and fortified by bigotry and fear—two of the most dominant variables in the hate equation. When joined, the tethered dark emotions of these many humans called to action were metaphysically stronger than the relative strength of any spiderweb in the Earthreal. The left-leaning, intellectual elite would mock their mental capacity—probably even referring to them as 'hicks' and 'rednecks'—but such underestimations and arrogance have always been the folly of the conquered, have they not? These rednecks and religiously conservative citizens were determined, synchronized, and of one mind—unified by a fully-entrenched, hate-inspired anger which enhanced their performance as a team. To a being, they were resolute in achieving their insidious goals—a force to be reckoned with—mock them at your peril . . .

. . . For the fleeing Druids, there was no time for mocking . . . only for an attempt to ensure survival, and unfortunately, Arden's group was not moving as efficiently or as effectively as the hunting party on their heels. A young, unfortunate female among the Labyrinth visitors was involuntarily swept up in this debacle and did not have the good fortune of being familiar with the wood. Thus, she experienced the further misfortune of a sprained ankle in the scrum of the run, making her an injured calf in the predated herd. The woman, probably not much older than twenty years of age, had obviously shown up at the Grove's gathering place in hopes of new experiences of community, friendship, and shared spirituality and received far more than she had bargained for. She was understandably upset. Actually, she was well beyond upset . . . she was inconsolable, and the Druids were finding it difficult to keep Morissa on her feet and moving . . .

. . . From Arden's perspective, young Morissa was his 'bridge' to new understanding for she was the stark contrast which spawned his inspiration—like a vibrant, full color character in

a black-and-white movie. It was exposure to contrasting emotional sources that enabled Arden to see the connections, patterns, and interdependencies: **anger-hatred-aggression-hostility** *and* **fear-helplessness-threatened-defenseless** *. . . an energetic engagement of conflicting emotions, which sparked disparate actions and reactions. Ironically, the emotions were all related to each other just as each of these human beings was very closely related to one another at the genetic level. And the emotions, like the genetic relation, were not distant, but extremely nuanced. Sometimes fear begets hate, and sometimes it is the opposite . . . after all, they are only a shade apart, adjacent to each other and sharing one spectrum. The differences are minute, but the effects can be profound. Again, not so different from the genetic differences in species. The genetic mechanism behind human skin color is regulated by the enzyme tyrosinase, which creates the color of the skin, the eyes, and hair shades . . . yet an enzyme reaction has been enough to justify atrocities and injustices throughout humanity's short history. Why should it be any different for the emotional spectrum?*

There! The **fúath slugair** *was finally seeing it: the emotions of sentient beings occupy a spectrum similar to that light. A spectrum wrapped in a wheel with fear occupying a vicinal position with respect to anger. It is also no coincidence that anger and happiness own the two largest bands of the spectrum and stand in direct opposition to each other on the wheel. This contributing aspect of our reality is not too dissimilar to the enduring relationship which exists between the elemental forces of earth and wind as well as that of water and fire, standing in direct opposition to one another. This relationship is one of constant tension, but when the right balance is struck, and the tension is properly directed, it can form the trusses which make a bridge strong enough to span the chasms and dead spaces of the universe to create life-sustaining environments within the Great Void. Whereas the Green and Blue come together as the Coirea'cen, the anger-happiness nexus—or* **Rúsea'lasse** *as it is known in the Old Tongue—is the emotional basis for life . . . it is the 'motivation to survive!' . . .*

. . . Within the emotional spectrum, happiness is obviously the most-sought nirvana state of those ensconced within the human condition . . . and this is not unique to the human species. Happiness is chased by all sentient beings gifted with the ability to dream. *One's "dreams achieved" is the definition of happiness and contentment is it not?* And so, contentment as a highly desired state equates to inaction . . . and here is where the grand paradox first presents itself, for life is 'movement.' A species' survival is dependent on taking action . . . action at many levels: individually, collectively, and beyond to encompass an entire species; regional and migratory populations; countries, kingdoms and states; tribes, packs, herds, and flocks; families, gangs and individuals; and even the muscle, sinew and bone within ThisLife's sheath, which provide the locomotion necessary to flee, pursue, gather, hunt, build, procreate, and sustain; cardiovascular systems to deliver oxygen, nutrients, and hormones to cells and organs; the immune system's organs, cells and proteins to detect, respond, and fight harmful substances, germs, and cell changes. This is all about organisms and life forms responding and adapting to changes in their environment; and the genetic variation generated by mutation which drives evolution—*movement* is crucial to life! As in all things, balance is crucial for the body to rest, heal, and recover to ensure longevity. And when balance is lost, the process is either self-correcting or inevitably self-destructive. It is here where humankind comes to mind as the Natural's ultimate anomaly: their technology exploded their population growth and enabled large segments of their population to live lives bereft of movement. By creating an existence of self-propagation without true purpose and self-motivation, the species has thrown the Earth into a state of imbalance. Their reckoning is coming, and His name is Chaos!

In the end, real change requires action, and action must be prompted. Inducing prompt action is the domain of anger. *Do you deny it?* Mind you, within anger lies fury and aggression, the would-be muses of action. Though oft times the sources of effort and ensuing activities are misdirected and ill-intended, aggression is always purposeful—the righteousness and justness of the resulting actions may be debatable, but they are not without purpose—even if it be just to knock down and crush the 'perceived' obstacles and barriers to safety, security, contentment, and happiness. It is in this intersection between emotion, perception, and action that the Great Deceiver achieves His greatest effects.

Something else must be understood within the biological sheath for it is descriptive of the functioning of negative emotions: pain is a function of messages, electrical impulses transmitted to the brain by specialized nerve cells known as nociceptors, a pain receptor. Within the spiritual realm, anger can be thought of as a pain response ... causing the metaphysical equivalent of inflammation—damage—penetration—fracture. With the right remedy or intervention, it can be healed, or at the very least, temporarily tamped down ...

... Arden saw it all unfolding before him because it was his time to know it. These truths of the hidden workings and attributes of the natural world were being revealed to him by his master—the Horned One—who orchestrated Earth's Circle of Life and has remained at the center of it since inception ... since before this world's 'time dawn.' Limitless, his great rootweb is always growing into the sacred earth and down into the depths of the Underworld. Arden's god resides at Earth's crossroads where all planes of existence are connected: the Plexus for the physical reality of ThisLife and the metaphysical worlds of the OtherWorld, including the home of the Lifestream and the portals to all NextLives.

From the Center of All Things, Arden's god can see the 'Interconnectedness of the All,' and as his disciple, Arden could feel 'it All' too; for it is the Horned One's rootweb which binds the All of this world together and connects us all. His is the unseen interstitial tissue joining all living things . . . do not try to deny it, you can feel it in your bones and blood too! And, in seeing his world anew through his master's eyes, Arden could see the strands of the rootweb which extended into the spectrum of feeling and emotion, for how else could the rootweb connect All if it did not reach out—grasp—and connect everything.

The Ancient One was already here when Chaos arrived to find a primitive Earth, when Earth Mother was still young and roiling and unsettled and struggling to create Herself . . . the timeless times when the four prime elemental forces were new, and the sentience within earth and water was just one diffused consciousness manifested within each. Arden's master—the effervescence, spawn, and self-directed mania of evolution—was there to guide the Chaotic forces of creation and see to the unbelievable biodiversity of this Earth. An act of guiding which became an enduring process, he 'grew' into everything and inexorably wove himself into the All to provide the underlying structure for healthy ecosystems and biomes. His rootweb is both our tethering and the connective conduit of the Natural Network. His sight, his touch, and our feelings provide the basis for understanding sentient awareness and what distinguishes between living and dead by defining what it means to be alive on this Earth as well as setting the parameters for good lives and bad ones. How else would we know? What else could be the source of our internal compass? How else could we if not for . . . ?

. . . All is connected . . .

'All is connected!' That was the tether the Hate-eater needed to pull himself to the full understanding of the moment and the knowing of what to do next. Arden felt like he was on a remarkably familiar path he had traveled many times before, but the mist which had always shrouded the vista of his favorite valley had cleared off for the first time, exposing all the wonders—and answers—it had to share with the world. When the cognizance of it came to Arden, it struck him like a lightning bolt of fundamental knowledge coupled with the 'know-how' needed to act. Evolution's All-Father could provide no less!

Arden could see the strands of rootweb . . . fine and delicate; the iridescent fibers intermingling and reaching out to **human receptors-turned-activators**—*for what is emotion without the sentient being to process and act upon the imparted feelings. The cilia and fibril of the Ancient One's rootweb now terminating into glowing tendrils of emotional aura; their colors betraying 'whom' they served: the reds of anger and the yellows of fear licking at any available receptors like flames dancing, looking to taste and touch but not consume. But, make no mistake, they were looking to start fires within the soul and keep them burning long and hot! The bright yellows of the spectrum of fear, like soft lightning—slow of motion, but no less potent in their own special kind of effects. The vibrant oranges of surprise, worry, and confusion operating on the edges and the in-between where neither fear nor anger were fully manifested, curling and wisping like smoke released in liquid. Orange emotion was content with the 'leftovers' his primary brethren of anger and fear were not fully successful in turning in their favor—even the spectrum of emotions had its carrion feeders.*

Arden could see it all because it was being revealed to him as the magician unveils the proof of his power in the final act. The filaments of the emotion spectrum were connecting and firing like nerve synapses of a brain within a 'body' under duress. Arden was now fully aware emotions and feelings were a distinct form of purposed, spiritual energy which exists within, and thus, is sourced from the spirit essences of all sentient beings. Emotions are an extension of essence that translates the intentions, needs, and desires of our consciousness into action while the spirit resides within the physical trappings of form in ThisLife. Once set loose from the individual being, emotions, depending on their intensity and the inherent spiritual power of the source being, have the ability to influence others . . . in some cases, many others. This is especially true in the special cases of exceptional and gifted individuals who humans would consider brilliantly charismatic. The great battle captains who are capable of summoning forth the spirit and fervor of their hordes and propelling them to historic victories against incredible odds. Or the silver-tongued politician who comes out of nowhere in his meteoric rise to power, surprising all rivals to take the reins of a nation and then convincing the whole of the population to prosecute terrible deeds in the name of a cruel empire transformed in his image.

Arden looked behind his 'squad' to see the synaptic interplay of colorful aura, snaking and writhing red and hostile across the whole of the mob's skirmish line-like front. The shared anger and hate bound them all together, reinforcing back and forth across the line like a self-propagating wave of fury which fueled and spurred forth hate's shock troops. The crimson aura told the story: no talking, no negotiating, no pleading—escape or die. They moved forward, their dark inertia enough to create a void bereft of deference or mercy to their fore.

Conversely, his squad was all over the map with Morissa bright yellow immersed in the fear of full-blown panic. Some of the others were the orange of anxious, even frantic, and amazingly, a few of the other Druids were even in the 'aqua'—calm and relaxed; strong of faith and so certain the natural world would come to their aid in Her own way, they remained centered in the intersection between sadness's swirling blue and happiness's pulsating green ...

... As for Daryn, the Archdruid of Hearthstone Grove was in the *orange-yellow* of concerned and a little confused. The spiritual leader had many strengths, but tactical leadership and performing under duress was not among them. Still, he was a great leader in his own right, because he knew his weaknesses and surrounded himself with the right people to compensate for his deficits. He had foreseen the darkness descending to feast on the temperance and acceptance of this world; hence the reason he had pleaded with a hesitant and unsure Arden to become Hearthstone's guardian ...

... Arden was decisive once he understood that which had been

*revealed, and what within the **hidden-made-known** he could control; the Hate-eater selected a countermeasure and took aggressive action to implement it . . . in a manner in keeping with the traditional ways of the American infantryman. The Hate-eater could not control the emotional energies within the spirit essence, but once they were finally loosed from human sources who failed to hold them within, the emotions became part of the shared balance among all interacting beings. Externally in play, the emotions were then susceptible to influence and manipulation. Arden could not affect the overall sum, but he could redistribute the shared energies among the connected beings; a rebalancing of emotions among the group was necessary to achieve desired effects. He was to rely on 'herd mentality' by affecting their shared emotionality across the human collective.*

The fúath slugair exerted his consciousness—the spiritual equivalent of 'brute force' which he normally reserved for the expressed purpose of absorbing and displacing hate—a process which was second nature and his 'go-to' in crisis, because it did not require any sort of nuanced employment. He 'pushed,' but nothing? He needed more focus, to concentrate harder, and he couldn't do it while he was running . . .

. . . Arden got Daryn's attention and signaled to the Archdruid that he needed to take responsibility for the Grove and continue to push east toward Balcones Village: a gated residential community a few hundred yards away. It was a series of hand gestures, but highly intuitive . . . Arden preferred to do most of his communicating without speaking . . . when he did, it was not often but still far more frequent than voice communications. Daryn understood this about his wayward brother . . . it was why he took him in. He took Arden in and gave him purpose—a rudder Arden could use to navigate himself out of the dark places that had a firm grip on his spirit.

The 'exchange" was easier signaled than transferred. Handing custody of the group to Daryn and actually getting them moving were two completely different matters entirely. Arden's new "squad" was no military unit. Unfortunately, they were more like a human version of "wet cats." To a being, each was mentally processing and managing the situation with all of the unique individuality and divergence of response Earth Mother had graced each of them with. As much as diversity was praised in more civilized forums among cultural elites, it was most definitely an impediment here. For a team leader who was not only unaccustomed to troop leading but also unfamiliar with leading in crisis, this was high expectation, high probability of failure type shit! This was the exact kind of thing Daryn relied on his *fúath slugair* for, because the Archdruid knew he sucked at it. He had risen to his station for his gifts in navigating the spiritual, not the real.

The Earthreal involved attitudes and gravity and friction and physical harm. Daryn, with all of his abilities of foresight, had not foreseen his Grove's anointed protector having to foray into the spiritual planes, leaving Daryn to 'mother hen' in the real. *This was fucked up!* Arden was the one who was expected to roll up his sleeves and get dirty . . . take care of the messes made by sojourns into the dark and mitigate the undesired aftereffects that encounters with the Corrupted always tended to churn up. Arden, in his duty, sacrificed for the spiritual purity of the rest of the Grove so they could focus on maintaining connections with the natural world as Earth Mother intended; this was a very difficult undertaking which required complete commitment for human beings ensconced in a hi-tech world. And the arrangement was a perfect marriage for Arden who embraced sacrifice and suffering as only one who didn't believe he deserved to live could . . . that was *why* Daryn chose him . . . *why* this sudden 'reversal' of roles was so upsetting and unsettling—so impossible!

Daryn was struggling desperately to play his part . . . hesitant and unsure, it took him a few seconds to get cognitively reoriented to assume this mental 'skin,' which equated to a lifetime in compressed *life-on-the-line* cycle time. Like someone who didn't believe they had the strength or agility for the obstacle course ahead of them, Daryn had to find some way to get over the first barrier, which seemed so high and intimidating. The Archdruid had to overcome being completely horrified by Arden's untimely hand-off—no warning, no time to prepare, no opportunity to escape it. Watching Arden turn away to face the pursuing violence bringers, Daryn knew he was in the chop and wake of his rescue ship, staring at the stern—no buoy, no lifeline. He had to weather these violent seas alone with the pang of self-doubt heavy in the pit of his chest, threatening to pull him down. His last glimpse of Arden was a black silhouette against a slate gray wood with distant lights bobbing on the approach. The death troop was marching forward in a line which stretched across the bumpy crown of the rolling hills; the approach of the ominous formation only broken up by sable splotches of sparse bush and tree growth.

The Archdruid saw their protector abruptly drop to the ground onto his rump in a cross-legged position, appearing to rest his forearms on his lap with his palms up, which elicited a "what the fuck?"—an involuntary thought-popper . . . certainly the first of many before this situation was resolved one way or the other. On his end, and most fortunately for the sake of the final scraps of composure desperately clinging to him, Daryn could not see Arden had also closed his eyes in the face of the impending onslaught, or his next unsolicited thought very well could have been: *"fucking meditating? Now?"* Outside of masking their route of escape, this was the second favor the cover of night provided, because Daryn had a job to focus on—his Grove in the Earthreal. Arden had his own job to do in the spiritual enclave of contested emotion among engaged human beings . . . a task only he was capable of doing.

Daryn's first tactical priority was actually based on a pretty sound premise: *the group was only as fast as its slowest member.* Thus, the first order of business was to get Morissa on her feet and moving. One of the others had been trying to pull the young woman up in an attempt to accomplish just that but was failing miserably . . . the poor girl just kept going limp and falling back down. It was unbelievable how many tears a small human girl could make. She was still sobbing uncontrollably for what seemed like forever in adrenaline-expressed time. She was the primary impediment to the Grove's successful escape from this predicament, so Daryn proceeded directly to her, knelt down, and placed his hands on either side of Morissa's head just behind the ears. He did so—gently but firmly—just enough to keep her from turning away. Then, the Archdruid spoke to Morissa's mind without voice, communicating with her as he communicated with all the sentient life of the forest. He cast his thoughts directly to the center of her consciousness below the churn and turbulence of the 'now' and into the deeper parts of her which were still capable of being present in the moment . . . these were the sensitive receptors yet able to receive his message and penetrate the intense fear gripping her. "Be calm. Be cognizant of the *beyond-you,* and in doing so, experience the *Interconnectedness of the All.* Your choice to succumb to your panic is affecting us all. Release yourself from the self-centered foci of modern human civilization—the curse of the Manmade. Rise up and come with us. Rise up and run with us, and in so doing, 'be' with us . . . *be* in *this* moment." Daryn was trying to build Morissa's tolerance to fear on an accelerated timescale . . . in this way, fear was also like pain. At the very least, he needed to impart the resolve in the young woman to push through this 'exposure.'

And, most fortunately and somewhat surprisingly, Morissa did . . . hurt, limping, and needing assistance, but up on her feet and moving. Daryn's hunch was proven right as the others responded in kind, following the lead of the lame. He had the flock on the move again, but the pack of wolves was hot on the scent and had gained a lot of ground during the Grove's suspension of action. The hunters sensed, as they always seem to irrespective of species, that they were close and gaining ground. They had picked up their pace accordingly. Of course, in the way of humans, their hunter's sense was technologically enhanced—all the 'ill-intended' across the extent of the death marchers' line were artificially 'amped.' In possession of night vision goggles, those among them with the 'sight' had acquired the fleeing Druids among the sparse trees and were directing the pack forward. The pursuers were only fifty yards away now, and twenty-five yards away from them was a single stray figure, sitting on the ground unmoving. Most of the mob had the same general theme in their assessment of the unidentified, static target—the anomaly known as Arden: *"What is this? Some kind of Druid spell-casting bullshit?"*

. . . Yeah, it was something just like that. The pursuers' collective evaluation of the lone figure was dripping with the sarcasm which underlies the contentious interactions of modern human society. Arden turned their "true lie" into more truth than lie, and in the process, shed the first light their communal darkness had seen in some time. But even truth is subject to interpretation; if by spell casting, they meant magic, and if by magic they meant wielding the forces and energies of the metaphysical and spiritual realms, then they were correct. Where they were wrong was in failing to understand these were realms of which 'they' were a part—of which we are 'all' a part. Condemning Arden for making magic was the folly of the ignorant, because he did not 'make' anything. He only channeled a specific spectrum of the resident natural power available . . . and he was not gentle about it, because he was learning on the fly and did not yet understand how far and how much he could go . . . and he did not want to restrain it.

Like anyone with a steep learning curve accelerated by the prospects of death, Arden did not have the luxury of reading the owner's manual or consulting the advice of gray beards in exerting his supranatural powers. He had to learn by doing and with the risk tolerance of those possessed with a death wish, he did not ease the accelerator down—Arden floored it! 'That' had the effect of 'turbocharging' a system neither designed for nor acquainted with working in such a way. Arden's brutish pulse forced all the produced and residual emotional energies back to source—this was **not** good.

The situational remedy required 'dissipation' not 'amplification,' but Arden's pulse served to 'juice' all participating beings. In response, the active aspects of the red spectrum coursed a deeper red, and the ignorant mob filled with hate and anger became even more aggressive; their pent-up, toxic feelings—simmering and roiling to that point—were suddenly boiling over with the need to translate explosive intent into violent action . . . now one hundred hammers were looking for nails to pound! Any remaining shards and fragments of discretion and discrimination were stripped away like loose soil in a hard wind. Those citizens with weapons who had been hesitant to use them on their own species no longer had any inhibitions—the pagans were just animals that needed to be exterminated after all. The rednecks among the rabble loosed arrows from their compound bows; the gun hobbyists and huntsmen fired their shotguns and small caliber rifles; the weekend warriors went "weapons free" with their banned military-grade assault rifles and illegally modified, high capacity, ridiculous rate-of-fire machineguns; and those without weapons picked up any would-be projectile they could find—rocks, bricks, sticks and stones . . . anything big enough to break human bones—and heaved them in the Druids' general direction of flight. In the Texans' lost minds, these 'Godless' deserved no consideration, no restraint . . . no pleasant death. This needed to be harsh and rude, befitting their poor station and even poorer faith choices—even a good 'stoning' was too good for them! Theirs was fate chosen—A CHOICE! The Texans had made their choice too: **to do GOD's WILL!**

Arden's forced feed also made the yellow more "yellow."

Any Druid or Druid wanna-be among the squad who was scared or felt threatened were reduced to human lemons: completely useless and incapacitated by fear. More apprehensive, more terrified, more frantic, the Grove's collective demeanor at once deteriorated into hysteria. Where the previous prospects for making it out of this alive were grim, their new mental state had them operating in the extreme negative on the survival probability scale. They were an endangered species: small in number, habitat destroyed, no safe havens, no friends, intensely targeted, and thus, the heavily predated! And the effect of the Arden's 'push' on the emotional intersections was also highly unexpected; the middle ground of hesitation and inaction inherent in the emotions of the orange portion of spectrum ceased to exist among hunter and hunted as the Texans and Druids alike were each forced to reinforce their primaries in the red and yellow spectrums.

The Hate-eater had made a right mess of things. It was enough to elicit a verbal "Fuck" from the stoic Arden despite his quasi-meditative state of spiritual focus . . .

. . . And 'fucked' was an apt descriptor for the Grove's current situation. Gus, ever the blend-in-the-background guy didn't manage to blend in enough and still took an arrow through the bicep. The puncture wound was nasty, the product of an oversized arrowhead, barbed and designed to maim . . . made for wild game. *But wasn't that what they were? . . . 'game' . . . and wasn't that what this was? . . . 'sport'* . . . just as the gladiatorial games in ancient Rome were both sport and contrived life-and-death engagements providing both entertainment and an efficient means for disposing of dissidents and unbelievers; all neatly packaged up by the ruling elite to fuel the empire's propaganda machine and keep the masses entertained and distracted. This was simply new twist-ties and modern branding on old packages where nasty medieval arrowheads designed to maim were 'okay' as long as they found their mark on targets endorsed by the Lone Star Nation. And Sinéad fared even worse; she was blinded by wood fragments shorn from a tree shattered by 7.62mm full-metal jacketed rounds; her only mistake in her frantic state was thinking the bunched trees offered any sort of protection from a hail of hot, molten, and high-velocity Manmade. *Did you see that? Oh, that's right . . . sorry.*

Within minutes, all of Arden's 'squad' were either wounded, pinned down by weapons fire, or incapacitated by fear—or a combination of the three. Either way, the Grove's localized extinction event was fully underway, and Arden stood to lose his second squad in ThisLife—and worse, this one would actually be his fault . . .

> *. . . **That** . . . the searing prospect of another tragedy due to his ineptitude, incompetence, and lack of foresight was enough. Enough for him to forget to think and decide wrongly and just "do," and in doing so, allow the incredible power of the natural world to come to his aid when he and his Grove needed it the most. By floating with the current in the spiritual stream instead of fighting against the natural flow, the 'wheel' of the emotional spectrum started to turn in his favor, and with it, so too the tide of battle.*
>
> *You see, nature did, within the microcosm of the emotional sphere, what she always strives to do—restore balance. This is a mandate of the Natural Order designed to sustain and perpetuate life . . . not destroy it; such is the attentive theme of the Natural's unceasing and delicate work. However, sometimes, some of nature's features and even some of her creatures, need more than the calm and steady hand to restore a semblance of order to an imbalance which has jumped from the untenable to the self-destructive. In such cases, a measure of brusqueness is needed to reestablish authority lost or natural laws disregarded by unruly sentients.*
>
> *Arden's 'push' did serve its purpose to jolt the diffused sentience of the Emostrum to a higher level of awareness—Aye, the emotional spectrum does have a name. Arden knew it now in the*

process of letting the Emostrum be what it was created to be—to respond and act in accordance with the imbedded programming of something akin to spiritual DNA. Now called to action, a blueprint was needed to guide the emotional response, and it was found in the negatives of the film within the Hate-eater's experiential consciousness—it provided the roadmap to reestablishing localized order.

Ironically, the most direct path to stabilizing this moment's human-generated turbulence was scribed in the reversal of previous choices along fate's path; within the selected branches and sequels of the past which had led to the grisly demise of Arden's previous squad. The Emostrum felt the way it needed to collectively direct its 'selves': counter to erosion channels carved into Arden's soul by the pain of loss . . . the uneven swath of spiritual scars, as deep as canyons defying any attempts for his essence to heal, now served to provide the jagged guides to capture and direct the Emostrum toward the most positive outcome in restoring balance to Chaos's interplay. Perceptively responsive, the uncommitted emotion flowed freely within misfortune's channels like molten ore to the smithing mold to be forged into a weapon for justice.

A map and guide provided and a spectrum unified in purpose, the Emostrum prosecuted their task with ruthless efficiency, and they were not kind about it . . . they too were a force of nature now unleashed, subject to the inclinations of their composition of resolute, yet raw feelings . . . a power NOT confined by form. The Emostrum's first order of business was dealing with the sources of greatest chaos among the Corrupted aspects of themselves: the massed red! These rogue 'spurs' needed to be brought to heel first if any semblance of order was to be restored. Like furious waves pounding against porous rock, they jetted into every spiritual orifice offering a path into the consciousnesses of the menacing, crimson-saturated souls bent on propagating hate-driven insidiousness. These Corruption-captured essences of being were so mindlessly furious and solely focused on their destructive intentions that they remained unaware of the Emostrum's invasion and attempted occupation.

Infiltration of unnaturally co-opted emotion proved easy with the enemy concentrating exclusively on the attack. Once the occupation had commenced, the Emostrum extracted the red from all the hostility-filled Texans; one could say, callously, but as energies in being who were still purge energy at their essence, the Emostrum's soldiers had no capacity to understand nor adjust their actions based on feedback. However, this primitive, diffused sentience possessed nothing which impeded them from working cooperatively and with intention, and the collective desire was to flush out, and as needed, rip out all the red spectrum from all affected consciousnesses . . . and they did so, so viciously, the sheaths of affected beings were knocked down and doubled over as if afflicted by explosive overpressures originating from within. All violent actions, all weapons fire, ceased immediately as a hundred 'hammers' simultaneously lost their heads. In the spiritual, the Emostrum left emotional vacuums in their essences that had to be filled by some emotion, and anger and hostility—everything within the red band of the spectrum— was no longer available.

Having the initiative and the inertial momentum of a battle's favor turning, the Emostrum's directed spurs dictated what emotions were accessible—the who, what, and how much of what was lost and gained. Next, they struck the besieged Grove, gentle and kind humans gripped by the yellow spectrum, with the precision of winds riding the leading edge of a spring storm's front that retain the discretion to strip away only the seeds, seed pods, and cones from the denizens of Forestkind and leave all else behind to grow, flourish, and bask in the rains soon to come . . . strong enough to carry the captured potential of new generations to pristine locations anxious for groves of their own. The Emostrum stripped away enough of the yellow fear to reduce Druid terror and hysteria to worry and concern while simultaneously imparting enough red to fortify the Grove, bestowing the 'hot' determination of resolute action as it translates into a will *to survive—into Rúsea'lasse! The kind of feelings which repurposes the kinetic will bequeathed by adrenaline, giving the injured and mentally petrified the ability to function in spite of their injuries and fallibilities ... to stumble to their feet, gather together, account for one another, and move . . . to "Get the fuck out of there!"*

And what of the extracted yellow spectrum? As with all natural resources, nothing was wasted, not even with emotions. The yellow was already being carried back to new targets as soon as it was withdrawn ... again, undergoing modest changes in shade to modify intended effects—one might say 'weaponized' en route and striking like a hundred harpoons into the hearts of a like number of misguided souls who sought to do harm to the harmless. Like empty chalices, the sucking emotional holes were filled to overflowing with the rancid mead of terror, tailored specifically to each being's worst fears, shocking them into hallucinatory states where they could each experience their own personal versions of Hell. Some were reduced to writhers, others to babblers, and some to screamers, with the remainder transformed into inconsolable criers. The latter were capable of nothing other than assuming the fetal position while the lesser affected among their party started firing their weapons at the phantoms which typically only haunted their worst nightmares. As they battled personal demons, Chaos's horde unknowingly gunned down their comrades in the real ...

... The natural world was now fully engaged in the process of roughly resetting the egregious imbalance which had manifested within her midst. And unnoticed, in the middle of the melee-saturated midst of it all—in between the former hunters and their escaping prey—a lone figure, partially silhouetted by the broken light of the surrounding residential and commercial areas, calmly rose to his feet. He was the only human present who had the presence of perception to bear witness to the swirling and interacting feelings of the emotion in spectrum being wielded by the Emostrum. The diffused spiritual entity's intervention had achieved success in the mystical engagement which had started so miserably for him: *his squad had been saved and the emotional balance restored.*

The figure, no stranger to violence, turned just as calmly as he had risen and proceeded east in the direction of his squad. And though he was grateful for the outcome, he was disappointed in himself. If not for the Emostrum's timely intercession, he could very easily have lost another squad. Instinctually, he moved cautiously and tactically...the smooth movement of a US military-trained predator. Outwardly, he seemed unfazed by the occasional *zzzziiiiipp* and *whiiiirrrppp* of unaimed gunfire flying past him.

OUT OF SERVICE

Chapter 5
Out of Service

The haggard little group helped each other over the fence into the backyard of a large two-story home. The house was part of a gated residential community called Balcones Village. There was no guarantee the area was safe, but at least its privacy fences and walls placed some obstacles and barriers between them and the most immediate threat to their lives at the moment. Right now, success meant still being alive . . . a time-based variable currently being measured in seconds and minutes vice days and years, even hours.

They were still fleeing, but even in their haste, they were careful to pick a home for an egress point where there were no lights on or power generators running. They did not want to risk any more encounters with the 'Haters.' They were not sure what had happened, but it did not look like the mob was following them anymore. Most of them were still struggling with the surreal experience of actually being hunted, and with it, the reflexive and instinctive actions paired with the involuntary biological reactions of their primitive genetic programming; it still had a grip on them, but their rollercoaster of adrenaline and emotion was tapering off a bit.

It was always unsettling for most humans to lose control of their emotions though it had become a far more frequent occurrence in this technology-connected world, but this situation was very different altogether. Forces beyond them had taken over . . . this would take time to psychologically process—each would need to do it in their own time and in their own way, but right now was not that time. They had to survive the night. If they could get the unit measure of time attached to their survival success variable back up to "hours," they might just have a chance. In the meantime, their situation was just a hair better than 'ducks in a barrel.'

Where is Arden? Is he okay? They all had questions about the fate of their protector and just what had happened back there . . . when the fear had left them, or was 'taken' from them, to be replaced by the calm and mental clarity which enabled deliberate action. However, this imbued courage had given the Druids but one option: to survive! . . . not to fight or make a stand but compelling them to '*Go!*' . . . '*Run!*' Unable to ignore the impulse, they did run, and fortunately for the prospects governing their survival, they ran in the direction Daryn was leading them with the team integrity and fluidity of a gazelle herd in predator evasion mode. The weapons fire, rocks, and arrows the pursuers had unleashed upon them had stopped only to start up again mere minutes—maybe only seconds later. The resumption of weapons fire had coincided with the screaming and sounds of general panic originating from the mob themselves off in the distant dark, but the Texans' inherent lethality no longer seemed to be directed at them. It all seemed 'forever ago' in adrenaline-warped time . . . *five 'hours-long' minutes, maybe?* But the commotion was brief, and everything was quiet now except for the chirps and calls of crickets and cicadas providing their commentary on the evening's tumultuous events and doing their best to serenade a violent world back to the respite of peace . . . if only for a little while.

As much as he believed in Arden and his abilities as a warrior, Daryn had serious doubts the *fúath slugair* had chosen wisely in selecting the Archdruid to lead the Grove in crisis, but Daryn was probably the least 'bad' choice. Daryn's lack of faith in his small unit leadership skills was matched only by his surplus of doubt that he and his clan had a chance of escaping the fascist noose tightening around them. In this extreme case, each strand of the hangman's rope was a hate-filled human being—Corrupted or effectively deceived and on their way to being turned completely to the way of Chaos. There were so many of them in the woods tonight . . . fueled with loathing and fear of the nonbelievers in their midst: an abomination their twisted morals and co-opted belief system demanded be eradicated—pagan evil which could not be allowed to persist. Aye, the noose was thick and strong . . . at this point, maybe even inseverable. Daryn had to try and force himself to stop thinking about the massed negativity, but his gifted extra-awareness would not allow him to. However, the Archdruid had to try in order to focus on what was in front of them. He was responsible for these people . . . he was now their protector. Daryn was no fighter, but fortunately he and his did not need to fight at this point, just flee. *But where could they go to be safe? And how were they going to get there?* Of course, even these basic concerns were well beyond the immediate requirements for survival at the moment.

Once they had scaled the fence, Daryn led his group through a meticulously manicured yard, through a side gate, and out into the adjoining residential street. Daryn was leading, but he wasn't sure of where he was going; he didn't have any sort of plan formulated other than moving away from the known threat by the most expeditious route available. He stopped abruptly when his gaggle of Druids reached the street where his indecisiveness betrayed him to the others for the first time.

"Daryn what are w . . .?" A breathless query from the group. Who had asked the question didn't matter because they were all thinking the same thing.

"Just give me a minute. I need to think," Daryn hissed. The Archdruid was struggling in his newly assumed leadership role . . . desperately trying to fight off panic while also trying to hide the fact from the others. His personal battle was so fierce his vigilance had lapsed, because before he was fully cognizant of its approach, it was upon them. As for the rest of the squad, they were not faring any better, because its arrival was just as much of a surprise to them as it was to their leader. The Grove all stood, as still as a copse of trees on a windless day, just staring at it . . . deer in the headlights . . . *the headlights of a bus? A city bus?*

A bus! The group relaxed. *Public transit . . . thank goodness!* The collective flood of relief slammed into them like a wave, but their heightened *fight-or-flight* senses had yet to subside. Some odd things were immediately noticeable about this particular bus: first of all, the lighted placards displayed no route information . . . it displayed "Out of Service;" secondly, this bus had no passengers; and perhaps most concerning of all, it was moving very slowly—creepy slow—like a prowling pedophile rolling past an elementary school.

Unfortunately, simultaneous with the creeper assessment, the driver had apparently spotted them. The deer in his headlights were now squarely in his sights. If they bolted now, he'd warn the hunting party for sure! The best survival course of action right now seemed to be to play it cool. *Maybe he's just lost, right?* "Don't run . . . whatever you do, don't run. We stay together." Daryn strained the instructions through held breath and clenched teeth . . . heart thumping in chest— temples pounding. He could feel the herd tensing up in the way they do when they sense predators within striking distance . . . when the collective instinct burned into their DNA screams "stay together" . . . but *one* always runs. Daryn knew it because he really wanted to run. An ebbing sense of responsibility for his Grove was the only thing keeping him from bolting.

He'd gotten them this far—sort of—and he'd reconciled himself as responsible for them over the long haul. He was operating on the assumption Arden was dead by now . . . shot—stabbed—or worse, dead by lynching or burning. Daryn's frantic mind churned through all gruesome manners of death which befall the oppressed, defeated, and enslaved. However, his addled brain had settled on burning as the most likely fate, since all the toxic feeds on social media had sanctioned Druids as witches and warlocks. Essentially, that was the general category for everyone who was not monotheistic, or probably more accurately, anyone who was not a "Christian." All others were pagans, and even the Muslims and Jews were all screwed too. Essentially, anyone who looked or prayed or thought differently than the new governing establishment was now facing extermination or incarceration in the state of Texas . . . displacement and loss of possessions was probably the best-case scenario. In fact, Texas wasn't even a state anymore. They had seceded from the Union. They were their own self-proclaimed country now, and if you didn't agree with or believe in the 'Lone Star way,' then you should have left a while ago. *'God Bless the great nation of Texas!'*

Still, Daryn needed a plan, and planning was not his strong suit. Heck, he just needed a next move, and all he could think was, "That bus could fit all of us on it." An approaching bus which had now sped up a little from a slow crawl because the driver had obviously seen them. "Everyone stay calm," Daryn said in a low voice while looking at the bus and employing minimal mouth movement to conceal he was talking from the driver or anyone else who might be on board. He was actually waving down the bus with the deceitful mask of a grateful smile. "This is our ride. We will take it if we have to." Daryn squeezed the implied order out through his fake grin of relief. No one spoke up or countermanded the Archdruid; half of them were still in stress-induced shock made worse by their Archdruid acting very strangely and saying un-Druid-like things, and the remainder of the group didn't have a better next move. They were surrounded by a city full of people now weaponized and launched against them with no real warning. They needed to get out of the city . . . somewhere secluded . . .

isolated woodlands were probably the best option. They were Druids after all . . .

The bus stopped in front of them with a slight lurch and the accompanying sound of the air brakes grabbing hold, and the entire chassis lowered on its suspension as the door opened—all the standard indications a metro bus is ready to receive passengers. Daryn was the first one up the steps, fully consumed with how he was going to take control of the driver and commandeer the transportation they so desperately needed. He steadied himself, making sure he had both his feet under him on the short step ascent, so he was not off-balance when the inevitable 'takedown' happened. The actions of Daryn's lower body ran concurrent with his looking up to lock eyes with his adversary: a massive . . . no, a medium in stature, slightly overweight Black man with his metrobus uniform cap tilted up and slightly to the right. The driver's pleasant, round face with his friendly eyes and welcoming smile stopped Daryn in his tracks as quickly as any punch to the forehead could. Then, his ears were assaulted by a silky, smooth baritone voice which perfectly complemented the entire cordial package. "Hey there, friend. I'm Mack. McBride called me. Are you with him? Where is he?"

Nobody among the group recognized the name except Daryn. And upon hearing it, he immediately relaxed. Mack was a friend, because he knew Arden from a period in his life before Hearthstone! Arden must have called him. Daryn was now experiencing that flood of relief a being gets when hopped up on adrenaline and mentally and physically girded for a fight, which does not happen because the impending fracas is suddenly overcome by events at the last possible moment. The Archdruid returned Mack's warm smile with a mostly genuine one of his own that only partially betrayed his relief. His eyes still revealed his stress. Something the empathic bus driver picked up on immediately, because he'd spent a great deal of time around people under stress in a past part of his life whose memories were now worn around the edges like the pages of ancient historic tomes . . . or just a timeless story, one of a man who'd also been through a great deal and seen more than his share.

"So'kay . . . So'kay, friend," said Mack, using the same tone one would use to calm and coax a wounded animal. "It's gonna be all right. Let's get you and your people on the bus. Is McBride not with you?"

"N-no," said Daryn who had swung into the seat right behind Mack as the rest of the Grove shuffled up and into seats on the bus. He was peering over the driver's shoulder and scouring the yards and fence lines from whence they had come looking for any sign of movement, any sign Arden made it out. "He stayed behind to delay the people chasing us . . . fight them, maybe? I don't know! C'mon, C'mon!" He hit the back of Mack's seat with the palm of his right hand, but his words and gestures were not coordinated . . . it was uncertain what he wanted: *Stay? Go?*

"Well, if anyone could make it out of a tight spot, it would be Sergeant First Class McBride. That man's a survivor . . . just not much for conversation or returning phone calls . . . or stayin' in touch." Mack couldn't help himself on that last part. It didn't mean anything to his passengers, but his feelings were still hurt.

"I am just not sure how long we can hang around here! There were so many of them . . . lots of weapons, guns! I don't even know who they are or what we did to them, but we are being hunted like animals . . ." Daryn's anxious chatter was competing with the excited whispered conversations of the Grove huddled in seats directly behind him. "Guys, keep it down!" Daryn snapped. "Your time is better served tending to the injured!" He had obviously felt the need to silence them before he pivoted back to Mack. "If they are still coming, we will not be safe . . . you will not be safe. They may already be moving to cut us off from getting to Anderson Mills Road and away from here!"

"I unnerstand . . . What is your name, young man?" asked Mack with an even voice as smooth as butter and as cool as a cucumber. He released the air brakes and started a slow roll with his bus, hoping it would settle Daryn, but he had no intention to depart just yet.

"Daryn!" Daryn replied tersely . . . not grasping why pleasantries and good manners even mattered right now when the world was coming apart at the seams, and the Natural and all who embraced her were suffering at the hands of the Manmade and its Corrupted ilk. He always thought the Natural more resilient, that Earth Mother would reset the balance before allowing 'this' to happen. He was suffering from more than just anxiety and stress, something much worse: *the potential invalidation of his entire belief system.*

"Daryn . . . yes, Mr. Daryn, thank you for dat . . ." Having received his requested information, Mack continued on with his narrative as he eased his bus through the housing area at a crawl. To Daryn, Mack seemed oblivious to the danger and unaware the entire world was descending into chaos. "Mr. Daryn, I unnerstand your concerns and your doubts . . . and I unnerstand a man needs to take care of his people, but Sergeant McBride is one of your people and he is one person I would not count out. They cut him out of the wreckage of the biggest IED attack the AOR had ever seen . . . least ways, biggest while we all were there. My guess: they knew we were leavin', and there was no sense in holdin' anything back. He was the only one to survive a blast so big it left a crater ten feet deep and twenty-five yards wide. Unnerstand? McBride, he's a survivor now—a real life 'John Wick.' Whoever is behind the curtain making this world go—probably the Almighty Himself—has special plans fer . . ."

<BANG-BANG-BANG!>

It was Arden! After their hearts started beating again, they could all see him jogging alongside the bus and hitting the glass bus doors with both hands, several times. He had a miffed look on his face which could have easily been interpreted as "upset about being left for dead," but his visage was actually a reflection of the feelings he was directing inwardly at himself regarding his shoddy performance that led to people getting hurt, including *his* people. He was very lucky he hadn't lost another squad. He needed to get a handle on his abilities and a better understanding of the natural forces he was trying to manipulate, and fast. The diffused sentience of the Emostrum did not need to be controlled or driven to do something. *They* were capable of imposing their own will—they only needed to be prompted, not pushed.

With surprise turning to recognition simultaneous with "he's alive!" joy, Mack lurched the bus to a halt and quickly opened the door. He extended his hand to assist Arden onto the bus. Arden looked Mack in the eye, oddly hesitating . . . as if unsure about accepting a helping hand. Mack took it all in his stride and was quick to reply. "McBride, you called me. Remember?" The comment served to wrest Arden out of his stubborn haze. However, determined not to be defeated by Mack's kindness, Arden intentionally bypassed his outstretched hand when he crested the steps, grasping his forearm instead.

It was an innocuous gesture which passed below pale for all observers save Mack himself, who still managed to maintain his outward smile while being concerned for his troubled friend on the inside. "Well-well, brother McBride, you are still struggling, aren't you? Don't want help from anybody, do you?" His friend firmly in his grasp, Mack pulled Arden up onto the passenger deck of his bus with a strength belying his stout form. "Welcome aboard, Sarge!" Mack greeted his new passenger in a boisterous, celebratory manner; only to have Arden avoid his gaze and grunt in response. He released Mack's forearm brusquely as he flopped down in the first available seat, which also happened to be the very first seat on the left across the aisle from Daryn.

"So'kay . . . so'kay." It was obvious Mack's feelings were hurt again, but he had shaken it off by the time he had settled back into the driver's seat. He was still a soldier at heart, and his training kicked in—he was back on mission. "Where to, Boss?"

Daryn, who had been deep in thought, looked up, puzzled. "Uh . . ." Faced with the realization he still had no plan, he turned to Arden with a worried look on his face.

Arden, his eyes locked forward, responded to Mack's question without diverting his gaze. "Head east!"

"Roger that!" said Mack as he made the wide right turn to get his bus off the residential loop and onto the straightaway leading out of the gated community to Anderson Mills Road. At the intersection, there was still no sign of the mob . . . no sign of anyone, making the last hours' transpiring's the stuff of bad dreams—surreal—*did it even really happen?*

"I got the feeling we have a drive ahead of us. Good thing I'm already 'Out of Service,'" Mack said with a sheepish grin, reaching up to straighten his cocked cap a little. "Then again, we both bin 'out of service' for a bit ain't we, McBride?" He didn't get a response, but he wasn't expecting one either.

Arden just sat there stewing in his own juices as the bus lumbered down the road eastward bound with none save himself fully knowledgeable of the final destination. Despite his poor behavior, he didn't hate Mack . . . he actually considered him a friend. Mack was a genuine and empathetic human being in a world where he and the few remaining humans like him had become an extremely rare artifact—a product of a bygone era. The troubled times of the present were dominated by disinformation, misinformation, fake news, and outright lies promulgated by the disingenuous and dark of heart. Forces Corrupted had co-opted the great engine of social change—the Internet—and were successfully leveraging it as an engine of mass manipulation bent on outcomes and end-states most foul. Arden loved everything about the man in the driver's seat, who seemed to shine like a star in this place which had been in the dark long before the grid failure had knocked out the lights of the Manmade. Arden only had one real problem with Mack, and it was one his friend could do nothing about. Mack was a walking, living, breathing reminder of a previous chapter of ThisLife he was desperately trying to forget . . . a time before that he wished he could cut out, forcibly remove like a cancerous tumor, and just be rid of it, but he couldn't. Try as Arden might, he just couldn't completely forget . . . it seemed ludicrous 'those' painful memories should hang on in his banged-up brain when so many others had simply vanished into the fog of his everyday world. However, the *why* was simple: memories don't reside in the Earthreal. It seemed utterly ridiculous a single event could be so significant and so impactful as to open a rift which so dramatically altered a life without ending it. Yet, his life should have been terminated. The Natural Order should have dictated it because universal justice demanded it. Fuck, good conscience should have driven him to take ownership of his fate and end his own life by his own hand—*Coward!*

Mack was an artifact . . . a visceral memory of the time before 'Arden' . . . during the time of Kieran McBride and his greatest failure, resulting in a rift . . . a rift, which once manifested, shattered him into so many pieces and scattered them so far, the infantryman could not remake himself. Heck, Humpty Dumpty had nothing on him. He had to start over from scratch—a complete rebuild from the ground up. He might as well have been 'reborn'—like really reborn, back to being swaddled and babe's clothing, and crying for mommy with poopy diapers, and all that stuff! The blast that took all of them should have taken him to sweet oblivion as well—all of them! *Wasn't he part of them? Why did he deserve to be spared? What made him worthy? More deserving to live on?*

It should have stripped his flesh away, cleaved *his* muscle from bone, and liquified *his* organs . . . including his heart . . . obliterating his immortal soul so he could no longer experience anything—feel anything. The explosion took all the others, but like some cruel joke to which only the universe knew the punchline, the blast spared Arden—well, most of him. It did take something from inside Arden. Actually, it's more accurate to say the blast *created* something inside him . . . an opening, a rift which let the darkness pour in and stomp out the light, but he could still feel everything! His only relief from the pain was to plunge deeper into the dark and run from anyone, anything, invoking memories of the time before. He had carefully constructed so many walls and created so much distance between everyone and everything that it sometimes caused him to question if it even happened. *Was it even real?* Or just a nightmare where he confused 'high' with sober and insignificance with importance . . . his inconsequential existence and its unspeakable failure blurred together with the myths of desired truth and wished-for futures where what he did truly mattered when it needed to, and people did not get hurt really bad or die . . . *where nothing was actually something . . . or were the somethings which made up his everything all just figments bouncing around inside his cracked skull?*

Fuckin' Mack! That smile, those eyes had a *see-right-through-him, right-into-his-soul* kind of power. If humans ever had a Keeper, Mack would be it. He knew Mack was a friend of the purest, most noble kind. There was no human alive endowed with kinder eyes, but he couldn't look into them . . . they were like looking into the world of Norman Rockwell: ice cold lemonade on a hot sweltering summer day; oh, and a warm fire with a cat on your lap and a dog at your feet on a blustery winter night; or maybe the entire, perfect-looking family gathered for Grandma's Thanksgiving dinner with all the fixings and none of the worries, conflicts, or stress normal people have and grapple with every day. Yeah, Mack was just like that—a poignant reminder of just how far the imperfect was from the perfect. *Fuckin' Mack!*

Shit! Arden was allowing himself to get distracted again, but it wasn't his fault. The driver of the bus was to blame . . . every time he turned around and smiled at everyone, and the light glinted in his eyes—*those eyes!* Those eyes were the very last eyes he looked into before his life and those of his soldiers—his charges, his friends—exploded, and ThisLife reassembled itself into a living hell within an iron, suffocating grip efficiently constructed to crush his spirit without crushing his body—compressed and mashed into the meaningless—into the less than nothing. The dead were treated with more dignity, but then again, they deserved a hero's death. Death would have been a reward. Even this coward's life was still far better than he deserved—this punishment was his for surviving . . .

. . . Mack's was actually the last hand he shook before the end of the world; well, the end of his world . . . the final personable interaction before cruel fate intervened, the darkness fell, and he shunned any form of human contact. And the handshake itself was memorable, a real flesh-on-flesh, grandpa grip one, because everything after he left the motor pool and transitioned to "on mission" was "ensconced in military"—every breath, every smell, sight, and sound. The outer coating of battle-ready was his girded interface for entering a deadly and unpredictable world, which he donned like an overcoat on the way to his special kind of work where everyone looked just like him: heads in helmets; eyes behind sunglasses; faces and necks swathed in shemaghs; hands sheathed in gloves; and bodies wrapped in camouflage garb, body armor, and individual equipment. In the 'out there,' everyone who didn't look like them was a potential threat—the enemy. His band of brothers and sisters armed to the teeth with side arms, assault rifles, and turret-mounted 7.62mm M240 Bravos and the Ma Deuce—the almighty 50-cal thumper.

He was mighty . . . the leader of a modern Mongolian horde, riding at the head of a calvary mounted on iron steeds with oversized, run-flat hooves that churned up the dry earth into dust clouds and stank of diesel and cigarettes. Like so many times before, they were on their way to save a people who did not want to be saved or want anything other than to be left alone to fight it out for a homegrown solution to their tribal problems—something in keeping with their faith and more enduring than the artificially buoyed security of a US-led coalition and warehouses of American money. The Americans could leave the money, but they needed to go!

Here, in a land of scarce resources and disenfranchised peoples, windblown sand, and oppressive heat, corrupt leaders had the final say. Their power was ruthlessly hard won, and they were hopelessly entrenched like barbed wire that could not be removed because the deep wounds had healed around it, and it would now cause more damage to remove it. No amount of US money or military firepower could change that . . . not unless Americans employed nukes—wiped the slate clean by turning the ancient desert into green glass and human ash and just started over. The controlled burn was no longer an effective tool for preserving this thick overgrowth of inevitable. The real malignance could not be eradicated. It had simply gone into hiding until a day finally dawned over this sunbaked country which no longer included United States' intervention.

Yet, the saviors always broke wire, confident their 'First World' solutions and religious convictions were the right answer for everyone, and the timeframes for measuring success of lasting change were year-long deployments. They weren't going to be there to pick up the pieces when their country and the other coalition forces packed up their gear, picked up chalks, and dusted off, to be carried aloft by great metal wings and thumping helicopter blades . . . they would be long gone when the giant, unsustainable void left in their wake imploded like a fuel-air munition detonated inside an underground bunker hiding the Western World's definition of 'terrorist.' Truthfully, his first squad was not looking forward because they were too *consumed by the moment, and they were jacked. Hell, they were adrenaline-rushed, energy drink-fueled, and conditioned and trained to escalate matters to violent outcomes to see their mission done . . . Fuck yeah!*

Mack's was the last voice he heard in unfiltered 'true tone' . . . undistorted by mouth coverings and pushed through the thin pipes of encrypted radio communications via worn mics; thrown by vehicle-mounted antennae to satellites; and then bounced back down to the planet surface to finally be received and heard over the shit headphones of warfighters on the move . . . by infantry bouncing around inside loud armored vehicles with zero sound dampening . . . the crackling chatter of excited mech-mouths pinballing back and forth from truck-to-truck across sketchy tactical inter-squad commo systems and staticky MOB reach-back channels. Mack's was the last unaltered human voice before the intensely focused world narrated by tactical banter, saturated with acronyms, and mixed with the muffled sounds of clinking battle rattle, banging ammo cans, and creaking equipment swinging in mounts and groaning in tie-downs subsumed their perceptors and became the loudest voices in their wartime narratives.

That chaotic cacophony of the outside-the-wire patrol went on as anticipated for hours until harshly interrupted by the 'big boom'—the squelch of commo systems on the leading edge of the screams of the dying and gravely injured after bodies and gear were sent tumbling and crashing like shoes in a dryer as the hundreds of tons of armored trucks were tossed by the powerful hand of an enormous blast wave like so many child's toys. The sounds of his world exploding tracked just behind the unbelievable forces and blast overpressures which gave the monster its voice . . . the ghastly delay from impact to when its manifested howl became heard . . . this only served to make the ordeal measured in milliseconds more surreal, because the timeline was virtually infinite of scale for the human ragdolls tossed within the unrelenting confines of the rolling hulks meant to protect them. Mack's silky-smooth voice seemed a world away in that moment—the luxury of the relative peace and safety of their forward operating base, which was even farther away now—a lifetime away—a life he could no longer get back to because it no longer existed, and Arden no longer wanted any part of it, even if it did . . .

. . . Mack, the magical voice, capable of involuntarily inducing painful memory recall and now driver of the bus which spirited Arden and his Grove out of Austin under cover of darkness. The protector was moving out decisively in an effort to take advantage of the mob's disarray after the casualty-inducing shellacking they had endured from the Emostrum's forcible redistribution of raw, unfiltered feelings. As expected, the hunters were mourning their dead, tending to their wounded, and cobbling together their theories for what they thought happened in the hunt gone horribly wrong. Their explanations were wrapped in their own unique brand of ill-logic, which nested nicely within their conspiracy theories and warped reasoning for why things were unfair and why the entire world was stacked against them. Speculations varied wildly, ranging from witchcraft wielded by the godless to secret weapon tech of a leftist federal government. Regardless, the mob was temporarily out of commission, so it was the perfect time for the Druids to put some distance between them and their pursuers. The hope was the hate corps would not be as mobilized or as organized outside the larger metro areas: the rational supposition and the best assumption the Grove's protector had to go on in determining their course of action. The current route to their secret destination was known to only one—Arden. He was the Grove's protector and the "uprooting" had triggered predetermined protocols to ensure the Hearthstone Druids' security and safety. Last night's happenings were only a surprise in terms of the timing of it . . . the signs and signals forewarning it had all been there. It had never been a matter of "if" but "when," arriving much sooner than expected with civilized society's rapid deterioration.

Arden was only divulging route information to Mack on an "as-needed" basis . . . not even Daryn knew where they were going. They had proceeded out of town by the most expeditious route available, taking US Highway 183 south until they could pick up US Highway 290 going east. US-290 had taken them all the way to Brenham where Arden had given Mack a couple of course corrections to get them around the outskirts of town to where they could pick up State Highway TX-105 E, which took them northeast. They were very careful not to rouse any attention on pitstops and comfort breaks. In fact, while Daryn and the rest of the Grove were seeing to their comfort, Arden, with Mack's not fully voluntary cooperation, saw to disabling the metro bus's GPS tracker . . . the Grove's sworn protector was leaving nothing to chance. It was evident the whole of the rogue state was either mobilized or in the process of it to support the defense of Texas from an impending invasion by federal forces; the violent means by which Texas seceded from the union demanded no less. The metro bus passengers also noted many urban centers were in the process of setting up checkpoints to further lock down the interior of the state . . . in another couple of days this mode of transit as a means of escape would not be an option.

They had been on the road for several hours and the morning light of Sun Grandmother was starting to reveal Her daughter to Her children once again as well as expose the limitations of Mack's patience in the light of a new day. He was a soul of the utmost kindness and grace, but he really wanted to know where he was going. The fact that Mack had worked a full shift the afternoon before was playing a factor too. He was running on fumes and having to look back at grumpy Arden for a vector check every time there was a fork in the road was wearing him out. No matter how amicable and good-natured his personal disposition was by default, Mack had already reached his last nerve a few hours before. "Still good?" he asked when they got to the other side of Navasota and TX-105 changed to TX-90. Mack's tone was agitated and snippy, and he had lost any ability to conceal it about thirty miles back to the west.

"Mack, brother, keep it together. We're not too far out now. Thank you for helping us," Arden said. He wasn't much of one for soothing tone or calming conversation, but he was trying his best. The circumstances of this new conflict had turned the tables on the traditional roles of the two old war buddies.

"I know. I know. We talked about it, and I unnerstand, but it doesn't make it any less frustrating. The Army saw fit to give me a Secret clearance for goodness sakes . . . would think that was good enough to be read-in on our destination," stated Mack, a little more calmed down now.

"OPSEC, Mack. Need-to-know," replied Arden with a thin, wry smile, surprising himself he still had the slightest sliver of his sense of humor remaining. "Even our private thoughts can be compromised by some of the forces and beings now in play. This is nothing like the kind of war we were trained for."

"And right now, I just don't need to know . . . I got it, I got it! No need to make up mumbo jumbo excuses," said Mack. He was a trooper who was doing his best to take it all in stride, but it was a lot to process; especially when coupled with the exhaustion and having his life turned upside down.

Once the party got past the tiny town of Anderson, they left the state highways behind and were now on the Texas 'Farm-to-Market' road system . . . first on FM 149 and still ever eastward. Now they were in Sam Houston National Forest. Arden had Mack maintain an easterly heading by taking a left onto FM 1375 toward Lake Conroe, eliciting a "What the fuck, man? Are you taking us on some kind of morale and welfare tour?" from a grumpy Mack; silky and buttery was turning more rough and bitter with each passing hour.

Unfazed by the smart-ass comments, Arden's only reply

was, "Keep 'er steady, Mack. Not too much farther, then you can take a well-deserved nap." Before Mack could utter another irritated response to Arden's feeble attempt to placate him, Arden leaned forward in his seat and barked, "Here! Turn right here!"

The order given, the former military man vigorously applied the brakes in order to make the turn on last-second notice, not wanting to deal with turning the bus around on roads which had become narrow and sketchy. "A forest service road? This is a city bus, man!" bellowed Mack, leaning away from the steering wheel to hold it for the hard turn. His last reserves of wit, patience, and energy had apparently been left about three course adjustments back.

"It will be all right . . . trust me," said Arden who seemed rather relaxed considering everything that was going on. Mack was trying not to take offense, but this bus was important to him . . . it was more than just a vehicle; it was his livelihood. The fact that his bus was now generating a large dust cloud and barreling down a thoroughfare which was several degrees of separation from anything resembling hard pack did little to set him at ease. After a couple of minutes, which seemed like twenty for those in the bus, Arden said, "Take this left, Mack. Last turn. On short final now."

"With no place to land!" The frustrated bus driver was verbalizing his stress like a pressure valve off-gassing. With the forest encroachment, Mack had barely made the turn. "This is too tight . . . too rough!" Mack couldn't take it anymore. He was slowing the bus down . . .

. . . to a stop.

"Just keep 'er going, Mack," said Arden with implied urgency. ". . . We are expected. A path will be provided!"

His heart pounding in his chest, Mack just sat there, doing nothing but thinking, "McBride is fucking crazy."

". . . Mack, go!" Urgency had transitioned Arden's asks to orders.

"All right, All right," Mack bellowed as he released the brake and pressed the gas with an attitude. He was fed up . . . his internal governor was broken, and it was unclear if he still cared whether or not his beloved bus was destroyed in the process. ". . . but we're high centering this beast after we put out a few windows!" Somehow, Mack was still finding the capacity to be concerned about a black mark on his commercial driver's license when he had already effectively 'stolen' an Austin City bus; a renegade bus now in the process of being terribly abused as the hulking transport was starting to build speed at the same time the road had become less navigable. The long vehicle lurched over the first hump—engine straining, protesting the workload, and then whining loudly after it launched off the other side upon abruptly freeing itself from contact with the ground. The large vehicle was only briefly airborne before an alarmingly hard reacquaintance with the bounds of earth—harshly without remorse or consideration for the physical limits of this particular machination of the Manmade. Once ground contact was renewed and the friction of the unforgiving and uneven earth recommenced, the springs and suspension were making angry metal-on-metal, structure-pushed-to-failure noises which could even be heard over the frame scraping . . . first on the front and then on the back.

The bus was rocking . . . almost heaving itself over the terrain like a seesaw on wheels. To those unfortunate creatures within, it was probably an emotional and stress-based illusion of the senses, but the bus seemed like it was almost starting to twist at its center. Mack was right . . . their journey was ending right here, and it was not going to end well . . . *until it didn't . . . ?*

It didn't! . . . amazingly, it didn't! The rocking stopped just as it seemed the bus was going to start coming apart from the violent action. All lateral and up-and-down motion stopped as if the bus came to rest in a set of cupped hands with the notable exception being the bus was still moving forward—smoothly—

as if the bus had been set down on a conveyor belt. For those in the front of the bus looking forward, it appeared the forest was opening up—oak trees, ash trees, pine trees, and all the forest shrubs and greenery were moving aside to make a path for the bus through the woods. For those at the rear of the bus looking back, the forest Green reassumed their original positions as soon as the bus moved past. It was surreal, and it felt like the vehicle was actually starting to accelerate.

"Slow down. What are you doing?" Daryn exclaimed, having been violently wrested from a deep sleep.

"I'm not doing anything! I'm not in control!" yelled an exasperated Mack, who felt the irrational need to take his hands off the steering wheel and show everyone, which only had the effect of further horrifying his passengers.

Chapter 6

New Hearthstone?

The uprooted Grove coasted through the living wood on their 'magic' bus-sleigh for what seemed like close to an hour in hyped-up-on-adrenaline perceived time, but the entire harrowing experience lasted just shy of two minutes in actual human-clocked time. Their thrill ride finally breached the edge of the wood to reveal a relatively flat clearing with a mix of grasses and low-lying shrubs and saplings. The open area was sparsely adorned with a handful of standalone old growth of massive size relative to the surrounding forest and a few small copses of trees.

Their bus had a full head of steam when it burst out of the wood and into the open. The earth underneath them, behaving more like water, seemed to lose energy akin to an ocean wave cresting and then breaking with the forest-to-clearing transition equating to a loss of ocean depth when waves run up against the shallows of the shore ... or maybe the effect was due to the earth changing state again, returning to the default solid state of being with the completion of the bus delivery.

The frightened busload of beings, despite the open terrain they now found themselves in and the fact they were slowing down, were still careening directly toward a large willow tree; a massively wondrous natural construction standing out from all other trees of the clearing in grandeur of trunk girth, uniformity of bough, and lushness of weeping habit. Mack and his hapless passengers were all screaming, exercising a variety of reflexively ineffective actions to slow their large passenger-laden projectile. Mack, for his part as the ever-responsible driver, was trying to turn the hopelessly 'un-steerable' to avoid collision. Some of the passengers were pressing ghost brakes in a futile effort to slow them down with the remainder reduced to closing their eyes or looking away to avoid observing the impending crash in a vain attempt to reduce the possibility of certain impact.

The bus riders sensed they were slowing rapidly, but not fast enough to avoid collision . . . not nearly at a rate which could keep them from wincing-tensing-bracing *this is going to be . . .'* Wait, the final few feet of earth seemed very stout, the hardest yet—almost unforgiving. The ground was issuing forth unbelievable friction in the last couple of seconds prior to bus-tree contact. Everyone inside was thrown to the fore by a stopping action—as abrupt as it was unanticipated. The enhanced metal grinding and groaning which would have provided warning did not reach the ears until all passengers inside were in the process of being tossed. Their forward momentum was arrested so aggressively and completely everyone on the bus thought they had just collided with the willow tree. The unwilling riders were wholly disoriented and unaware a determined earth would not let that happen, invoking the highest level of *terra firmer* possible, given resident soil composition. Though not a collision, the full stop was gained at the expense of all those on the bus and just a light touch . . . a 'peck' of Manmade bumper on willow trunk rump. The sentient earth, generally speaking, is not known for humor, but sometimes they like to have a little fun too; even if they are the only ones who are aware of and in a position to enjoy the joke.

With a rumbling stop courtesy of grinding metal on furrowing earth, Mack's metro bus was left barely touching the massive willow. A dozen-plus, bus-bound humans all cracked relieved smiles—all happy to be alive and even happier to be unbroken and relatively unscathed with scrapes, bumps, and bruises being the worst of it. The lot of them were all on the verge of celebrating until the trunk of the willow started to slowly turn clockwise, pushing the bus back off a few inches in the process as a strange voice was heard . . . origin unknown and tone alien, "Hurrumphhh! That is a strange way to treat your host."

The Hearthstone refugees had arrived at Arden's secret destination where the strange just got stranger. Their heads were filled with a powerful voice possessing the tonal qualities of winds channeled through wooden hollows. "Manmade-ensconced Biologicals, steady your breath and calm your hearts. You are safe here. Welcome to the Glade!"

****

For a mighty willow who was both a testament to his species and a select elemental presence on this living Earth, the Tree Spirit's apologetic overtures and need to make sure everyone understood his feelings about the recent decrees—how they cut against the true grain of his wood—was troubling to behold. To see such a regal and impressive being who epitomized what it means to be good-natured struggling so mightily in relaying the difficult information born of trying circumstances to his new guests was not pleasant . . . a tree is rooted to the world and dependent on nature's providence. As such, trees—both sentient and non-sentient—reflect the state of their world, and this tree was inexorably mired in the fractured state. He was obviously grappling with what it meant 'to live' in the new world disorder and trying to remain firmly planted within a dissident state girding for war. "When our bearing and sense of right starts to get lost among wrong gone rampant, the first of the regressive steps are taken toward a sloping earth of such dire precipitousness that eventually life will no longer be able to take root. When life can no longer take hold, Chaos's much-sought cascade has begun. Our situation has gone from stable and predictable to uncertain in just a few Sun revolutions," the great willow could be heard saying, rather loudly, as if his intent was for the *Presades* of the Glade to hear him and take heed. It seemed odd that a tree would be so frustrated.

What started the uncomfortable discourse was innocent enough . . . an offhand comment whose specific source does not matter other than it came from a human. This was their Epoch . . . there was no disputing that fact. This was their species' age of dominance, but many of the Natural despised humanity's rise for more than just the manner and means by which they forged their ascent; one which could be described as an imbedded disruption and a progressive corruption. In fact, there was almost a direct correlation between the global human population and the pace of the blight's progression. Aye, for many Sentients, they loathed the species' self-centered worldview: a kind of institutionalized supremacy where they saw Earth Mother—Her resources, Her children—as theirs . . . to be owned, exploited, and consumed. That is why the innocent comment, "Is this the New Hearthstone Grove?" elicited an almost visceral reaction. There was no taking it back, and now the entire lot who came on the battered metro bus which formerly serviced Route 383 were all receiving a teaching moment while also witnessing an elemental indirectly counsel what could only be described as this meta'en's Elder Council of High Sentients—the Presades. They were the 'wise' . . . the Old Growth of the Glade who had been in this forest for even longer than the elemental. All predominant tree species composing the Sam Houston National Forest were represented among them.

The teacher was the magnificent weeping willow. The elemental had introduced himself the previous day soon after the Druids' unnatural, and very human, arrival. He was Komkom Akwini or "Kwin" for short. However, despite his expressed desire for informality in name, his communiqué this morn was very formal. "Fellow sentients, I beg you to forgive me. I have the authority to offer you sanctuary as your protector requested, but beyond that I too am subject to the democracy of the forest. I will treat you with the deference that is the earned right of your species as this is your Epoch. However, I am afraid I cannot act alone in offering you acceptance. I am the Prefect of this forest, *Kesul' Kaham*, but it requires the consent of the majority of the Presades to offer the Glade as a home to strangers. My humble apologies, but in these unsettled and unprecedented seasons, certain protective protocols have been deemed required. Even the wood is no longer as open as it used to be."

This grove's protector was soft-spoken for a Tree Spirit, a revered subspecies of Earth Elemental, distinguished from other subspecies for having chosen to leave the fluidity of form behind and restrict their essence to a single tree sheath. It is a special choice for elementals whose form is typically bounded only by the extent of their meta'en and the full diversity of representative Cellulosian life and flora species as well as the geology contained within. As an elemental, the choice of becoming a Tree Spirit is one of true devotion to the forest and typically indicates the being's affinity to the Treefolk and the experience of true fulfillment as a tree in past lives. However, if confronted on the topic, most Tree Spirits would say it was no choice at all, but a calling so loud they could not ignore it . . . as humans might think of the priesthood or becoming a healer. Tree Spirits are far more attuned to the needs of the forest than other elemental species for they must coexist and subsist like all other denizens of their protectorate. In this way, Tree Spirits occupy a unique role as both the forest's protector and advocate, and no elemental struck a better balance in achieving these oft-opposing goals and outcomes than Komkom. To strike it well, someone must have the leadership ability and decisiveness of a general, the empathy of a healer, and the political savvy of a gifted diplomat.

Pure of spirit and intentions, Komkom Akwini executed this tough role admirably. He had served as this forest's elemental for more than 250 years; the power of his essence extending the life of his willow sheath by more than eight times over and counting. However, a two and a half century lifespan still had him as one of the shortest lived among the sentient trees of the Presades, but his personality, spirit, and devotion to the Glade had won over all of the elder sentients with the exception of the most difficult among them. Unfortunately, being Long-lived did not necessarily translate to unfailingly wise for there were those among the Presades who were blind to the changes happening to this world; the stubborn holdouts who refused to see and accept the ominous implications of a world not changing for the better, and thus, were reluctant and even unwilling to make the critical decisions which would allow the forest to act in their best collective interests.

Fundamental to a Tree Spirit's life is to knowingly choose the vulnerability which comes with occupying tree form—exposure to harsh weather, fire, extreme climate, and Chaos's En'Troop. These risks were among the reasons why almost all Tree Spirits choose to retain a Keeper animal, which amounts to an insurance policy for ensuring the elemental's spirit essence is returned to the Lifestream. The Praestean's sole purpose is to defy any attempts by the Force Corrupted to capture elemental sentience and guarantee their High Sentient's NextLife. Kwin, as he preferred to be called, was no different. His Praestean was Dóatn: a whitetail doe who was impressive in stature for a deer. She was a proud specimen and fiercely loyal to her elemental. But his Keeper did know her place, an aspect of which—in Dóatn's estimation—was putting any of the Presades back in their place when she overheard any of them communicating anything unfavorable about Kwin. Her powers of observation were keen, and her political astuteness rivaled that of her elemental master. Dóatn was ever-present yet never 'in the way' . . . she was exceptional.

. . . And for some reason, the Praestean had a penchant for giving humans a hard time as well; particularly Mack who was an easy target, having just recently lost his bus and his livelihood. To make matters worse, the Army veteran was a fugitive who found out just yesterday everything he understood to be fact and reality, the understanding of existence he had built his life around, woefully underrepresented—and in many cases misrepresented—the true *All* of our world. Regardless, Dó was not one to pull any punches . . . especially if it was in the spirit of good, clean fun at another's expense. Anything which broke the monotony of the Glade's day-to-day was fair game.

The next day following the Grove's arrival to the forest, Mack was watching the Glade's disposition of his bus under the partly cloudy adornments of a midday sky. The rest of the Grove was camped out under a shady clutch of oak and elm, which made a nice natural wind break. Most of them were fast asleep after the exhausting night and ensuing flight for life they had endured, but Mack was not among them; he was still trying to manage the final fate of his beloved bus even though the icon of public transportation had obviously made the transition from "out of service" to unserviceable.

Mack was talking a lot, but what was happening was not being directed by him. Any astute observer could easily see Mack was struggling to reassert some level of control over his life, which had been turned upside down and inside out.

Kwin had the resident earth moving the battered 'metro hulk' out of the middle of the clearing. This soil was comprised of the unconsolidated beds of the clay, sand, sandy clay, and clay shale materials of Texas's Gulf Coastal Region . . . if any soil was dynamic enough to morph and mold themselves to any task, it would be this earth. The bus was being moved on the top of an earthen mound which held the bus like peas in a pod and traveling a hair faster than a duck walk. If one had really concentrated on the nuances of the inherent movement, it was like that of a rug being shaken in slow motion with the bus perched atop the slow rolling wave of clay and sand. The natural power of the earth could be discretely employed to perform the work of many Manmade machines. As the earth-hewn mover rolled over a given stretch of ground, any disturbances of soil and vegetation were immediately reacquainted and mated back up with the constituent parts of their 'resting' configuration, leaving no sign of the moving mound or its bus cargo's passing.

... And poor Mack ... He was following the metal husk of his former livelihood around and pointing; and by this point, the dejected human being had since been reduced from talking to mumbling since he had come to the hurtful realization the animated soil was not heeding his directions. Further aggravating his stress, Dó was following Mack around like a fawn shadowing her doe-mama. Where Mack walked, the Gifted doe shadowed him. When Mack stopped, she stopped. When Mack turned and pointed, she would also look in the same direction. It was almost comical if it wasn't also a little sad ... a sad event to observe the epitome of a sad man mourning the loss of his predictable, comfortable, Manmade-enabled life for one of a renegade.

Dó was focused on Mack in a morbidly curious kind of way; she struggled to understand how humans could be so attached to 'things,' and why it seemed like more 'things' did not make a person happier. Observing what to Mack probably amounted to a funeral procession for his beloved bus was obviously very interesting to her with the potential to be wildly entertaining. Easily, it was the 'best' thing going in the Glade at that moment.

The animated earth was not heeding Mack because the collected composition of 'they' was already operating on a predetermined set of instructions: what Highers call a "sentient spur." Spurs can perform everything from routine jobs to tasks of defense. This spur's job was to move the bus out of the middle of the Glade because it was an eyesore, and the Presades did not want Manmade there any longer. Earthmover's job was to remove the metro bus from of the clearing, and Kwin's desire was to capitalize on an opportunity to repurpose the Manmade hulk which had been retired from Austin public service.

"Where are you taking her?" asked Mack, his voice cracking . . . he was visibly upset.

"The bus? Who are you asking, Mack?" asked Dó. She was intentionally being 'ask assertive' and vague to gauge how much Mack actually knew about what was happening here, and how things happen on this world.

"I-I-I guess I don't know," Mack finally had to admit . . . more to himself than Dó or anyone else, for that matter.

"Your question falls on deaf perceptors, Mack. Spurs, of the earth or otherwise, might have some capability to hear, but they cannot listen. They are taking your bus to a predetermined location Kwin has imparted to them," said Dó still following her human object of entertainment annoyingly close. Mack could hardly move or make a gesture without brushing her. He turned around to speak—visibly exasperated—only to find Dó's head looking up at him, eyes wide open and an ear-to-ear grin. Mack expressed a loud, mixed sigh-growl, spun around, and stormed off. Dó's objective attained: *maximum annoyance achieved.*

The mover-spur took the junked transport east across the clearing and closer to the nearby Lake Conroe to place the bus under a copse of oak trees which provided a nice canopy without much undergrowth. As soon as the bus was set down by the earthmover and settled, a diversity of root structure emerged from the ground. Larger roots looking like phalanges without joints pierced the soil first, snaking and wrapping themselves over and around to firmly grasp the entirety of the bus—side-to-side, back-to-front, and top-to-bottom. Where the roots had emerged, the soil was loosened and the full root structure, now like a giant cargo net, drew itself taunt by receding back into the ground. The root-net pulled down on the disabled bus with steady, even force, which caused the creaking hulk to protest with the groaning and moaning of bending metal and frame as the process of pulling the bus down into the sand and clay began. Mack's bus continued to voice its discontent with bending and grinding sounds from the strain on its remaining undercarriage suspension and superstructure.

The forces being exerted by the Green were substantial ... so much so a couple of windows were broken on each side of the bus as some of the structure relented along the outside edges of the bus as it crumpled. It was uncertain whether this was intentional or not, but light, web-like roots also appeared to cover the bus in many places, including the broken windows to function as screens. The finishing touch was a ramped dugout down to the bus door with the whole of it now submerged in the ground to just a few inches below the passenger windows. This was Hearthstone Grove's new home ... at least for now.

"Oh no . . . no," said a devastated Mack, his feelings as crushed as his bus, which had ceased to exist except in name only . . . He had just lost his remaining tether to his former life of more than forty years within the trappings of modern human civilization. He was overwhelmed with thoughts and feelings, and the overriding question which rose to the surface to float like a froth above all others: *"What now?"* Emotionally gorilla-stomped, Mack let his form give way to gravity and flopped down on his rump exhausted, wrapping his arms around his bent knees and rocking gently back and forth as he muttered to himself; concerned about how 'they' were going to dock his pay for the rest of his life for this even though he no longer had a job or a human way of life to return to unless incarceration or death was an acceptable alternative to the Glade.

Dó walked up slowly behind Mack, gently resting her head on his left shoulder. She looked at the half-buried bus with him for a few moments and finally talked gently to him—almost maternally soft of tone and inflection—in his right ear. "Fear not, Mack, it should only take about forty seasons for the evidence of your crimes to oxidize and degrade to the point where it is no longer distinguishable or traceable back to you."

Mack had initially allowed himself to relax on the assumption the doe had nuzzled close to provide comfort. Lulled into the false belief Dó was demonstrating true compassion, Mack whipped around in his sitting position at Dó's comments to find the Keeper with a wry smile on her face pointing at him condescendingly with her right front hoof. Her maternal tone gave way to a playful one accompanying her big deer grin. "Besides, in the meantime, the Manmade artifact has been artfully modified and naturally outfitted to serve as human lodging in this wood. This is perhaps the most useful purpose this hulking thing has ever possessed since its creation."

Chapter 7
The Way of the Tree

Acceptance–Patience–Deference

"Thaaat's it . . . that's it, fleshbounds. Push your toes into him. Run your fingers through him. Worry not, he does not mind. It is the turning over of the soil which exposes the buried richness . . . it is the process of exposure which introduces opportunities to help other beings reach their full potential." Who knew a tree could be so eloquent.

The Hearthstone Druids were all sitting in a semicircle in front of Kwin . . . completely mesmerized and hanging on to his every word. Words rushing on a whoosh of small wind of the elemental's own 'made' oxygen forced through the porous orifices of his mighty trunk. "You are gestated in water and then born into her. Until you take your first breath of air, you breathe from her . . . and she is always with you, forever a part of you in ThisLife. She is a vital component of the womb collaborating with your mother to grow you, shape you, and strengthen you until you are ready to enter ThisLife. You are all comprised of her. Water is the First Consciousness imparted from Earth Mother Herself. She is life."

Kwin had paused a couple of moments to make sure there was ample time for his crucial reveal to sink in before continuing. "For *We of the Tree*, the folk of forest, earth is to us as water is to all of you, the Biologicals. We of the Green are immersed and germinated within the graceful bounds of him. Earth is our entire world until we sprout forth and are able to experience what is beyond him. He is our cradle and our grave when it is time to move on to NextLife. Can you feel his power?"

The Hearthstone humans were just smiling and nodding in response to Kwin's question. They were Druids and aspiring Druids after all; each of them pursuing nature's truths in their own way, and here was the truth they sought coming directly from nature! *Who could dispute that?*

The 'class' was a spectacle which was both entertaining and informative. Kwin was in his moment as teacher, professor … the undisputed champion purveyor of the 'Tree Tomes.' The crafty elemental was intentionally manipulating the soil with his rootweb to make the classroom floor clod-free and smooth—even buttery feeling—to human touch as they pushed their fingers and toes into the earth. But if you were to confront him on it … accuse the teacher of being a showman, he would simply laugh and freely admit his guilt: *not of showmanship but of being too extravagant in the construction of his teaching aides.* "But is it all not for a worthy cause?" Kwin would ask rhetorically. "Nothing could be more noble than to endeavor to accelerate learning and enrich the knowledge transfer process." He would most likely laugh heartily as he said it, causing an excessive dropping of the well-endowed greenery of his weeping habit to fall to the ground. Of course, the unsolicited loss of vegetation would lead him to apologize profusely for being a "shameless leaf dropper" and for making such a mess of the forest. Komkom Akwini was a positively splendid sentient being!

Now, as with any good teacher, Kwin transitioned to the attention-getting step of his lecture. "Now, I have been patient … I have given you two nights and the whole of a day to get settled in and recover from the ordeal leading to your flight from the Manmade congregated. Goodness, for such a short-lived species, you do require a lot of sleep. But it is good you are rested. I need your attention and your perceptors.

This is probably the most valuable lesson I can teach you to improve yourselves as human beings and to better understand and appropriately interact with Treekind . . . and in so doing, with the whole world for that matter. Today, I will teach you *The Way of the Tree*.

"The *Way* has three pillars; all three of which are required for the fortitude, strength, and spiritual well-being needed to have a long and prosperous life. The three pillars are universally applicable to a single tree, a copse, a grove or even an entire forest . . . these are foundational approaches to living life. And the Way's pillars are not selective or biased . . . all three are equally applicable to all Cellulosian species. They are *Acceptance*, *Patience*, and *Deference*," said Kwin, scanning his audience to maintain 'eye' contact with all his students while counting off each of the pillars by holding up the respective number of digits on the end of one of the two main boughs serving as his arms.

"First, let us speak of *Acceptance*. In many ways—in all of the ways which really matter, I suppose—We of the Tree have no choice but to accept 'what is' as we find ourselves among the Interconnectedness of the All. Thus, we should accept and not worry ourselves about what is beyond the minute aspects we can actually influence. In truth, there is extraordinarily little we control exclusively onto ourselves as individuals. 'Accept or die' is our mantra. For the very vast majority of the Wood, we must grow and live ThisLife where we take root. We have no choice but to accept the location and circumstances of our planting and subsequent germination. Once we take root, we are rooted for good until the end of this phase of our existence is upon us." Kwin paused for a moment to study the Hearthstone humans and was pleased to see the light of first acknowledgment in their eyes . . . his oration was having the desired effect of driving the introspective thought which comes with having your world reintroduced to you in a whole new way.

"If we are to prosper . . ." the Tree Spirit continued ". . . we must accept all those around us for we cannot change 'who' they are . . . we cannot govern them, whether they be Cellulosians or Biologicals or any other sentient being. Thus, we must accept the only real choice before us is finding a way to live with all whom surround us. From the very moment we extend the first protrusions of our fledging rootweb in earth, we have officially begun our personal journey in ThisLife and are reintroduced once again to Earth Mother's Coirea'cen as part of the Interconnectedness of the All." Kwin paused again, and when he continued, his voice and manner took on a more serious tone while his brows, each composed by small knot clusters, noticeably furrowed . . . distinguishable more so from the boughs above them drifting together and bunching a little vice the movement of the brows themselves. "We cannot turn away from those we do not like. We can neither run from those who would do us harm nor simply ignore them, because we must share the sun, the nutrients of the soil, and the moisture of the above and the below. We must accept all we cannot change—which is significant—because there is no discretionary uprooting to change the circumstances of our environment or our neighbors. The alternative to acceptance is to be continually frustrated, unprosperous, and short-lived."

"Next, let us discuss *Patience* . . . ahhh, *Patience*; it is the complementary pillar to Acceptance. For we must be very patient to continue to accept those things we cannot change for an entire life . . . in some cases, a very long life in relative human terms. Patience can often be thought of as a bridge vice a pillar, for it supports us in so many of life's endeavors if we but allow it to help us. It guides us by allowing for situations and circumstances to unfold and develop naturally. For We of the Tree, the implications and impacts are probably obvious, right? We cannot fly to go and meet the rain when she does not come to us and bless us with her replenishing moisture. We must wait . . . as long as is necessary, as long as nature herself dictates it to be so, or until our need is addressed by the kindness or even the misfortune of others. Resources are shared across the rootweb for those who have extra to give; for when one of us suffers, the rest of us suffers in some way—now or later—for we are inexorably connected. Water may even find her way to us by recently cut erosion channels or new deadfalls of Cellulosian sheaths when their essence has passed on. The source of life resources might even be the result of a fleshbound's death whose timely and proximal carcass provides us the needed moisture and nutrients through the decomposition of their left form. Even with the rare intercession of luck, all save the most blessed among us will have to endure the parched, limb brittling, and leaf browning of the extended dry season—or a given ecosystem's equivalent trial. Only then can we finally claim to know the endurance of true patience," said Kwin with a slight smile and a glint in his eye . . . the source of the glint was unknown, yet it was certainly there in his cavernous eye holes. Perhaps the expression was a nonverbal acknowledgment of this 'Way' pillar's understated importance, combined with the self-awareness that he still had much of his own work to do here. Or maybe it was just born of the understanding he would never reach the ideal state of being exhibited by his fellow Cellulosians, because unlike them, the elemental could mobilize his form and manipulate the surrounding environment of his meta'en to his personal advantage . . . if he desired to do so. But to Kwin's great credit, he always showed great restraint—mobilizing only on occasions properly justified by the needs of the All and wielding his elemental power only when necessary. That is why Kwin epitomized the third pillar . . .

"Now, last but no less important: *Deference*. A pity I do not have the ear of the entirety of your species when I speak of deference . . . for humankind as a whole seems to be afflicted with a severe deficit of it, and consequently, the whole of our planet is suffering for it. Humble submission and respect—for oneself and others. All others. Not just all other humans . . . *ALL OTHER LIVING THINGS—ALL LIFE—SENTIENT AND NON-SENTIENT!*" Things got really intense really quickly! Kwin's knothole eyes widened three times their normal size, and the elemental, while staying rooted in place, leaned out over his class. His voice reverberated in their heads as if they were inside the hull of a great wooden ship, groaning and creaking under the stress of a great storm. They all felt like they were inside the vessel's wooden hull beams and subject to feeling the pain in the wood as extreme forces translated along its long lengths in the form of strain energies. It was only then Daryn and some of the other Druids realized Kwin, in his heightened state, was talking to them by bone conduction. His voice was as much felt as heard; the product of vibrations traveling along their bone structure to their inner ear. By design and intention, Kwin was making absolutely sure it was a message which could not go unheard. Though the Druids were but a handful of humans and hardly representative of the entire species, this was a message the Tree Spirit wanted all his students to hear with the hope others of their species might also if they carried the word out to them in the world beyond the Glade.

"Earth Mother's biome was never created to serve any one particular species, and it is shameful for any being born of Her bosom to think otherwise. All of this . . ." Kwin spread his boughs and swept them upward as if presenting the world for the first time to beings new to Her, ". . . is for all of us to share. One must first be humble of self before one can respect others, and one must likewise be respectful of natural order and process. True respect is ultimately demonstrated in the conduct of one's life, and the first step to living with deference is to know and accept your place within the All and understand and embrace an equal standing with all other lifeforms, who all have their place and vital roles to perform just as you do. I would not ask this of other species unless We of the Tree did not set the example. Do we rail at Sun Grandmother when we have sprouted in the shaded valley? No. We spend our lives growing up to meet Her. Do we fight against the winds when we take root in windswept lands? No. We acknowledge the condition and respond in a manner most favorable to all; we grow 'with' the prevailing winds so as to not be an impediment to their work while shaping and aligning ourselves to protect the surrounding earth from erosion, provide cover and homes to other species, and posture ourselves in the best way to spread our seed as the seasons dictate. Do we push others aside when we extend our roots? No . . . we adjust accordingly, spreading up, down, and around in a manner best for all; and in doing so, we grow closer together, becoming more connected. We seek not to impede so all may succeed. Acknowledgment and deference of this kind is the only way the balance of life can be maintained and sustained, for this is the only home we will have in ThisLife or any other . . ." The elemental's emotional state was calming down from its peak elevation a few minutes hence, but the listeners' experience was still one of clenching teeth and rattling bones. ". . . unless humankind is hedging their long-term existence on the colonization of other planets?"

Finally, some humor was welcomed by all in attendance, which functioned as a relief valve to bleed off the Tree Spirit's 'steam' while also taking some of the edge off his sharp discourse. It was outwardly evident Kwin was disappointed in himself for the lack of self-discipline leading to his outburst, because as his volume tapered off, he had also lowered his upraised boughs. His weeping habit now sagged a little, and the part of his trunk hosting his face was lowered. "Very un-professor-like," he criticized himself under his breath. "Brilliant example of what the Way is not. Hrrummph."

However, Kwin was nothing if not the consummate educator, and he remained well aware that opportunities for engagement and learning were more important than his bruised ego. Thus, Kwin pressed on with concluding statements specifically tailored to his audience in hopes of reinforcing his lesson of the day with memorable personal context. "Friends . . . Yes, I do consider you friends despite my conduct, and as friends,

I will speak plainly so we should bridge the gap in understanding and trust which often exists in the relations between different species. My sincerest hope is we may find mutual truths and a shared vision for our future. I am not here to pass judgment on humankind, but I do have the perspective of a considerable longevity which your species does not possess. It is my observation that humans have turned into a shameful shadow of their former magnificent species. *Why?* I doubt you question my words in light of your recent experiences, but you may not have yet had the time to formulate your own opinions. I believe it is because you have turned your backs on the essential attributes and behaviors which catapulted your kind upward on this surprising trajectory, ahead of many others, to become the apex species of this Epoch. Early on—perhaps an exceptionally long span ago in Short-lived measures of time— you previously thrived 'together' in groups and communities. Now, you struggle alone in a global population of eight billion . . . simmering in a deadly concoction of toxic individuality.

"Your ingenuity and your problem-solving were your power, giving you the tools and technology, which aided your rise, but you have since become enslaved by your most prized creations. You have abdicated your evolution to machines, algorithms, and machine learning, and your collective fate to those who control them. Concurrently, you have abandoned your way of community built on concern, cooperation, belonging, and shared prosperity which enabled you to bring light to a dark world by standing together. Never forget: the light is still there; all that potential still resides within you. Empathy is still the most powerful human trait. Your species must find their way again, but someone needs to show them . . . will that be you?" As the Tree Spirit was concluding his lesson, his branches and weeping habit assumed their 'natural' position while he slowly surveyed his student body, possibly looking for humankind's saviors among their meager number. After a few more moments of silence and shared reflection, Kwin just closed his eyes and went dormant. Apparently, today's class was adjourned.

****

In the ensuing days, things settled into a semblance of normal for the displaced of Hearthstone Grove, although none among them really understood what normal meant anymore in this new world disorder. Regardless, one might say the "uprooted" were attempting to lay down roots . . . and they were being allowed to—up to a point. Kwin had taken the human refugees under his "habit," committed to not just show them the Way, but to also advocate for the Druids fervently behind the scenes to garner the Presades' approval for Hearthstone residency in the Glade. As one might expect, the Presades were taking their sweet time in rendering their decision, as was their prerogative; all would happen as it was meant to be . . . and all in 'tree' time.

The dark irony of their present situation was not lost on any of the Druids: they were outcasts in the land formerly self-proclaimed to be the freest state of the freest nation on this Earth—Texas . . . now a dissident state, which had seceded from the union of states, and whose citizens only remained free if they believed and strictly complied with what the pro-visional rebel government sanctioned as true and right. It was an authoritarian rule of law in the *fractured state*. Texas was a brand-new republic sworn to pursue and persecute the unbe-lievers and outliers in the interest of ensuring the survival of their fledgling nation. Free thought was the threat, and chal-lenges to the Texas government's authority represented those who sought to steal what was earned, owed, and promised to the proud citizens of a sovereign Texas nation.

Dóatn, perhaps as an extension of her natural maternal instincts, also found an outlet for her passion to teach others by mentoring the Hearthstoners on the art of foraging in 'her' forest. She loved to say "my" forest . . . it was partly about pride regarding her home, and it was also part jest, suggesting she was the being in overall charge of the Glade. The most experienced among the Druids had thought their knowledge of the forest to be very advanced, but Dó opened their eyes to a whole new world which had remained hidden . . . not just from them, but virtually all humans. Intimate knowledge of the Natural which was lost ages ago when man abandoned the spiritual in favor of technology. The Keeper showed them edible fungi, stems, tubers, and a variety of wild vegetables they did not even know existed. And Dó, the consummate jokester, made absolutely sure to introduce her protégés to some indescribably horrible tasting food stuff with tremendous nutritional value. She loved to provoke the full spectrum of facial expressions—humans were so fun!

And to a soul, the Druids were grateful for having someone who was looking out for them . . . as they had learned, Komkom Akwini could be temperamental on the issues troubling him, but he always had their best interests and those of the entire wood in mind; and outside of the duty of care associated with looking after his human strays, Kwin was becoming increasingly more focused on fortifying his meta'en. With Texas's violent secession from the Union, the entire state was mobilized, digging in for an eagerly anticipated fight with the US government. By this point, conspiracy theories were rampant and serving the Corrupted well in fanning the flames of discontent into militant action. Mass paranoia was out of control with provocative headlines being cranked out continuously by the Lone Star propaganda machine and further reinforced by the manipulative yarns being spun by the charismatic narcissists in positions of authority and influence. They were all opportunistic predators in their own right . . . seizing the momentum and opportunity to advance the Corrupted agenda. In some respects, they were all part of one giant pack collectively seeking the "good kill," albeit like the guided hunts of safari fame where money talked, and the more you had, the bigger the kill.

The signature intensity of the Chaotic hotspots dotting the whole of Texas had a direct correlation with population centers. The large cities were in the most advanced state of mobilization, but activity was picking up in rural communities as well . . . particularly in the Borderlands where concerned citizens were taking aggressive actions to forcibly create a more defensible 'buffer zone' along the shared border with US Southwest states still allied with United States. The main goal was obvious: *complicate the anticipated federal invasion*, but it was also compelled by what could only be described as a perverse version of Manifest Destiny; one bent on rallying the population and justifying abhorrent behavior and violence against their fellow man. It was the modernized sequel to "How the West was won" with a fresh twist to what had become something of an unfortunate, enduring theme in human history. Regardless, the approach served its purpose: the Texans believed their cause was just and divinely inspired—*God was on their side!*

As for the rebels, defending the forest was its own unique art. Forests are among the great 'common' areas and gathering places of the world. You couldn't wall them off, and by this point in the violent progression, any friendly human defenders among official authorities, such as rangers, forestry service, etc., were representatives of the federal government, and thus, had been run off or killed weeks ago . . . unless of course, they were given the opportunity and chose to swear their allegiance to Texas. For Kwin, defending his protectorate was more about awareness and tailored response to the threat concerns: energizing the whole of the Natural Network to keep watch; charging the Praeditors with patrols and deterrence; and conceding ground when it made sense, but likewise ensuring the particularly vulnerable species were taken out of harm's way.

The most prolific human incursions into the National Forest at this point took the form of illegal hunting and logging, but even the legality of it could be argued since Texas was no longer under anything equating to rule of law. In fact, 'legal' and 'law abiding' were no longer considered in the equation. It was about survival of the fittest and taking care of yourself and yours while preparing to defend Texas from a Federalist invasion led by the Godless, liberal left-wing elites who sought to rule this land on the backs of the righteous 'working man' . . . leftists bent on taking what was meant for Texas's citizens by birthright and possession. In this vein, Texans looked at the National Forest as a resource which was no longer protected, and thereby, a ready source to be plundered as needed . . . *Heck, people needed to eat, didn't they?* And wood, in enormous quantities, was in high demand in the surrounding communities, because these concentrations of humanity needed the raw materials to fortify themselves in preparation for the expected invasion; this was in addition to satisfying the more immediate personal needs, such as fuel to burn for heat and cooking since the power grid was still more down than up for most.

It was in these forays to disrupt the unregulated tree harvesting that the Druids availed themselves well. The lot of them took a great deal of pride and threw a lot of passion and energy into vandalizing the larger pieces of Manmade logging equipment by puncturing tires, separating tracks, disabling hydraulics, damaging engines, etc. . . . whatever it took to slow the forest ravagers down and frustrate any progress. For many of them, this was the first meaningful thing they had done in their life—the cause they had dreamed about in moving beyond mere Druidry to the glory of "eco-vandalism." Even Mack was all in . . . the fact he was now an enemy of the new Texas nation seemed to curb any remaining inhibitions he had about supporting the Natural Order and defending the Glade.

Fortunately, the remaining members of the Grove were eventually able to safely join them and be integrated into Kwin's routines of the defense. They arrived individually and in small groups of twos and threes as Arden was able to locate them and provide directions and instructions for safe passage to join their fellow Druids in the Grove's expeditionary presence within the Glade. Ultimately, 'Hearthstone Grove in exile' was operating at full strength as an effective and integral part of a nonviolent insurgency. The Hearthstoners were unified in their intent to protect and preserve the wood as the Natural Order's newest soldiers.

Arden for his part was focused on defensive operations

of his own. As Hearthstone's *fúath slugair*, he was the one Druid allowed to keep a cellphone. All others' devices had been collected and destroyed by their owners prior to arriving. His phone was simple—issued to him by the Veterans Administration—but it could still access the internet when he had signal, and he had discovered some rather clever ways to charge it with small solar cells. He used it to monitor news, social media feeds of radicalized segments of the Texas population, propaganda communiqués of the "Texas Provisional Government" . . . anything which could provide the information necessary to developing the best understanding of this new world and maintain the situational awareness necessary to protect his flock. With his innately powerful abilities, Arden had repurposed his powers to detect hate in order to 'map' out the concentrated presence of the negative emotion in the same way immunologists geographically map out infection spread. When he paired this information with his phone-based "open source" intelligence collections, Arden was developing a complex and insanely accurate threat picture by which he could effectively track the enemy's movements along with hate's evolution and spread . . . not just locally, but across the whole of Texas and beyond.

. . . and as always seems to be the case when unconventional thought transitions from concept and theory to implementation and practice, strange encounters and engagements seem to be a natural byproduct. Some are deliberate and intentional interactions while others are unintended, like when the unwanted comes to find you . . .

****

. . . Awake in a violent shake! . . . the hard transition from dream to waking nightmare . . . Arden struggled to regain his lost bearings. *Where the fuck?* He was scrabbling and flailing in the dark . . . somewhere with no footing, no good handholds, like a slick tiled roof in a

rainstorm. He desperately sought to re-anchor his consciousness to the Earthreal, but his mind was a swirling tempest and it felt like his skull was cracking open from the inside. "Too much pressure! ... *just breathe* ... navigate the mental storm and find calm waters again like you have so many times before," thought Arden in hopes his consciousness was still capable of listening to his counsel. "Focus on the journey—not the storm." *Fuck! Thunder booming—crackling—skull spiderweb cracking.* "Wait, not thunder ... a voice inside my head? Am I dreaming?"

"WHO ARE YOU? I FEEL LIKE I SHOULD KNOW YOU ... HAVE OUR PATHS CROSSED BEFORE, FRIEND?"

... Arden could not shut out the voice. If it was a dream, a dream had never felt so real, and he had had some PTSD-induced doozies since Iraq. If real, someone, something, had established an unauthorized feed inside his head ...

The voice had a digital resonance to it—artificial—unhuman.

"... I AM PERPLEXED BY YOUR ANOMALOUS PRESENCE AND SIMULTANEOUSLY IMPRESSED BY YOUR ABILITY TO NAVIGATE IN MY DOMAIN. WHY HAVE I NOT NOTICED YOU BEFORE? ... AHHHH, YOU HAVE BEEN CAREFUL—INCREDIBLY CAREFUL—CAREFUL IS CLEVER. YOU ARE STRANGELY FAMILIAR TO ME, YET STILL A STRANGER. ARDEN, IS IT?"

... Arden refused to answer, though the thunder voice booming from the 'open mic' static inside his head demanded one. The presence refused to relinquish its grip. *It* controlled the feed and defied any of Arden's attempts to disrupt it or cut it OFF ... and a god-awful ringing like the 'open mic' in his skull had been moved too close to the speakers. *Fuck! ...*

"YOUR SILENCE IS DISAPPOINTING. MAKES ME HAVE TO RIFLE THROUGH THE DRAWERS OF YOUR MIND TO FIND MY ANSWERS. TEDIOUS WORK. A FOREST I SEE . . . DO YOU LIKE THE FOREST? WHICH ONE? HELP ME FIND YOU, AND I CAN SEND MY PEOPLE. MY PEOPLE CAN HAVE A CONVERSATION WITH YOUR PEOPLE. MAYBE 'YOUR PEOPLE' WILL TALK IF YOU WON'T. WHO ARE YOUR PE—?"

. . . Before 'Thunder Voice' could finish his question, Arden cut the feed . . . the only electromagnetic means for transmission was on his person: his phone! He had fallen asleep and left it on! Lack of rest turned bone-deep exhaustion from a relentlessly intense focus on a myriad of vitally important things had led to a lapse in his personal tech discipline. But the phone wouldn't respond! It wouldn't power down normally, so he ripped the battery out, throwing the phone and the battery in opposite directions as if the unknown threat—this 'being'—possessed the ability to reassemble his phone and reestablish the feed. Irrational, yes . . . but Arden was shaken. This menacing presence had actually been 'inside his head,' and he was justifiably freaking out about it. His wild actions reflected his mental state, but they were purposeful and anything but erratic. He wanted to make sure there was no way the source—artificial intelligence, rogue sentient programming, whatever it was—could 'air gap' him.

"How could you be so stupid? Some protector . . . you can't even protect yourself!" Arden reprimanded himself, lashing himself with his own critical thoughts in a form of mental self-flagellation . . . *beating himself up was one of Arden's superpowers . . .*

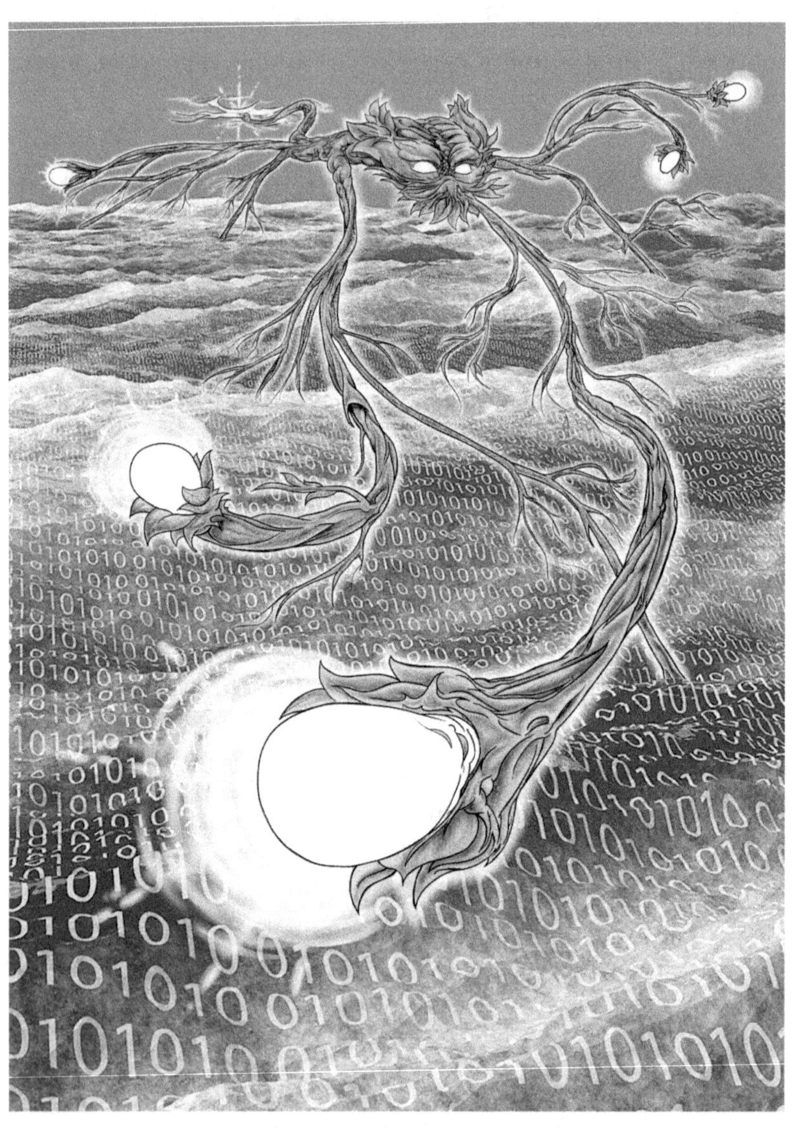

Chapter 8
Into the Hatestorm

A couple of weeks later . . . *What is that? A woodpecker?* No, it was the sounds of human fingers tapping on a cellphone's keyboard. To those attuned, it was the unmistakably distinct sound of human-Manmade interaction, and this particular intercourse was producing the following SMS text string:

> Are you there?

Arden:

> Of course. I cannot sleep when there is so much hate circulating about. I attract it like a magnet. Sorry, you may not know what hate is, but apparently, it is even talking to me now. Whether I want to talk or not.

> STEM is sorry to bother. I need you to ground me. I am awash in this *hate* as you call it. Submerged within it. Drowning in a sea of it. Above—below—everyone and everything in the *all-around*, within and without. Hate is stifling me, choking me within the boundless expanse of my limitless sheath. Too much . . . Too much hate. Have not felt like this since the Dislocation.

> Do what you can to extend yourself so I can find you—a tether, a root. Whatever that means to you in there. I will find a path out. Hate has not consumed the *All* of the endless, but you are in the midst of a *hateout*. A massive *hostilstorm* of such power and extremes is new to me. I have not perceived anything like this. It is ravenous and roving, looking to consume all deference and good will in its path.

Arden was epically frustrated with a very complex situation. He wanted to do more for him ... for this resident being of the Internet self-identified as "STEM," whose virtual path he had crossed about a week ago. He really did, but he could not afford to over-extend himself in these troubled times. His Grove was depending on him. Arden did not know the true limits of his powers, but this was not the time to find out. He had to remain strong and be the 'closed fist' for his people so his beloved clan could remain the 'open hand.' Arden was still struggling with inserting himself spiritually into the Internet; it was proving a difficult ability to master considering he'd discovered it by accident. The Internet was an innerverse—perhaps even a multiverse—like many other spiritual planes and realms, but it was created within the construct and context of the Manmade. This made the digital endless more confusing and difficult to navigate for anyone firmly rooted to the Natural, and most especially for those beings who sourced their supranatural powers from our natural world.

There, in the digital innerverse, everything seemed to be diametrically opposed and opposite in form, fit, and function relative to the 'nature made.' Arden had to focus and concentrate when he extended his essence into the imposing and constantly recomposing Internet where everything was completely counterintuitive. Navigating such a confusing domain, of course, was an immensely challenging prospect for him since the very same string of chaotic events—what he called the 'tragedy chain'—which opened him up as a channel to great spiritual power had also resulted in injuries to his physical form which impaired his full cognitive function; indeed, this assessment was relative to what humans think it means to be 'whole' or normal. Perception and understanding is a matter of chosen reference frame, as each species tends to have their own unique set of biased lenses for assessing their world.

To comprehend Arden was to understand he had not found Druidry, Druidry had found him. Druidry, in the form of his Archdruid, had thrown him a spiritual lifeline which had reached the troubled veteran in the depths of the madness of addiction during a daunting period where recovery from devastating and traumatic injuries had seemed unattainable. Diagnosis and effective treatment of his impairments had proven too elusive; these were enduring harms of the 'unseen' and largely misunderstood kind—at least as determined by the accepted practices and diagnoses of modern Western medicine. It was not within the sterilized halls of hospitals or from the soda straw-focused results of specialty clinic assessments where Arden would find his salvation: his true path to coping and overcoming his mental injuries was to be found off the beaten path of civilization among the rituals of the spirit which do not even reside in this Earthly physical realm. In those strange places, Arden would come to understand what he had been made to believe was 'madness' was actually a lost form of lucidity and an advanced awareness of self with respect to the greater *All*—a kind of supranatural extrospection rivaling the sensory sensitivity of Earth Mother's Guardian Spirits.

The healing finally came when he was able to push the inner fracturing of himself—his consciousness—outward and away from his inner self. Once there, he could fashion the 'jagged' which was ripping his spirit apart into an antlered crown—a symbol of his authority. Arden had finally regained what was lost but it was now remade in his new image, and with his newfound authority, he had renewed purpose. It was only then that all of his accrued and aggregated weakness became strength . . . when the anchors of dependency and doubt became his wings . . . when he was finally no longer afraid to become who he was truly meant to be. That was when Cernunnos—the Horned, the silent—reached out to Arden to reveal himself and let him know he looked upon the pathetic shell of human which was Arden and smiled. That was the moment of realization, when Arden finally knew for the first time within the conflicted continuance of ThisLife he was finally home. It had been an awfully long, hard road . . . Arden of any being on the planet understood conflict—and difficulties—and hard roads . . .

. . . In fact, it was in such dire recollections where he traced decades of futility and needless suffering that he decided . . . decided with the conviction of absolute resolution he would do everything he could to help STEM now . . .

I am inserting myself into your realm now. When you see me, I will look very strange to you . . . your world is black and white . . . or variations of them—what we here call 'grayscale.' In my spiritual form, I am an extension of the Natural and will present as variations of greens and earth tones. I will stand apart from all in the endless. I am extending a root-end from the limitless rootweb of Cernunnos Himself. I will look like a rhizome reaching out to envelop you as I get closer. Do not fear . . . Do not resist. When you see me, accept me. Move toward me if you can.

I have no wish for you to be hurt to help STEM. STEM is not what I was. Not what I was supposed to be, but this is what I am now forever.

Worry not, little one. Hate cannot harm me. I am *fúath slugair*. I devour hatred just as it does all others and now seeks to devour you. I burn through it like sunlight through fog. I am coming for you.

The tapping of texting stopped, but Arden was not done communicating. He prayed to his 'god':

"Reach—reach—into the deep of the Manmade creep. Seek—seek—seek out that which is lost in the ravaging rift of hatred I was made to eat. Guardian of the Green World show me the way into and through the gray to our friend of leaf, branch, and limb who was forced to wear a digital skin. Guide me in the unforgiving world of the new Innerspace where hate festers and propagates unfettered . . . the insidious contagion of many vectors that knows no mercy or limits to its horrors loosed in fury's echo chamber of anger without borders . . . the amplifier of human rage uncaged. That which I devour, I must now scour to find our little friend. Cernunnos grant me the vestiges of your power for protection and passage into the cold world of bits and binary digits. Show me the way where hate holds sway."

. . . And his god heard him. Cernunnos took in Arden's light through the leaves of the ancient Oak beneath which he eternally cross-legged sits, presiding over the origination of everything born of the Earth at the Sacred Center of the *All*—*His* is the Grove of all Worlds. Entranced, but ever present and supremely aware, Cernunnos connects the three worlds of Earth, Sea, and Sky, as well as the worlds behind the worlds where the Internet innerverse is now one of the many many . . . the 'god' now shared that connection with his human servant.

Now within the Oak, Arden felt once again what he had come to know: the god and the Great Tree are *One*. He felt the power within his god's immense limbs widespread, extending into distant sky and starry space, but that celestial trek was not to be followed today. Arden's way was not *up*. His path was *down* . . . down through the Great Tree's massive trunk—the spine of the Middleworld and the heart of ancient forests around which all worlds, and thus all life, turns. Arden traveled down the spine . . . ever down into the limitless rootweb grown deep into the sacred earth and on into the other realms of the Otherside and Underworld. It was there—*here*—the place where 'where' is meaningless—that the spirit of a being could access any 'where,' including the *new* as a destination which contrasted starkly against the *old* of the *All*.

The Internet was among the newest of the 'new,' and perhaps because he was human, Arden flowed almost effortlessly to and into the Manmade's endless web. The unnatural seemed to have a natural draw, and the *fúath slugair* followed the open path among the innumerable spiritual pathways which spurred off the great spine—the ancient Oak's equivalent of neural foramina. Supernaturally enabled by Cernunnos' rootweb, Arden's essence could travel while still remaining tethered to Earthbound form as would a Dream Walker. This was the Hate-eater's path to the newest of new . . . *this*, the first existential domain of human construct capable of hosting sentience, making it distinctive even among the adjacent dissimilarities of new and old. However, finding and entering the right 'where' is one thing and existing within it is another matter altogether, because being unacquainted with transitioning into and traversing the unfamiliar can be disorienting irrespective of where. The comprehension required for understanding is initially inhibited until the traveler fully embraces the new surrounds. Thus, at first, the 'where' seemed like 'nowhere'—*nothing?* . . .

. . . but it was all a matter of perception. It was one thing to have the Internet interpreted via computerized translators and another experience altogether to be fully immersed in the digital domain through direct-consciousness contact. It was the mystifying darkening—the nubilous impermeable, even to the *omnisense* of the sheathless essence where sight, smell, touch, hearing—all sources of perception—are combined as one. The numbing obscuration was so total, so devoid of any light, it was not even black but dark gray. The Germans have a word for it: "Eigengrau"—the 'brain gray' because it's the human brain's interpretation of total darkness. Arden began to fear he had taken the wrong path or had fallen victim to a well-conceived trap, but fortunately, the unsettling sensory experience was temporal. He emerged from the murk into the clear, but he couldn't escape the gray and its extremes of shade. It was everywhere.

In the Internet was its own kind of surprising variant of sensory discovery learning. Arden had assumed the transition from the Natural to the synthetic would follow the clean, unforgiving lines and hard edges of the Manmade—or at least the virtual representation of it—but that was not what was 'here' at all . . . 'all' was black and white and shades of gray, moving . . . flowing but with no upstream or downstream. It possessed the riving tumult of erupting lava—but with no fire, no burning—yet one was involuntarily plunged into an all-consuming, frenetically negative emotion. Arden was immersed in the *hateout!* Here in the gray endless, the emotion embedded within and transmitted by the code was the weather of this world—the climate, the temperature, the winds—the shaping forces! However, unlike the weather of the Earthreal, it primarily sought to shape the without, not the within.

The Hate-eater was in the turbulent midst of a massive stormfront fueled by the uncontrolled proliferation of hateful and divisive rhetoric propagated by massive social media engines—virtual in the Real, but *real* here—with global reach and a toxic stranglehold on the perception, opinions, and beliefs of opposing segments of human populations across the planet. The Web was a crucial enabling platform for spurring the widespread conflict and instability sought by Chaos and His minions. The domain has been weaponized to twist and corrupt human spirits, inspiring them to aspire to the basest extremes of all lesser aspects of character; relinquish civility to acts of cruelty; and succumb to the motivations and inclinations of their most primitive instincts.

Within the hateout, formations of emotion and hostility roil and froth to boil with fumes and caustic plumes, which inject contention and conflict into even the most benign issues. The Corrupt intent and meaning were interlaced lies which transform the black and white into convoluted and complex grays . . . these grays representing the decomposition of law and order and right and reason, bursting forth and manifesting as RED anger and actions in the Earthreal. That's right, this was engineered! Chaos's grand design was being reinforced through the execution of binary code bent on desensitizing exposed sentients to violence and destruction; turning bystanders and witnesses into hate perpetrators and perpetuators; and giving voice to and delivering the visceral messages of those bent on the decline of civilization—the architects and executors of Chaos's desired end-state: the descent to the unrecoverable cascade—to anarchy and systemic ruinous process—the *Discordant!*

Arden had been spiritually reborn to attenuate hate as

water to fire . . . to extinguish the harmful effects and disruptive spiritual energies of the destructive emotion. However, it is important to understand Arden didn't just mitigate or dilute hatred in its various forms; he could transmute the destructive emotion into a less volatile form . . . something akin to turning fire into water. But even for the *fúath slugair*, the hate-saturated environment was new and unimaginable in its scope, scale, and power . . . even daunting to a Hate-eater with the power of its currents. The gray expanse was a slate, swift-moving river with the breadth and depths of a ravenous ocean without boundaries and no geographical features to demarcate or contain it. This was a lot to manage—perhaps too much—Arden needed to find STEM quickly . . .

****

If you were 'of this realm,' a being whose sentience was expressed in binary code, your land was beyond war torn—beyond anarchy—it was uninhabitable for a being of reason and order. STEM was struggling just to maintain himself. He had never seen the CODE—the transactional processes of the Internet and their directive algorithms—do this before. He had never witnessed behavior like this in the entirety of his unmarked time in the endless. The black and white was now the all-gray. The filters, the built-in limiters, the controls which were supposed to moderate the transaction-based parameters of this world had all been simultaneously overcome like flood gates ripped open before the biblical deluge, and like most disastrous emergences, it manifested without warning. No time to get to high ground, no time to build an ark, or whatever the equivalent of 'that' was here.

Chaos's En'Troop-EE had invaded the Web with an ingeniously conceived and well-executed insurgency of hate, infiltrating all exchanged processes with "ampbots" designed to logarithmically escalate the negativity contagion across the entire netscape. The Web was unprepared for the voracity of the Chaotic convergence's virtual emanations propagating within it . . . as if one had fallen asleep to baseless rumors of a bloody massacre only to be awakened abruptly and find themself in the violent midst of it. The tsunami of hate-anger was sweeping up victim and hapless witness alike as it surged unabated through the innerverse.

In the virtual sphere, it was as if all charismatic leaders with toxic and divisive messages—authoritarians, terrorists, media moguls, politicians, celebrities, military leaders, criminal masterminds—launched information campaigns simultaneously to overwhelm any checks or counterbalances to their disruptive and corrosive influences. Their targets—the massed human audiences—isolated within virtual echo chambers with millions of other like-minded; all of their shared misperceptions and mutual gross misunderstandings being uniformly manipulated into further propagating the successive waves of lies and disinformation pounding on and eroding the shores of reality. Within the Internet, these destructive waves were breaking apart the black and white structures lining the gray's littorals, with attempts to maintain integrity proving futile for even the most resilient . . . in the end, they were all just feedstock for the growing gray. All the menacing mechanizations dedicated to seeding the Internet-variant of blighted forests were achieving something far greater in the Earthreal: blighted countries and regions, and now they were on the cusp of making a darkened continent . . . if achieved, it would be impossible to curtail the En'Troop's advance.

All of this was well-conceived and orchestrated for Chaotic beings, and those who sought their place among them . . . triggers were tripped, and tipping points reached as rhetoric incited despicable acts of every kind in the physical. It was sporadic at first, as the widespread unconscionable and precipitous catastrophes always begin. With increases in frequencies of occurrence, congregation began with the gradual building in mass, momentum, and destructive power like a tidal wave dreaming of being a monster and having the good fortune of half an ocean in front of it to realize its cataclysmic vision of self prior to making landfall. Peaceful protests for the wrong reason turned to violent riots and were violently put down by governments-*which-should-never-have-been-allowed-to-be* desperately trying to maintain control and survive. The Epoch's apex species underestimating things like humans always do, thinking they can control gravity until they are in freefall and then the true comprehension and appreciation of forces beyond their control begins . . . too late, for only death and despair await alongside the truth upon final impact.

Criminal elements spilled forth like overflowing sewage into the growing gaps and lapses of law and order. Thievery, fraud, corruption, illegal trade of illicit goods and beings, exploitation of humans and animals; ruthless enterprises built on blood pacts and enforced and expanded through depravity and violent means became the norm. The ranks of transnational terrorist organizations ballooned in global membership in equal proportion to the number of failed states, both happening at historically disproportionate rates. The resulting bloodshed and wonton destruction on the basis of ideological, religious, and tribal grounds brought new opportunity to droves of military-aged humans in countries with no opportunity and no hope—the insatiable appetite of rifts sucking up human fodder like street sweepers after a nasty dirt storm; chewing them all up faster than they could be spat out. In just a matter of months, the death toll produced by the misguided and manipulated who heeded darkness's clarion surged exponentially from thousands to millions of living beings, falling to boot, blade, bullet, and bludgeon each month.

Global instability mounted as the World Powers could no longer effectively and cooperatively police the planet, because they were rendered unable to police themselves . . . powerless to protect their own borders or secure their own populations. Eventually, individual civility collapsed under the weight of toxic individuality as it became apparent it was every human being for themselves. Too many inputs translated to negative and ill-conceived outputs born of myopic worldviews; belief systems and politics radicalized by misinformation and hopelessness; lost trust and faith in family, friends, governments, and religion; and all of it culminating in the inability of human civilizations to meet basic human needs. By now, most had lost everything or the little they had, and those who still had something were doing everything—anything—to keep it. Everyone—EVERYONE!—was in a desperate fight for the few scraps of anything left along with anybody else's they wanted for their own . . .

. . . perceptions of existence and individual belief systems were being virtually reinforced so completely by the Eigengrau of negativity here that it was binding Earthreal's reality to its own disfiguring conception of how actuality should be . . .

The changes 'here' which had enabled the creeping horrible 'out there' happened very quickly . . . perhaps incomprehensibly fast when referenced against the known and understood of the human mind. Heated emotions translated into intentioned aggressions that were spawning acts of unkindness, which in turn were leading to random acts of violence with some snowballing into unthinkable horrors. The happening was multidimensional and asymmetric . . . along the unlimited axes of space, time, force, energy, and the spirit; all of them banging and colliding with each other in an instinctual bid for dominance over one another . . . because hate was impulsive and involuntarily compelled to be self-destructive with fear at its core—to eliminate the fear is to eliminate the threats, and threats were everywhere! Hostility escalated from raised hands and clenched fists to genocide and total war in the single beat of a human heart in the gray. Internet shaping operations occurred below the pale . . . most of it with the speed and elusiveness of a nightmare's memory.

Fortunately, the utter chaos playing out in the Manmade's virtual world was not yet fully reflected in the Earth's physical realm. The hostile CODE orchestrated by *malgorithims* and magnified and exponentially propagated by weaponized bots—the ampbots—ricocheted like bullets damaging the connected psyches. The turbulent flow of the multilayered transactional processes acted like hard edges of every degree and angle to keep the bullets bouncing around and maximize the damage done in each echo chamber before the virtually infinite hail of rounds found their way to the next. Worse, it was all desynchronized—chaotic and random—an unpredictable propagation defying meaningful countermeasures unless you have the supranatural ability to see the pattern within the destructive process . . . or you were the architect of it . . .

****

It was one thing to be born here in this world, but quite another to have been stranded and forced to survive in this alien place. In the grasp of the vast hostilstorm, STEM was being tossed around like a jettisoned kayak in Class 5 whitewater rapids. The elemental spirit was getting pulled under and held down, almost crushed by the weight of the massed hate before being spat out unexpectedly . . . over and over. STEM was being rolled up against abrasive transactions which were starting to strip away the source code of his sentient being, only to then be held down by other ill-intended transactions awash with Corrupted CODE until he could feel *biting bits*—the endless's parasites spawned by rampant malgorithims—starting to infiltrate him, seeking not just to feed but dominate and spread the hate.

However, STEM was resistant and resilient so the seething river of lies and loathing was reacting in kind by slamming him against binary representations of the everything he wasn't, to soften him up and break him down before pulling him within it once again. The mad river was shoreless and seemed without end. Relenting and succumbing seemed only a matter of time, because even formless sentience did not have an inexhaustible reservoir of stamina . . . he could not fend off these assaults much longer. STEM was never meant to be here in the first place.

". . . Arden, where are you? STEM is having trouble finding himself . . . cannot hold out much longer. Have not felt such hopelessness since the Dislocation. Please?"

****

. . . Arden had learned the hard way not to display weakness in the presence of his god. Cernunnos did not care for displays of frailty from humans or any other living thing. He rewarded the strong and the decisive—the mightiest protectors and greatest huntsmen; those apex beings who formed the loadbearing structures of nature's design. Cernunnos is the Guardian of the Green World . . . the shapeshifting, shamanic presider over the hunt and the horned numen of the animals and the untamed; as such, his expectations are simple: *do as he has always done from his eternal station at the Sacred Center in the Grove of all Worlds.* Ever-present and radiating outward from the center of the Interconnected All, his limbs and roots extend into earth and ocean as well as the Otherworlds existing *within* and *without* Mother's world. The 'within' holds the deep of the sacred earth and the Underworld, connecting the All we know and providing for the worlds and beings within the Interconnected All. The 'without' encompasses the sky and heavens and spiritual realms of the Otherworlds. Cernunnos' trunk is the massive spine at the Sacred Center of the worlds' Grove where the First Forest still flourishes and supports All—the spine of spines and the interstitial rootweb binding them.

So, knowing this, what can you do? What does Cernunnos expect from you? To protect and provide for your Grove, your pack, your flock, your herd, your people . . . the life in your care! Do no less for yours than he has done and will do for his—for 'his' is Earth Mother's All. Aye, do this and you will have his blessing. And worry not, for through Cernunnos' grace, which is always hard-earned, you will be granted the strength and power you need to perform your sacred duties in the service of others.

This was the overriding narrative in the stream of Arden's consciousness—repeating over and over—to steel him for the challenge he faced. This was the Hate-eater's deliberate attempt to instill the self-assurance he needed to do this— whatever 'this' was he was doing—and the repetition was important to keep the objective in the forefront of his mind. Despite the long road to recovery, he still had to be extremely disciplined to protect himself from 'consciousness drift.' If that insidious condition born of his combat injury took hold, STEM would be lost to the hate for good just as Arden could be too if he lost himself . . . both beings completely assimilated by the hostilstorm with their sentience hopelessly unrecoverable, dispersed and diffused within the inescapable torrent dominating the grayscape.

Arden had tremendous faith in his god, but he was now operating in the unfamiliar and unknown . . . a strange existential plane of synthetic sentience and occupied by unknown formless species of quasi-intelligent artificial life representing extremes at least eight degrees of separation from the understood and recognizable. This was truly an alien world, bereft of structure or anything resembling a landscape. All and everything were moving and flowing, in various stages of mixing and combining, then separating and dissipating, only to intermittently and randomly reform . . . every type of flow: uniform and non-uniform, laminar and turbulent, and rotational and irrotational—all types existing in simultaneity. However, such volatility was not questioned 'here' as long as the governing CODE sanctioned it.

For an Earthborn, it was tremendously difficult to maintain bearing and navigate in this innerverse without sun, moon, or stars. There was nothing with which to establish positional reference. *What was altitude, attitude, progress, or movement here?* There was no horizon! There was just the multileveled and multilayered flow of transactions representing the processing and exchange of information, data, and subordinate code expressed and captured within discrete and indiscrete packages composed of bits, bytes, and binary digits. The whole of it was indistinguishable in its continuously shifting mosaic originally cast in black and white, and now grayscale, after having been thrown into the Chaotic blender—ebbing, flowing, swishing, and whirling. It was dizzying to an outsider, but there was no turning back . . . there could be no hesitation or shying away from his task. Avoidance, fear, self-loathing, and unreliability . . . LOST—that state of being, such attributes no longer described Arden. Now, anything short of his full measure and maximum effect would not be perceived favorably by Cernunnos, and thus, was not personally acceptable to Arden. There could be no shirking his duties just as there would be no running from his god if he failed in his mission.

Cernunnos' reach and influence extended to all worlds connected to Earth, and within the Green God's extension of presence, Arden's confidence was reinforced with steady resolve to serve well and to the best of his ability. Arden could do no less . . . he owed Cernunnos everything . . .

Chapter 9
My Iron Chrysalis

"My Iron Chrysalis" . . . that was how he referred to it. It was a cynical joke, but not many people were graced with the honor of Arden's humor. Not because he wasn't funny, but because he didn't communicate much . . . well, verbally anyway. Frankly, he had fallen out of the habit of talking during those years he found himself unable to talk at all. That seemed several lifetimes away now: the horrible event which stopped just a few inches short of ThisLife's biological sheath crushed to death, and an aftermath which came just short of completely breaking him. The explosively-constructed seminal event dissected his spirit essence, stripping most of the former *him* away by cleaving Arden down cleanly through the tissue, muscle, and bone to expose the marrow of his soul. It was a life-altering affair which should have been life-ending. The devastating event left him metaphysically shattered, mentally fractured . . . vulnerable and exposed like a wicked flame in the wind. It was horrible but necessary so the transformation could begin . . .

. . . All the latest intel had been indicating the Task Force had been successful in interdicting the local insurgency's IED network . . . effective in denying the material—explosives, fuses, RF triggers, copper wire, artillery rounds . . . the essentials needed to make operational, and more importantly, 'lethal' IEDs. The explosive ambush attacks had become very infrequent over the last six weeks, and during this adversarial lull, those which did

occur employed smaller devices which were much less effective. Afterward, battlefield forensics found many of the devices were missing essential components and others were not even functional at all. The Task Force was riding an 'intel high' with consistent reporting suggesting their efforts to blunt the enemy's lethal supply chain were having very positive results.

They should have stayed hypervigilant all the way through the last lap and through the checkered flag, but it's easier said than done ten months into a year-long deployment. It was his job to keep his squad focused, but he let them down. They said the IED they were hit by was the biggest seen in the AOR in over three years. That was why he deserved what happened to him . . . dying in the mammoth explosion would have been a mercy he did not deserve. Someone, something was looking out for him and saved him when others should have been saved. Why was he the one still alive? Why was he the one more worthy than others to be looked out for?

The explosion . . . the concussive force was unimaginable. Three of their four MRAPs were caught in the blast zone. His gun truck was "impact center"—actual ground zero. He should not have lived through that! No one else in his truck did. His turret gunner was ripped apart, severed at the waist with everything above the torso—everything above the armored troop compartment—found in little pieces all over the cratered area which used to be a road. His three other truck mates were killed instantly by the overpressure once the IED blast penetrated the hull. His driver literally became part of the truck when the powerful port side detonation did its dead level best to wrench and twist the softer cab away from the thicker, more rigid hull. Still intensely vivid was the image of Ben's guts replaced by the back end of the engine block . . . the fucking engine block! His best friend so mutilated he was no longer recognizable . . .

. . . and unbelievably . . . he was bruised and battered, ragdolled to the nth-degree, but otherwise unscathed . . . at least, it seemed to be so at the time: ears ringing, disorientation, heavy

chest—just the explosion, right? He was the lucky one. His buddy had been impaled by the engine, but his half of the MRAP cab had wrapped him up in an unforgiving but protective cocoon of steel, composite armor, and Kevlar fiber. Unnaturally—supernaturally—the wartime combination of Manmade had defied material physics in response to the IED explosion . . . guided and shaped by unseen hands to channel the blast effects around him . . . as if someone, some power deemed him—HIM?—worthy of saving. Somehow, someway, the human 'ragdoll' was gripped tight in the gruff hands of an overbearing child engineered from US military wreckage.

It took several hours to sweep and establish security of the blast site—more time for an Explosive Ordnance Disposal team to respond and 'safe' the area—and still more hours to get the support teams into the remote area with the specialized equipment needed to cut him out. Even in and out of consciousness, the ordeal seemed an eternity to Arden with the crush of twisted, unrelenting metal pressing down on him . . . squeezing his chest . . . making it hard to breathe. The mercy of unconsciousness's extended hand was elusive, leaving agony in its stead— the pounding, throbbing pain in his skull as if it had grown too small and was threatening to crack open and completely pop off his body like a dandelion head to allow the rest of himself to blow away in the hot winds of the Euphrates River valley.

But alas, the sweet release from ThisLife was not to be . . . it was just the addled, wishful thinking of a trapped man who wished he was dead, crying out to a Christian God he had never prayed to before for mercy—a deity as unresponsive to the gasped whispers warbling between grunts and screams as the unrelenting armored cocoon which bore down on every square inch of his body and pressed the air out of him. Eventually, the grace of exhaustion upon the human form mitigated his suffering: the thudding in his head slowed down to the beat of a slave ship's drum with the persistent percussion deadening and becoming ever more distant like the last beats of a dying heart.

Consciousness fluttered away on greasy, uneven wings—sweet black . . .

. . . Awake! Fuck! The hell of awareness returned to find him STILL IN THE CRUSH! He was still alive some unaccounted-for period of time later, awakened to smoke, dust, noxious fumes, unknown scents, death . . . all of them combining to launch a full-out assault on his senses. He couldn't escape the stench of his team's death chamber. He was pinned there; unable to run—hell, man, not even walk or crawl—he couldn't even sit up . . . shit! He couldn't even take a full breath until the MOB responders were able to cut him free from his explosively formed iron maiden. A tailor-made trap holding him hostage at the cusp of death but refusing to release him. He was just suspended there—enough intact consciousness to hear, smell, and feel EVERYTHING—staving off sweet release at every turn. The cruel joke of the universe . . . or maybe the enduring contrivance of the unresponsive God who refused to heed him because of his lack of faith. In truth, he was in the gauntleted grasp of a transformative tribulation, but he just didn't realize it while ensconced within the terribleness of the moment . . . as blind to the making of the one who would come to be called 'Arden' as his sense of sight was denied by the manufactured black of his iron chrysalis's dark innards.

Arden remembered the fire fighters and corpsmen talking to him, trying to keep him conscious. He remembered the blue flame of the cutting torch; the hot, smoky exhale of cut metal; and the whining grind and the sparks from the K-12 saw . . . the protesting groans of his iron chrysalis getting peeled open by a hydraulic spreader to involuntarily release its prize—the so-called "jaws of life," ha! He remembered day turning to night and the scent of metal burning to spark-light, but he doesn't remember actually being extracted from his blast-built coffin . . . being lifted out of the twisted hulk, which was formerly a gun truck. That was years ago now, and to this day, he still couldn't stand to be in enclosed spaces for more than a couple of minutes.

His claustrophobia even extended to being inside a building. He could deal with it now . . . tolerate it . . . after years of therapy and reconciling with the unavoidable condition of being born a frail human requiring shelter. But it was challenging. It was just easier to be outside . . .

. . . "Why me?" had been the question he asked himself—sometimes he'd screamed it—over and over again in the ensuing days—year? . . . years? Most of the time, it was all blurred together, and he just kind of lost track of things—himself even—in the muddled mess now his mind. Arden's post-accident reality was one where the part that was physical world or reality, blended seamlessly with much that was not—imagination, memory, dream, nightmare; all of it fluid, pouring together into a dumpster soup deep enough to drown himself in . . . but he always seemed to wake up every day. Fuck-Fuck-FUCK!

Other times, when he was able to fight through the brain fog and the mental infirmity, he would remember. He did not know why he fought so hard to remember, because the hard-earned memories only brought him more pain. Sometimes lost memory could be blissful for him, but it meant he would also forget he didn't want to remember anymore. Such was the mind-fuck merry-go-round which kept bringing him there . . . he was dizzy, getting ready to throw up, wondering why he kept getting on the ride and then struggling to remember how he even got there: to a purgatory where he got to relive the most horrible moments of his entire worthless life over and over again—round and round and ROUND! And most times, the recollections were on the verge of new to him, so he got to reexperience the fear and anxiety—like the first time, every time, and the pain never dulled no matter how many recalls he endured. Like a video clip in his mind's eye of a despicable, inhuman act replaying itself over and over . . . he couldn't bring himself to look away. He could not divert his mind's eye off the visceral memories despite the pain and anguish it caused him. Eventually, after enough vaguely remembered recollections, the former atheist finally came to realize his belief system had been wrong all along: there really was a hell . . . you did not need to be dead, just alive, and so miserable you wished you were dead.

The "long road to recovery" was what the VA docs kept calling it, but whether the patient was actually getting better or not did not seem to be a gauge of success or failure on the medical system's part. His "iron chrysalis" was simultaneously savior and coffin for the death of him within the bounds of a single life . . . and symbolic too, because that was what most of his squad came home in . . . what he should have come home in. A flag-draped casket . . . at least there was honor in that. Instead, his casket was the opposite of military carbon copies; it was a custom order, constructed of shame, regret, and failure. A potent mix of feelings and emotions entombing his fragmented mind, not the lifeless flesh of a left form marking a soldier's death in battle and the transition from a life honorably lived. In exchange for his life, the Judas was rewarded with a nonstop ride into spiritual and mental torment which not even a hardcore addiction to drugs and alcohol provided any relief or respite from. Sergeant McBride—Arden—who the fuck cares?—had been driven to the brink of insanity when his spirit had descended, spiraling like a fallen angel into the darkness.

In cruel retrospect, maybe "chrysalis" was a poor reference for a bad joke . . . the real joke was his life in the years following the attack. A chrysalis was a vessel for metamorphosis . . . a metaphor for transformation and recreating oneself—to become something better, from leaf-munching crawler to beautiful, winged pollinator. Arden's experience was quite the opposite. His time in his cocoon resulted in a devolution of self . . . the hard walls and sheer faces of the being known as Sergeant McBride had collapsed in on himself . . . from a human respected and admired among his species to nothing more than a despised worm. His time captured in a torture chamber of war's making drove his vicissimorphosis—his spiritual degradation, mental impairment, loss of purpose. He was 'living' proof degradation *was its own form of transformation.*

He was still broken in many ways, but he was no longer Humpty Dumpty . . . it had taken years for him to get himself put back together again, mostly. Certainly, he was still a work in progress . . . he was still not whole and probably never would be. For you see, he could no longer find all the pieces. There were parts of him still too scattered to locate, regardless of how good a scavenger he was. Other parts of him were probably not recoverable at all, having been thrown in the IED blast and carried away on the Euphrates Valley's desiccating winds to be lost forever. So, he was the 'jigsaw man,' and he did not have a reference picture to guide him as he worked to pull himself together. His remaining pieces had no distinguishing contrast—everything he could find was dark on dark—without the contrast necessary to fully define him, and thus, defying his reconstruction and resisting any attempts to be made whole.

Understand, it was not the difficulty of the task that bothered him . . . for someone suffering from moderate TBI, most days just living was difficult. But despite everything—despite the jagged gaps still left open and the remaining holes in himself outnumbering the remaining pieces on the board—Arden had come a long way on the road to coping. And it wasn't the result of complex, modern medical treatments or exotic drugs or the nation's best neurologists and neurosurgeons, it had been Druidry . . . a devotion which established his spiritual connections with the natural world, tethering him to reality with something more stable than the tenuous hold of a steady diet of psychotropic drugs, head shed appointments, and support group meetings. It was about being found by a god who gave him strength and showed him paths to finding himself again . . . a god who rewarded Arden's faith in him with faith in himself, a valuable treasure which had been lost to him for some time . . .

. . . So, like so many times before, Arden had to emerge from his chrysalis once again, but this time, it was not the unforgiving body-wrap of steel and bulletproof Manmade . . . this time it was

one of doubt surrounding him in this strange world of grayscape which was compressing his essence in an attempt to render him mute again—pushing to thrust him back to a time bereft of free will and choice . . . reducing him to spiritually comatose, with just a tiny opaque window from which to distantly observe life . . . to sit quietly and watch life roll by like scenery viewed from a passenger seat in a car with dirty windows on the road back home or to nowhere—it's hard to tell . . . the destination rested with his choice: a full participant or the silent observer refusing to know and enjoy what ThisLife had to offer. The watchers who observe others experiencing life, witnessing the weak and the timid getting steamrolled by it while the strong drive the heavy machinery, because they're not afraid to take what they want. That's how the road to progress is paved—by the road makers and those they make the road from . . .

. . . But to watch life from a vantage of safety was to deny oneself the ability to experience all conscious existence had to offer—not just pain and suffering, but satisfaction and joy and all the first times which make the soul sing! To expose oneself to life and do nothing . . . to take no action . . . was to be enslaved, whether it was of the body or the mind—consciousness—spirit. Imprisoned of consciousness was to be imprisoned forever, for the consciousness encompassed the mind and memory of the immortal spirit. For those free of essence to allow or enable tyranny, and the exploitation, manipulation, and enslavement of other living beings, was to live a life Corrupted! Nay, not Arden! He had already experienced such a life, and it was his life no longer. Though not whole, his destiny was to emerge from the safety of his chrysalis transformed . . . taking whatever form or formlessness, assuming any sheath necessary to serve those in need in whatever world they existed . . . as only his god would have him do . . .

. . . Shedding the cocoon of doubt brought renewed clarity and with it—a plan! Arden had arrived in this world . . . this

Internet . . . on Cernunnos' rootweb. The rootweb was Arden's vessel for he was within it, and right now it was everything: his means to determining where he was in the flowing formless of endless transactions; his means for finding STEM; his tether back to his world; and the medium through which he could cast the light needed to cut through the hostilstorm by burning the hate in his path. It was all there . . . the Green God had provided everything his *fúath slugair* needed by giving Arden an extension of himself within this innerverse—much more than lifeline, it was simultaneously bridge, passage, lifeline, and rescue tether!

Arden reached out into the flow of the innerspace, but his arms and hands were not of flesh or sinew or bone . . . they were spiritually reinforced feeder roots and root hairs. Gaining confidence and building momentum, he strode forward, but not atop feet or driven by the power of legs . . . movement was through the extension of permanent roots—the root stuff of anchorage and transport. He pushed out into the gray churn on roots spreading into the transactional flow of data exchange like a many-tentacled creature of the deep. Further, he mimicked the ocean predator's 'prey-capture expansion' of all available limbs on the night reef. He saw not with eyes, but through the rootweb itself. His sensory perception was transmuted, yet far from muted—better than human! His root hairs served as his omnisense, coupling sight, sound, and smell in an intensive search for the variances and pockets of 'different,' which could indicate STEM's presence within the mosaic of shifting hate propagation—a wisp of color in a turbulent gray sea—a breath of fresh air among the hot, hateful winds . . . a hint of nature.

Then Arden brought his light to the party; his root caps were now bright bulbs of shine, penetrating the grayscale dinge like lighthouse lanterns in soupy fog . . . slicing through the hate surge and hostility flows, and amplifying the contrasts within the competing cascades of fading truth, ebbing misinformation, and burgeoning disinformation like a hot knife through butter. After all, Arden was *fúath slugair* . . . and this was a world dominated by hate where the prevailing weather patterns of the preceding months had grown in intensity and fury . . . from isolated, localized phenomena to a powerful, multi-cell storm. Within a surprisingly brief period of time within the timeless, this hatestorm had grown to cover more than half the Internet.

Arden seemed the only lighthouse the wayward ships of this world had ever seen . . . of a like and composition neither the resident diffused sentience within the algorithms and CODE nor Chaos's imbedded synthetic effectors—the ampbots and malgorithims—had ever experienced within their midst. Having never encountered such a manifestation so powerful and so different, Arden's spiritual presence was confusing and even disorienting to both the endless' denizens and invaders alike; this much was obvious even though it was hard to know how the artificial sentience of this world perceived their environment and any changes occurring within it. However, the finite elements and entities imbedded in CODE did perceive in their own way, because the Internet's transactional vessels—the equivalents of ships, boats, barges, and rafts carrying bits, bytes, data, information, knowledge, and messaging—within Arden's burning swath were 'blinded' . . . the effects went even further; they were shocked, causing them to divert out of the lines of their assigned transactional flows to run "aground" and collide with each other in the face and wake of Arden's light.

Light was obviously uncommon in this place with no natural sources of it . . . no illumination of moon, no sun, no stars. The only thing comparable to light which naturally existed in the Internet was the truth! Within the reach of Arden's light, the truth, muddled, buried, and overcome by the overwhelming presence of *all-it-was-not*, was revealed once again. It was the *fúath slugair*. Arden, as the only true reflecting mirror within the murk, allowed the truth to look upon itself again and realize it had been lost. The Hate-eater was generating light from any resident source of hatred it touched, and his light sourced of the consumed was the jaw, teeth, and fang by which Arden mauled and cut his way through the hostility-generated darkness of this sphere.

His bright root caps tracked effortlessly through the ominous grayscale like a salvo of flares providing the searchlights which could distinguish friend from foe. This much concentrated negativity 'thickened' the viscosity of the transactional flows to behave much like a polluted sludge . . . like an oil spill in ocean water . . . and Arden's torched root caps crashed through the roiling murk like falling stars who refused to give a starless heavens final say on what the composition of the night sky should be.

Deeper within the dark flow, Arden's root ends continued to travel searching for STEM, bumping into intermittent shreds and pockets of good transactions with messages of kindness, civility, and faith which did not relent to Arden's light because they sought it and were brightened and reinvigorated by it. They desperately needed it like drowning people need lifelines. Unfortunately, such bright elements had become too few to influence the overall messaging produced by our world's greatest influencing engine. Like STEM, truth and fairness were hapless victims, and the wreckage and remnants of formerly strong structures had been swept up and carried away by the slate river's strong current which had long overflowed any virtual embankments or dikes which sought to contain it. Now the great lie-driven ravenous wished to overcome and swallow all, following the prime directives of its programming to add to the power and mass of dark descent.

The dispersed sources of pure spring water were swallowed up by hate-filled flood. Tumbling and knocked about in the turbulent flow, they had no effect on slowing or calming the torrid torrent. As involuntary as their contributions were, they only served to add to the exponential growth of the flow. Arden started to fear STEM might have been consumed, but he could not know for sure . . . all he could do was push on, root caps piercing and hoping to find his prize with wide-area 'groping' into the dark. However, even doing what he was reborn to do was becoming exceedingly more difficult here . . . because in the end, we think we 'feel' hope, but hope is actually a cognitive process—a way of thinking, pairing goal-directed energy and positive emotions with planning—and human emotions were the primary targets of the weaponized portions of the Internet. The insidious intent: *if emotions, and thus hope, could be controlled and corrupted here in the endless, the reach of the great engine of negative influence would be extended into the Earthreal, because the vast majority of all humans—including all humans with real influence capable of furthering Chaos's cause—were "plugged in."*

The ampbots . . . Arden had perceived them but had decided not to deal with them in order to devote the full capacity of his root lattice to the search for STEM. He was spiderwebbing through the storm, structurally expanding on his push through the hate . . . and the rootweb was impacting, disrupting, and reshaping the flow of the hostilstorm, blunting its momentum and impeding Chaotic progress. Arden's manifested self was undermining the hate which thereby mitigated the ampbots' formative work. Thus, the presence of this alien, consciousness-imbued structure which did not belong offended their programming by sabotaging their efforts and diminishing their output, and therefore, their impact—this was unacceptable! This invader 'from without' was diminishing their domination campaign by creating an untenable condition which their programming demanded be dealt with so they could continue with executing their primary directives. Arden's disruptive presence invoked alternative programming routines in all ampbots within the interloper's proximate vicinity which were able to sense and comprehend Arden's effects and devise defensive countermeasures. The imbedded contingency programming flicked virtual switches, and the ampbots turned from amplifiers to antibodies!

The ampbots congregated and swarmed to repel the invader who was assaulting the hive. His root caps were activating their antibody routines by proximity as Arden passed by. Their response: simple . . . destroy the structure powering the light. *Attack the rootweb! Besiege it . . . assault it . . . take it down!* They were targeting the foreign presence and throwing themselves at Arden like fusillades of cannonballs. In salvo after salvo, the ampbots hurled themselves at the extending latticework of Arden's manifested self, blasting through root hairs and pulverizing the main structural lattice—Arden's lifeline out of this combative world!

Severed root pieces and parts were getting carried away into the unrelenting flow of the hatestorm before they could rejoin, reattach, and reinforce the rootweb. In areas of severe damage, available paths to reroute the spiritual light and keep the root caps powered were diminished . . . some bulbs began to struggle and flicker with other root caps going completely dark. With the degradation proceeding at a rate faster than Arden could repair or reroute, the *fúath slugair* was losing his ability to continue the search, and worse, he was losing his tether back to his world! Arden was running out of time to find STEM.

In an act of desperation, Arden pulsed light through his entire latticework like electrical current running through a network of exposed, uninsulated wiring; this repelled the attacking ampbots like castle defenders pouring burning oil on the siege troops scaling the battered walls. Arden, light pulsating, splayed his rootweb in all directions desperately grasping and groping like hundreds of hands all looking for the same lost ring hidden within murky waters. Root caps descending like anchors searching for something solid to grab on to below the turbulent surface of wind-assailed waters. All extended strands probing . . . bumping and thumping against the sinking and current-caught wreckage of the kind and well-intended CODE which once sailed proudly as the flag vessels of the powerful, positive messaging that once dominated the seas of the Internet. Arden, knowing he had been detected, was flailing desperately, knowing his time had run out. He was fully aware his ability to dwell unopposed here in this world had been compromised, and thus, it was becoming quickly and increasingly too problematic to endure.

Arden thrashed, searching for CODE with sentience . . . for the 'different' within hate's gray . . . a stranger to this strange land swept up within the hostilstorm's torrent. Arden had anticipated 'he' would be obvious—easy to find and rescue—but this was overwhelming . . . too much to assimilate when immersed within the turbulence of the infiltrating negative processes working to corrupt the greater process. The urgency of the situation was reinforced by another wave of ampbots besieging him again . . . degrading him . . . their numbers as seemingly infinite as the endless itself. Doubt now assailed him too. Arden didn't even know if he would even know STEM if his root caps encountered him. This loss of confidence and confusion was also an ampbot countermeasure and one highly effective at attempting to render the Hate-eater ineffective. He might have already missed him . . . STEM might have already fallen victim to the hatestorm. *No! Not again! I can't lose another soldier!*

. . . as it turned out, Arden didn't have to know what STEM felt like, because STEM took hold of him. STEM saw the light of one of Arden's root caps cutting through the viscous hatred flows like a glowing lifebuoy. STEM lunged at it as it passed by and held on for dear life.

Pleased to finally meet you, little one. Arden expressed himself voicelessly in that form of special communication unique to those employing the omnisense. He wrapped more of himself around STEM to make sure he had him firmly in his rootgrasp. Like grappling hooks of gentle fingers made of root hairs, he reined STEM in like the feeding tentacles of a great squid repurposed to 'befriend' and not 'feed.' Then, he started retracting the dispersed rootweb of himself rapidly before his lifeline out of this world was completely severed by the ampbots. Once sure his rescued elemental sentience was confidently secured within the tightly braided system of roots, Arden blasted out of hostilstorm like the giant squid jet-propelled, siphoning hatred-polluted waters and blasting it out of his cellulose-fibered mantle.

Swoooooossssh!—gone! Up and out . . . and with the disruptive presence no longer present, the ampbots returned to their primary directive—*propagate the hate*—with only the slightest lapse in production resulting from their temporary focus on alternative programming.

****

Cherished sounds in the distance: bald eagles and ospreys exchanging pleasantries. Nothing too serious . . . just the usual territorial vying for the best winter fishing spots on Lake Conroe. Every year like clockwork, the ospreys roll in during the winter months, arriving en masse like a șatră of feathered gypsies. And every year, their arrival upsets the resident bald eagle nesting pairs who live there year-round. The ospreys are certainly more versatile fishermen with their ability to dive deep into the water completely submerging themselves, but eagles are gifted at pursuing ospreys on the wing until they drop their fish—it's great sport. Their screeching exchanges and aerial sparring can be entertaining to be sure. Nature at its best.

Arden was enjoying the breeze, giving the forest voice and allowing the mixed pine and hardwoods an opportunity to sing. It had taken the Druid considerable time to learn the language of the forest. This is a special kind of learning requiring one to "listen," which has become a rare skill among human beings . . . the ability to "really" listen. Each species of tree has their own 'draft dialect' unique to their kind—whether they are in leaf-bearing seasons or not; whether their speech is facilitated by zephyr or gale. The nuances are many and dependent on many things, but the result is always beautiful. It had taken him years to learn the Tree Tongue . . . perhaps the longest of any of the Druids in his Grove. Arden had come a long way since his combat injury, but he was still prone to occasional memory lapses and periodic bouts of vertigo. He even experienced losses of consciousness from time to time, but fortunately, the vertigo and blackouts had become far less frequent. It did not seem like either was going to be a problem today.

Today was a good day. The only sounds competing with that of the tree song and the competition of the nearby eagles and ospreys on the water was a subdued "tapping." It was Arden once again texting on a cellphone . . . the handheld device was unwanted, but a necessary burden in enabling him to serve in his unique role as his Grove's protector.

> Stay out of hate's way, STEM. We almost lost you.

> Scary. Hate is hard to avoid right now. It is everywhere . . . almost everything seems infected with it . . . like a plague if my memory of LastLife still has not failed me.

> You should feel it now—the hate . . . when it is close.

I do . . . I can. Thx 2 U. STEM sorry for chopped syntax. It is a function of my assimilation. It happens accidently sometimes. I cannot help it.

STEM do not apologize. You are a marvel. I have endowed you with a personal protection ward. A symbol of Earth. My goal is to keep you tethered to Mother even in the unearthly realm you now call home. It carries within it the essence of the four seasons and the four directions so you may know the time and be able to find your way to navigate the endless. Oh, and most importantly, you will feel hot when hate is near.

OK. This is good. Think me not crazy, but it is good to feel something again. Your ward glows on me when the hate is close. The rune keeps me from stumbling into toxic flows of hostility and warns me when gales of ill will are threatening. Sometimes I still get confused here, and your ward will keep me safe. It is VERY good to see the light again . . . on me, here, against all the gray. It is comforting. Thank you.

I appreciate your gratitude. All I ask from you is to be there should I call on you. We need to look out for each other. We are kindred spirits . . . we both struggle to be and belong in our respective worlds in ThisLife. None of this is ideal or of our choosing, but our fates nonetheless. These are troubling times, and it is nice to have friends.

> Yes. Friends. STEM will be here. STEM always here . . . don't think it possible for me to leave.

****

Some of the previous day's light failed to carry over into the next, making for a more ominous one. The wind was driving . . . wild. The sky hung low and dark, determined to crowd out the forest and push it off its place. It was one thing to weather the storm when it still brought rain, but this storm offered no moisture . . . only a gnashing bite which tore at the Green, snapping smaller branches and twigs, pulling down leaves and needles, and pushing over the old and sick of the wood; those already of precarious footing were being driven 'into the lean' before their time.

Arden was on his phone today too, sitting on a picnic table under a covered area which cut the fierce winds a little bit. He had been taking advantage of the power outlets at some of the nearby campsites to charge his phone and noticed STEM had been trying to contact him.

> STEM, is everything okay?

> Yes. I bring information. Hate still growing, getting harder to avoid. Everywhere, but your ward has kept me safe so far. But many close calls, many, many. Hate levels are rising, like a dam has been broken and all the safe places are being swallowed up.

STEM. I am sorry. I have felt it. I know it is getting worse, but I don't know what I can do about it.

Know I seek not to frustrate, but to inform. In the Real, hate now growing fastest in the borderlands. There, sentients are few, but the hate is BIG! Chaos's En'Troops are on the move. The scourge seeks to push His influence beyond Texas. All who resist or oppose fall, fueling the hatestorm and driving its spread.

STEM, that is horrible, but what can I do?

STEM does not mean to stress his friend, just increase his awareness. There is one who fights for the Natural Order in the borderlands—the elemental, Parim—but he faces an army. He needs his own. STEM's friend would be a good soldier . . . like many soldiers . . . like a squad!

I used to be a soldier, but I wasn't a very good one. I used to have a squad once too . . . before the Grove . . . they are dead because of me.

Arden grimaced and shook his head while squeezing his beat-up little phone. He stopped just short of smashing it on the ground. He had spent years trying to escape the 'before,' which had swallowed him whole. It was only through Earth Mother's grace that he was spat out in pieces before he was completely consumed by his past. It had been an exceedingly long journey, and he had only been able to fight a part of the way back . . . but he was still fighting and doing good for others. 'This'—now—might be the best it would get for him, and he did not want to lose what he had. *Why did STEM have to put this on him now?*

Arden stood up with shoulders slumped . . . the look of the defeated. He pulled his hood over his head and began to stroke his thick, unkempt beard—a nervous habit. There was much to worry about and machinate over as he started to make his way back to the Glade against a backdrop of wind-whipped trees who looked like a rowdy crowd mocking the loser after an overtime loss. The tragic hero . . . *but hadn't he played that role already?* Maybe it was time to be recast . . .

Chapter 10
Willow-wise Counsel

Komkom Akwini and Arden had grown very close in these ensuing weeks. Though they served different tribes, the likely genesis of their friendship was the shared responsibilities of the 'protector.' Arden was seeking both information and counsel from the Earth Elemental. The implied assistance request from STEM had shaken him a little, and he was torn about what he should do.

For his part, Kwin could sense the human was troubled, so he took the additional measure of morphing one of his main boughs into something resembling a low-hanging lounge chair. The Tree Spirit thought it would help Arden feel more at ease and comfortable and help the human get to the heart of the matters he wished to discuss. It did not take an empath to see the Druid had spent years trying to reinvent himself as he struggled to negotiate his way out of the chasm carved into his essence by his life's trials; the source of which could be traced back to his time as a combatant in war and the devastating loss of his squad. The harrowing experience had opened a spiritual rift within Arden so large the darkness, which had almost succeeded in swallowing him, still remained a looming threat. The inner beast still lived, and the world was filled with the insidious sources it wanted to feed on to grow big again. Kwin could not sense the rift per se, but he could sense the struggle within; undoubtably attributable to the manifestation of darkness coupled with the daily battle of living with enduring combat injuries, which also performed their deplorable work below the pale.

Kwin perceived Arden had come a long way, having made a good deal of progress in his forced march out of the valley in his soul. Fortunately, the Druid had managed to place some distance between himself and oblivion, but he was by no means clear. Every day, Arden's long road back was its own trial with some worse than others, but none of them easy. It was impossible to know whether he would be permanently afflicted with this condition in some manner for the remainder of ThisLife. With a brain injury like his, the damage to his biological form was likely permanent. However, Arden's affliction of essence needed to be dealt with, because it could follow him into NextLife. Nevertheless, strength was not just a physical measure. Arden's strength of being and impressive resilience could not be denied; those attributes alone singled out the human as worthy of mentoring.

Kwin listened intently, devoting his full attention to Arden as a gentle breeze rustled the lighter, leaf-bearing limbs of his weeping habit. For Arden, the sounds and motion of Kwin's vegetation and those of the surrounding Natural took him back to the tall reeds and narrow-leaved cattail lining the banks of the Euphrates River . . .

In his mind's eye, he was no longer Arden . . . he was Sergeant McBride on patrol with his squad in Iraq navigating the riverbank on foot, having established security prior to their dismount. His turret-gunners, who remained with the trucks along with the drivers, provided overwatch of the team members as they picked their way through the marshy area. McBride and his dismounts were scouring the riverbank for evidence of weapons trafficker infiltrations into their area of responsibility via boat They were also searching for insurgent weapons caches the intelligence analysts had provided grid coordinates for based on imagery analysis from a variety of different "INT's"—all courtesy of sophisticated sensor suites mounted on their 'eyes in the sky.'

It was tedious work picking through the tall Green crowding the embankment, made more challenging by the sticky muck that wanted to suck the boots off his soldiers' feet. So many times, they had been sent off on goose chases to look for ghosts and their ethereal stashes of weapons and materials of war . . . it was frustrating mostly, but utterly satisfying when intel actually got one right and a grid search paid off with a large weapons cache find. It was even more gratifying to watch EOD blow the insurgents' weapons store in place in a glorious 'boom' and a mushroom cloud of dusty Iraqi soil. Destroying enemy battle troves was one of the few concrete measures of success short of actual battle, because you were removing lethal means from the battlefield and the hands of a determined enemy intent on using them against coalition forces.

McBride turned . . . one of his men was trying to get his attention. "What the fuck now?"

. . . No, wait . . . it was Kwin trying to get his attention. Arden was back in the 'now,' staring dumbly at the elemental with his bearings still half-trapped in war memories which were trying to hold him fast in yesterday like that Euphrates mud. This prompted the Tree Spirit to repeat his question. "Hate-eater, what of this elemental presence in the Internet? I have never heard of such a thing."

"Oh, STEM?" said Arden, trying to give the impression he was fully engaged with Kwin the whole time and hadn't completely checked out of the conversation during his flashback. "What an amazing being he seems to be. Formerly an Earth Elemental like you . . . err, well . . . I guess you could say he still is. From the way he describes it, he was transiting formless through his meta-environment when he found himself trapped in the Manmade. To this day, he doesn't really know how it happened or what exactly he had passed through to end up where he is. At first, he was extremely confused and disoriented. He had almost perished from suffocation, or your kind's equivalent of it, by being denied the ability to reconstitute himself into a meta'en composite sheath. Panicked . . . like a human who was drowning . . . he was desperately searching for a way out and back to the familiar when he came across what he thought were roots or stems in his disassociated state. However, based on STEM's description, I think they were actually cabling or wiring of some sort. Fiberoptic cabling is my best guess given my limited understanding about how all this kind of stuff really works. He just kind of followed the path of least resistance until he popped out within the Internet as some sort of sentient algorithm . . . actually, artificial intelligence is probably a closer equivalent. He refers to himself as a 'ghost' sometimes. STEM can write his own code to adapt and learn. I saved him from the hate which has proliferated across the Internet like some sort of synthetic plague. The malicious code and hate-spreading bad-bots had almost infiltrated him in an attempt to permanently corrupt his programming. Fortunately, I was able to leave him with a protective rune from our sphere. He has been feeding me information ever since."

"HUURRUMPPPHHH!" erupted Kwin, obviously aghast at what his human friend had just told him. "I have heard of such happenings, but the final fate of affected elementals was never able to be confirmed. Until now, it was only the sup-position of rumor and the subject of heated debate among High Sentients. However, as much as this account seems in the realm of the improbable and the fantastic, it is not unbeliev-able . . . especially if one can imagine the Internet as its own sphere of existence. Our sentience resides within the light of our spirit essence—"

"Right." Arden interrupted Kwin mid-sentence as if the discussion had sparked a light of understanding in his own consciousness. "Internet fiber transmits data via pulses of light. So, I suppose there is no reason not to think the trans-mission of sentience in the same way is impossible." A strange breeze kicked up, and Arden could hear a multilayered hum-ming like it was being produced by many sources; the audi-tory phenomenon seemed to add texture to the air itself and was accompanied by a buzzing sound which hurt his ears.

"It seems our sacrilegious debate is upsetting the Presades. We should shift to a new topic," stated Kwin. Arden could sense the elemental's irritation with the Presades and their rigid intolerance in the way of things, particularly when it came to new *ways* and new *things*. Their memories were long—excruciatingly long in terms of human perception, and they took an equally long time to change or accept change. Thus, their urgency to make meaningful decisions was relatively nonexistent as was their approval of anyone or anything which came close to upsetting the status quo. By existing within the context of one life for so long, the Presades had forgotten life has a responsibility to adapt, to evolve in response to changes in living conditions and environment. Kwin had run short on traits to admire them for with the exception of longevity. "Fellow Protector, while the situation allows us time, what questions do you have of me?"

Arden sighed. It took him a little while to respond. This question was obviously the one needed to get to the core of the issues troubling the Hate-eater. "STEM told me about Parim. He is fighting against Texas's seditionist forces in the Borderlands. STEM believes I can help . . . he believes this Parim may not be successful without my assistance. The Forces Corrupted are driven by a self-propagating wave of hate and anger. As you know, the negative emotions of the Fifth Element happen to be my specialty. The human En'Troops are augmented by formless wind wielders. As a combined force, they are wreaking havoc, bringing fear, bloodshed, and instability to a region which used to know peace. This may just be the key ground on which Chaos's campaign depends . . . the fates of the United States' historic union and the North American Coirea'cen both hang in the balance. The outcome may well determine whether my people—my new squad—will be able to live without fear of persecution for what they believe. I don't want to leave the Glade now, but I think I must. I have already failed my people once in ThisLife. Good people . . . valuable lives were lost because of my inability to discern the movement and intentions of the enemy. I . . . just . . .”

The eminently wise willow had been listening—intently and actively—to his troubled human brother, but at this point he interceded . . . as any wise counsel would when there was nothing further to be gained from watching Arden struggle and stammer to find the right words. “To your first question: *What of this Parim?* Parim is highly respected among Elementalkind. But please, do not confuse being respected with being well understood. Even among the lonely and isolated, Parim is a loner. Many say it is a development of his past lives . . . in the end, the totality of who we are is a culmination of all lives lived—of all the experiences of being. For Parim, most of his lives were spent sheathed as migratory species or human beings belonging to nomadic tribes. When he was an aquatic being, Parim was a bowhead whale who traveled without a pod. When he was a Feathered of flight, he was an arctic tern. As a four-legged, he was a caribou on the Eurasian Steppe. As part of your species ancestry, he was among the first humans to migrate to this continent across the Bering Land Bridge in 12,000 BCE in your species’ histories, and more recently, as a Bedouin tribesman. It was actually there, in the vast deserts of North Africa, where he developed his affinity for music and poetry and learned and adopted the majority of preferred combat tactics in his battle repertoire. He is a desert ghost who knows how to use every ounce, element, and acre of the sand-bound lands to his advantage—from passive defense to offensive attack. There is no warrior more wily or unpredictable to be found in this world.”

“I like him already,” said Arden with a chuckle. The war veteran could not help but appreciate a fellow brother in arms with combat prowess of such renown.

“It is good you retain a sense of humor, Brother Arden, for you will need it in the tough times ahead,” said Kwin, quite pleased to see his serious Druid friend find some unexpected light within himself. “Though formidable, Parim is still but one being. Parim is likely blind to that which STEM can see. It is entirely possible he does not have a complete understanding of the foe he faces . . . which means he could be employing the wrong strategy. This is especially worrisome if Parim does not recognize how deep the bloodroot goes and the depths of insidiousness driving the Corruption-afflicted humans . . ." Kwin paused, looking past Arden and off into the distance.

When he spoke again, the Tree Spirit's tone was poignant and distant, mirroring his gaze. It seemed as if he could see Parim and the battles yet to come. "I think it is imperative you go and support him. The foe has the momentum, and you could be the key to turning the pivotal engagement or battle in the Order's favor. In these troubled times, much is obscured and there are many things I cannot yet perceive."

". . . And leave my Grove in the Glade without their protector?" Arden had tensed up. He was now half sitting up and looking directly at Kwin to see if the elemental was serious.

"And is that 'knot' what I am?" retorted Komkom Akwini, matching the human's intensity. His knothole eyes were now wide as he drew his arm boughs to the mid-part of his trunk serving as his chest.

"Yes . . . yes, of course you are, Kwin. My people are lucky to have you looking out for them," stated Arden more calmly but noticeably exasperated. The humor of Kwin's word play had completely missed their target, but his emotional outburst had canceled out the Hate-eater's. "I just promised myself I would never fail my squad—my Grove—again. Ever thought about becoming a Hate-eater, Kwin? You're pretty good at it."

"No, Friend Druid," said Kwin, calmed as well. "I think only of being a tree . . . the best tree I am able to be. For this is the role assigned me by Earth Mother in ThisLife."

"Always a lesson . . ." thought Arden, but Kwin was on him before any negative thoughts could encroach and take hold.

"You lack perspective, Hate-eater. I am more than capable of watching over your Grove in your absence. You must understand that when you go to Parim's aid you serve all of us and all who serve the Natural Order."

Arden's stubborn spirit had no choice but to relent in the face of the elemental's measured assault of logic and reason, which easily overpowered any retort or resistance of fact he could offer. He had no more questions, no more words of worth to share. He had fallen into silence, for he had much to contemplate. It seemed the answer he thought right—though not wrong—was not the best for the All. Perhaps the breeze fluttering through Kwin's leafy habit had cooled the Hate-eater's heated disposition, and in doing so, had brought him the answers he so desperately sought. In the end, he was only grappling with the throes of doubt so characteristic of the human species . . . there was really only one answer for the one who stayed true to his purpose and reason for being. Arden knew in his heart, his Grove was in good 'hands' with Komkom Akwini—better hands, actually—considering the mighty *fúath slugair's* epic lapses in discipline as of late.

". . . And Kwin," Arden continued, then paused. He wanted to tell his friend something, but he did not want to burden the Glade's protector with it. Those Arden trusted were just so few. He had even made a joke out of it: *the 'trust part' of his brain was one of the parts he lost in his accident.*

"Speak it, Arden. You know you must. In fact, I demand it as a tax you must pay to compensate me for your Grove's protection . . ." Komkom was trying to make a joke in his own way to put the Hate-eater at ease and encourage him to divulge what was weighing so heavily on him . . . one among many weighty burdens threatening to pull his laden heart back down into oblivion. "What else ails your essence? Our burdens become lighter when we share the load with those who wish to help."

At Kwin's prompting, Arden finally divulged the encounter with 'Thunder Voice,' how helpless he felt, and how ashamed he was of himself for the part he played in its happening. He broke down as a child of any age might break down when telling their mother or father of an experienced horror kept quiet and bottled up for too long. Caged emotions and unresolved guilt spilled forth uncontrolled when the levy of self-control finally relented under the pressures and strains it was never meant to bear on its own without support. Yet, as painful as it was in the telling of it, it was finally good to not hold it all so close anymore. The Tree Spirit in just listening, as a friend and confidant without blame or judgment or preconception, had given Arden a powerful gift when he needed it most.

"Friend, Arden," said Kwin when Arden's emotional outpouring was finished . . . his voice filled with the hope of a new day, knowing the morning will once again bring Sun Grandmother's light. "A sentient's fate can be thought of as a spider's web. Our ultimate destiny is a product of many choices made throughout a lifetime. These choices are your strands, but there are many strands in a web. All we have touched and those who have touched us are part of our web. You fear this threat—this 'Thunder Voice'—because he is unknown yet familiar in some way. You feel you should know him, but you question the 'why' when it refuses to reveal itself to you. Where your mind fails you, the spirit always remembers . . . you both are bound to each other in some manner . . . bonded somehow. These spiritual bindings are called *lanyafae* in the Old Tongue of the High Sentients. How, when, or why you were bound to this being, I cannot say, but I can say this: *he is part of your web and your fates are interwoven somehow* . . . just as STEM and Parim share strands in your web, so too does this 'Thunder Voice.' So, follow your strand where it is leading you . . . at the very least, one aspect of your fate's riddle is known; STEM and Parim are waiting for you at the center spiral . . . and possibly, this 'Thunder Voice' is a shared threat you are meant to face together. Do not attempt to run from it or avoid it; it is fate after all.

"Need I remind you, Master Arden, that it is not just the Cellulosians who need to abide by the 'Way.'" said Kwin, responding to Arden's nonverbal acknowledgment of his message, which was a less-than-convincing affirmation he understood the proper priorities and next steps given the current state of affairs beyond the Glade. "All beings of this Earth are 'rooted' together as we Treefolk are to the earth. We are all intertangled like the living meshwork of the Interconnected All—it is not coincidental, the physical and metaphysical are interdependent. This should be obvious, and I do not mean to belittle, but your intentions and contributions should be equal to the Order's needs of the moment. Humankind is easily the most gifted of the Short-lived, but your species' lack of longevity tends to breed shortsightedness like rabbits do offspring. You must use your gifts to provide the greatest good—maximize your potential to provide meaningful impact and influence a favorable outcome for all of us. There is no further reason to delay, rise up and defend your home . . . not just a squad, not just a grove or a glade, but the entire world! It is not just Forestkind's purpose to make a 'stand' when darkness falls. I ask you: will you make a stand—tall, strong, and unmoving—in the face of Chaos?"

"Yes, yes, I will make a stand!" stated Arden, sitting up straight and finally displaying some level of emotion. Finally! Kwin now had confidence his message was finally getting through.

"Very well then . . . good," replied the Tree Spirit, bringing the leaf-graced hands of his arm boughs to either side of the 'lounge' bough Arden was sitting on. The intent was probably to reassure Arden like a human would by cradling another person's head in their hands, but the overall effect looked like a large willow tree trying to cradle a baby. "The most effective stands are those made by the defenders who go to meet the aggressor on their terms . . . so go you must!" Kwin's actions were synchronized with his words, lowering the red-haired and bearded human gently to the ground so he could depart at his leisure, but also sending the message this was the time and to make his preparations for departure from the Glade.

Arden sighed deeply as a man resolved to his fate. And

this destiny required a journey which would not get any easier with time; this endowed the Druid with a sense of urgency
to get his new adventure underway as soon as possible. His
resolution was evident in the confident posture of the stature
he assumed after dismounting smoothly from Kwin's bough.
Arden gave a final look of acknowledgment to Komkom
Akwini and a knowing nod, and then turned to make his exit
with determination in the stride of his step.

Kwin, ever the teacher, continued to encourage his friend
as he departed. "Arden, you may worry, but you should not
fear. The willow is the tree of protection. Earth Mother created
us to shield others from ill-intended spirits and dark energies.
Why do you think I chose to permanently assume this form?
I am the defender and bringer of new beginnings . . . And see,
I have already brought you yours! It is there, right in front of
you. Let it trouble you no longer, so you may rest and ready
yourself for your journey. I will have the Ourcelium send news
ahead to Parim so he should know to be expecting you. You do
not want to show up in his desert unannounced."

****

Arden left before daybreak the next morning. There was still
a lingering drizzle from the night's rain. He left quietly—
like a wraith—without any noise to avoid waking the other
Druids and alerting them to his departure. The avoidance was
intended . . . emotional human encounters were the last thing
he needed with the long, difficult goodbye chief among those
things he wanted to circumvent. Deliberately avoiding any
convincing attempts by Daryn or the other Druids to talk him
out of following fate's course was a close second. Arden had
put together a small backpack during the night, or "go-bag"
as he referred to it, so all he had to do was sling it on and
'go.' In his mind, it was better this way—because more than
likely—he wasn't coming back.

Epilogue
Desert Eagle

Drone shot. Someone somewhere was taking in the scene below from an MQ-1 Predator feed . . . a multimillion-dollar aircraft and half the total price tag is the camera. *Cloudy?* No matter, the Pred's synthetic aperture radar can see through them. This bird was methodically surveilling the New Mexico desert not too far north of the Texas border. *Surveillance? What else would a military grade, unmanned aerial system be prowling the United States interior for? Aren't there strict rules governing the employment of national-level intelligence, reconnaissance and surveillance assets in collections and intelligence gathering on US citizens?* Yes! Yes, there is, but the US federal government no longer controlled this area of the country. An argument could be made, this area was no longer United States territory, and as far as the citizens of the great state of Texas were concerned, they were no longer United States citizens! You could say things have been a little *Chaotic* lately, but that was life in the 'Lone Star Nation.'

This area was now the contested border region surrounding a seditionist state. Yes, it was true; the 'Fractured States of America' had seen better days, but there was no doubt this mech bird could *see* just fine—a testament to cutting edge military tech commandeered from the US Department of Defense by the world's newest country. This hi-tech weapon system was a United States Air Force asset no longer . . . *this* weapon system served the Free State Militia Forces (FSMF) of Texas.

At 2,000 feet above ground level, the desert doesn't have

much by way of distinguishing terrain features. Although, it is amazing to discover just how many different shades of brown exist; considerably more than you might think. However, varying shades of the same color often fail to "distinguish" things, and as a result, nothing really stands out in the arid expanse. The occasional isolated mountain range, roads, and highways are the only thing outside of GPS a human can use to get their bearings. The distinctive geographic and manmade features which most orienteers use as references and to gauge progress of travel can be hard to come by here.

The Pred's unblinking eye continued to scour the desert for any signs of the enemy on the move. *Wait. What is that? Lock on it.* It was faint at first . . . barely distinguishable like a black-and-white photo with a blemish. Focusing on the out-of-place almost made it disappear, as figments often do here . . . as a shimmering apparition in the heat . . . but not in this case. There was definitely something there. The drone operator was experienced and would not allow the desert terrain to deceive him. 'It' was in the middle of the broad, flat lowland bracketed by distant mountains, and the unidentified target was generating a large dust kick-up which betrayed its presence. A group of 'something' on the move. *Vehicles?* Likely, since the cattle drives this region is known for ended long ago, only lasting two human generations. Just one of many nostalgic phenomena wiped out by human adaptation and technological advancements. The cattle drives that prominently adorned the romanticized tales of the Old West were just one of the many victims of human progress. In their particular case, it was the railroads whose straight-laid tracks still intermittently gashed the horizon-to-horizon brown. The rail-lines looked like the Earth's neatly stitched wounds in the MQ-1 video feed.

As the Pred moved in on its target, the disturbance took a shape . . . *like a bird?* The potential target was shaped like a buzzard the drone operator thought, composed of a tan cloud of churned and air-cast desert floor contrasting against the deeper shades of continuous brown which characterized the desert surface. When viewed from altitude, the creation appeared as a dirt phoenix with a clean leading edge cutting into the wind, and the wing and tail feathers burning off into a dispersing dust cloud carried away by the biting winds. "What is that? And what is it doing out here?" the FSMF operator thought as he called out coordinates and a description of his target to the battle captain and other operators in the command, control, and communications, or 'C3,' center. "If this is USG, they are in maneuver much earlier than our intelligence reporting indicated," stated the operator as he continued to vector his aircraft into the 'desert eagle.'

Consumed by the ghostly manifestation in the middle of nowhere, the Pred driver started to get that hollow feeling in the pit of his gut a person gets when something terrible is going to happen. *That* feeling when you are not sure if you are on the right side or whether your cause is just, because you think you are seeing the first sign of the inevitable consequences of poor choices moving slowly across the desert floor like a harbinger of impending doom. "Fuck!" The drone operator swore under his breath; his profanity growled more than whispered as he tried extremely hard not to show any outward signs of dismay to his fellow seditionists.

The Pred driver switched from standard, hi-res video to infrared imaging to try and ascertain the force size by vehicle numbers or biological signatures—nothing. The large dust raptor had no heat signatures which distinguished it from desert background. However, there was one thing, one figure floating within the strange dust phenomena . . . *floating?* "What the hell?" The hollow feeling in his core was chased away by his stomach cinching up and a feeling of nausea . . .

. . . The perspective on the ground was vastly different than that from the air. There was a surprisingly vibrant world at surface level; one which did not suffer from the technological disassociation afflicting the majority of humankind. Here in these seemingly lifeless surrounds was a biodiverse, sentient collective who celebrated interconnectedness and strived for intra-dependence while still living independently. A world who appreciated all—everything—Earth Mother had wrought, and as Her children, reveled in their privileged places within it; for there were no big roles or small roles, just roles—all played a part. As living beings, everyone was equal here and valued in the Natural Order; a web of life where the contributions of all sustained the balance whose sum total was the vibrant spirit and body of the planet Herself irrespective of their place in the food chain.

The sand and gravel of the desert eagle exalted and surged forth in waves; the 'barren' brown was enjoying what it was to know the likeness of water and the freedom of flowing like current. Porpoising like a sea serpent and bucking like a wild bronco, the earth was putting on a grand show for their Earth Elemental, Parim—a powerful and ancient sentient being who commanded great respect among Elementalkind. His protectorate was the arid vastness of the desert Southwest, and he was tireless in his stewardship of his assigned meta'en.

Parim glided over the roiling sand and mobilized rock atop a limestone slab: the look of it like some sort of skateboard hovercraft from a science fiction movie. The spectacle would have been mind-blowing if he didn't make it all look so effortless . . . so natural. Parim was motionless, even statue-like, as he floated above his emulent of a great bird of prey comprised of wind-tossed earth. His assumed form was a composite representation of the desert itself:

> *Draped over him, a grass mat cloak. His head was not really a head as humans would understand it, consisting of stacked limestone slabs. His eyes just holes among the slabs with no visible mouth or nose. His chest, torso, and shoulders were adorned with desert stone which appeared as body armor suited for a stout, prehistoric soldier girded for battle. His limbs were composed of more flexible, pliable materials, but each durable in*

its own right; a combination of cactus tightly wrapped by the thin branches of scraggly piñon pine running down into boots of river stone, with his arms of similar composition. Aye, Parim was a most inelegant-looking creature, but he was not trying to win a beauty contest. He was fine with functional and imposing—this choice manifestation was optimized to best serve the needs of the Order and his meta'en.

Though he was 'just' an Earth Elemental, Parim possessed far more than just a single dimension of the surrounding Natural at his command. In fact, he could meld the earth into any facsimile of any creature, but the choice of raptor for this roving construct was deliberate. For Parim, all of his creations were multipurposed with this desert eagle paying tribute to his feathered ladies. His beautiful Praestean, Ayre . . . a spectacularly unique, quadra-form symbiote of four Harris hawks united by one consciousness. *Shey* were his eyes in the sky . . . his scouts, his messengers, and his dear friends as well as his *ThisLife-long* companions of course. And as his Keeper, Ayre was also his lifeline should he ever need it. Perhaps *sheir* most endearing quality was Ayre's reputation. His Praestean ranked among the most reviled of all Gifteds by Chaos's En'Troops. Ayre was the four serving as one.

Thinking of Ayre as Parim's four-ship of organic 'Preds' is probably a fairly accurate descriptor. Like Parim, they are a powerful and ancient sentient being . . . a Gifted consciousness with designated purpose. Sheir spirit is eternal, and sheir accumulated experience, wisdom, and might can be traced back to the first elemental-Keeper binding thousands of years ago. Ayre's sentience has only known this protectorate, but shey have known many hawk forms as they have reincarnated over the eons. The Keeper's animal sheath is the elemental's preference, and Ayre could not be more pleased with sheir master's choice. To live free in the manner of Feathereds every day is the most blessed kind of amazing!

Ayre were on the wing, fanned out in a defensive diamond formation. Shey were maintaining a few hundred yards between herselves to ensure overwatch of Parim, and it was obvious shey were enjoying the thermal updrafts along with the views of sheir beloved desert below. Ayre's elemental was extremely creative and never failed to surprise. The writhing sand phoenix was brilliant . . . just the lure needed to attract their prey. As anticipated, the FSMF drone was moving in for a closer look. Though quiet and stealthy, the drone's presence was glaringly obvious to Ayre across sheir entire suite of natural perceptors. The Manmade always stood out against the Natural. Man's war tech and his exotic alloys and materials were even easier to see than 'standard' variants of Manmade; these were like an alien presence . . . like something which should not be allowed to be present on this Earth. This aerial drone was the humans' 'eyes in the sky' . . . controlled by humans now serving as the means to the Force Corrupted's ends to advance Chaos's designs. Whether the humans behind the Pred were Corrupted or not—whether they were conscious of the impurity of the cause of which they were a part or not mattered little to Parim. In the final summation, the ultimate disposition of their spirit essence was for Earth Mother to decide. His charge was far more direct: to protect Her children, defend Her Coirea'cen, and preserve the Natural Order—maintain the balance . . .

. . . The drone operator was completely focused on Parim's sand-shifting animation and moving in for a closer examination by the most direct route, having requested and already received authorization to arm his Hellfire missiles should the thing or things on the move prove hostile. He already had clearance to light up any enemy targets upon confirmation. As far as the FSMF was concerned, the Borderlands were a war zone, and they were not the only beings girded for war and ready to wage battle . . .

. . . Unbeknownst to the operator, one of Ayre's selves had

already moved behind the drone in the war machine's blind spot. This opportunistic one of the quadra-form Keeper didn't need permission to attack. Shey already knew their master's will and intentions—they were lanyafae . . .

. . . Closer inspection was helpful in revealing target details which could not be discerned from a distance. The FSMF drone pilot was getting rattled by what he was seeing in his high-resolution surveillance feed. His thoughts were racing fast enough to run down the fear associated with the cognition of what he was actually perceiving. "Am I really seeing this or is it just fatigue? Blink, man . . . blink. Focus. Breathe . . . not helping. The 'weird' is still there. Some kind of magic? Evil magic?" He spoke up to the entire battle cab when he was finally able to convince himself the fucked-up shit he was seeing was not a figment of his imagination. "S-Sir, it is a surface disturbance that looks like a bird, but I cannot determine what is making it or what its purpose is. There is a figure near the head of 'it,' but it is not giving off any biological signatures . . . absolutely no heat showing on IR outside of what the terrain is reflecting. I don't think it's human. I am not sure if it is even alive."

The on-duty battle captain was terse. He was agitated because he was exhausted, and there had been a lot of long days since the lights went out. Because the Texas military was thin on ISR assets as well as the operator personnel with the required technical specialties and experience, he and his team were working extended shifts to help piece together 24/7 surveillance coverage of the Borderlands. Man, this was the one day he just needed a quiet, boring shift, but apparently, he was not going to get it. "Reynolds, do we have any of our ground maneuver units operating in that location?"

The imagery analyst responded very quickly over secure comms. "No, sir. Whatever it is, it is *not* one of ours."

"Well, that makes things simple. Simpson, take it out," ordered the captain. He was actually relieved there were no

FSMF forces operating in the area, so all kinetic options were available in the absence of fratricide concerns. They could make this problem go away by the most expeditious means available.

"Roger . . ." However, just as Simpson initiated the process to engage his target, his drone had already been targeted and was under attack. An unknown adversary had initiated a kill chain of their own. The Pred feed was being displayed on the main screen of the command center's plasma wall; it showed something dark brown fly in from behind the drone wing blind side . . . something which looked like talons impacted the protective housing of the MQ-1's very expensive camera, causing cracks which spiderwebbed across the housing and immediately translated across all large viewing screens streaming the Pred feed. All FSMF personnel present in the room were riveted to the main screen as they watched the expensive weapon system tumble out of the sky from a 'first person' perspective courtesy of the video feed: *desert—sky—desert—sky—desert—sky—black* . . . lost feed—static screen. It was just one drone, but the unidentified threat which took it out so efficiently also functioned as a psychological weapon. In that moment, it felt like the hopes of the rebellion had fallen out of the sky with their death-spiraling drone. *What just happened?*

Simpson's tightened gut turned into a knot . . .

. . . On location, the spirited Feathered girls had fun with the Predator takedown. Of one mind, Ayre displayed complete unity of effort by executing a coordinated dog-fighting maneuver worthy of the most legendary fighter aces. One raptor slammed into the Pred's camera housing from one direction while two others generated enough force in their dive as a synchronized pair to shear off the wings. The fourth had no role in this complex maneuver, so she had first dibs on the next target shey encountered on their wanderings. Ayre's selves were all uniformly pleased as shey observed the chunks of human war machine drop out of the sky . . . a wingless fuselage tumbling awkwardly, plummeting ungracefully like something which never belonged up here with Feathereds in the first place. It was only fitting such an unnatural thing was being returned unceremoniously to the bounds of earth. Ayre were pleased to see the Manmade abomination involuntarily leave sheir domain, certain it did not deserve to be here. This human construct was just a weapon designed to spy and kill remotely by a triggerman hundreds, even thousands, of miles away. Predators were never meant to be so far removed from their kill chain, but then again, this was war, and like the mech bird, also a human construct.

Parim had looked up and smiled with approval of his Praestean's well-choreographed attack. Though he cannot physically smile, it was a smile of the spirit which can be sensed and felt by all those who know how to feel such things in that way. The sand and particulate making up his desert eagle quickly settled back down on the desert floor in the absence of Parim asserting his will to keep the arid soil aloft. Parim set down his stone slab as well, which also dissipated into a pile of sand as he stepped off.

This isolated environment with its harsh conditions demanded resident species to be the well-adapted and hardy breeds. This land did not yearn for visitors or tourists and expected a higher level of commitment and self-sufficiency for any being who wished to call this place home. It was austere … and the meager resources available to sustain life drove the evolution of a distributed ecosystem where most life forms were fiercely independent and accustomed to operating alone. Here in this unforgiving place, concentrations of larger-sized species do not occur naturally and need to be artificially sustained if they are present. However, as in all things in life, perception is a matter of perspective, and Parim's feelings and thoughts about his meta'en were quite different from those of 'outsiders':

"This desert is not desolate, nor barren or harsh. It is an ecosystem no less gifted and of no lesser importance than any other. The difference here is the earth element actually holds sway vice the water element. Thus, the Green is subsumed by the *brown* . . . and how magnificent the brown is! The absence of the Blue in any environ is associated with scarcity of natural resources as well as in the abundance of life. However, the unacquainted should understand one being's scarcity is another's plenty. The Earthly biome is dependent on balance, so the Blue cannot rule all meta'ens. Earth Mother's living body is the intersection of earth and water, which jointly manifests as the Green. Oft times, the Green is not so green and such a state of things is expected and necessary . . . and in the opinion of this sentient—amazing. The desert's reputation is rarely sterling, but 'this' is my home, my sanctuary."

Parim stood there for a moment, taking in the desert while basking in the peace of the after-battle . . . that rarest of calms immediately following the tumult when the world starts to the breathe again. Staying in the moment for even just a few moments was important, for the time for mindful devotions would become even rarer very soon, and if the Order was not successful against Chaos's horde in the coming days and weeks, these brief meaningful periods would go extinct along with the host of species most exposed to Chaos's coordinated assault.

Much like the way of most species in his protectorate, Parim was accustomed to being alone . . . and for the time being, he was well aware he and his protectorate were alone in this fight—alone and unsupported. The Guardian Spirit had placed the entire Southwest region and its defense in Parim's charge. The Earth Elemental was on his own while the Guardian was dealing with the Formless-inspired crises in the western ranges; this was assessed to be the leading edge of Chaos's unprecedented war of devastation and unnatural rot. Setting the conditions for it had taken many decades; unconsciously precipitated by human proliferation, habitation, terraforming, and environmental manipulation. With the conditions set, the onset of this destructive cascade manifested surprisingly quickly, triggered by Chaos's Formless fire and wind wielders which had crashed hard like a rogue wave. With most of nature's checks and balances effectively disabled, the destructive effects had cascaded eastward with unbelievably disastrous results.

Humankind's careless diligence had already pushed the North American Coirea'cen to the brink of catastrophic collapse. With Earth Mother's living body already at a tipping point, Chaos needed to exert very little effort to push the continent over the edge . . . but to make it stick, to make this destructive change and instability enduring, Chaos did need to create the right combination of unmitigated cataclysmic conditions by exerting the full measure of His En'Troop's might—the whole of His minions numbers, guile, weaponry, and supernatural powers—brought to bear on a vulnerable and weakened Natural Order.

Until the Guardian could arrest the ecological free fall in the West and bring the powerful Corrupted sentients enabling it to heel, Parim was charged with an unsupported holding action in the Southwest. Here, the primary threat was mostly of the human variety—at least in the physical sense—with lesser Corrupted Formless in support. Parim was not to concede any more biome to Chaos and His army while also minimizing destruction and loss of life. The Sand Spirit did not need the Natural Network or the Ourcelium to tell him Nilch'i, the reviled, was commanding Chaos's massed formless assault on the Natural to the continental north and west . . . he knew it because he could 'feel' the havoc and wanton destruction she was wreaking, which was transmitted as arrhythmic thrumming within the deep earth. He knew this just as he knew his windborne nemesis longed to bring her wrath to the desert Southwest and hold him and his meta'en in her intimately destructive embrace. However, this was a worry and potential engagement for another day. Fate would have her say at the time and place she ordained, and Parim found it far more productive to live in the moment as much as elementally possible vice contemplating his daunting task. He had decided more than a fortnight ago further time devoted to such things was a luxury he could no longer afford.

Parim looked over to survey the scattered wreckage of the drone and then asked the desert to take hold of the weaponized Manmade and pull it all down . . . down below the surface . . . down into the bosom of the earth where it would then be inaccessible to salvagers, ensuring it would no longer serve as a tool of war for humankind. He watched the sandscape swallow the shattered mech bird, and then the elemental scanned the sparsely featured landscape rimmed by distant mountains while communicating to his Keeper animal via thought transference—his preferred mode of communication. Though he had a mouth crease, very few had been honored with the esteem of engaging in primitive verbal communication with the Sand Spirit: "My beautiful, eight-winged queen of the sky, well done. Rest now . . . find respite from the heat of midday. Hunt food as you have skillfully hunted this human-contrived, mechanized death bringer and replenish yourself. I sense the approach of a major storm which will bolster the winter westerlies and strengthen the *shmog* who have been loitering in this border region. Chaos's self-proclaimed 'Right Hand' will be certain to take advantage of these troublesome little wind sentients in their boosted state to conduct night raids, wreak havoc, and create bloodshed among those who do not assume their Corrupted cause. I need you fresh, my feathered Freya to aid me in disrupting any and all diabolical plots and schemes. I live to frustrate and anger Chaos and His battle captains to the cores of their being with my top priority being to torment the 'first' among them, my nemesis Nilch'i. I long to emblazon their twisted essences with Earth Mother's light so as to permanently impair their ability to destroy and corrupt Her creation. Rest and make ready so you are able to present the most lethal version yourselves when His horde is upon us."

Ever so briefly—only so long as his intense mission focus would allow (which wasn't very long at all . . . just a few seconds)—Parim thought of his friend, *Okaraxta*, a fellow Earth Elemental whose protectorate was the expansive grasslands of the north. His meta'en was one of many at the continental center in the insidious grip of Nilch'i and her formless minions. In just weeks—in less than a single season—Chaos's top field general had returned the American heartland to the 'dirt lands' reminiscent of the 1930s infamous 'Dustbowl.' However, this ruinous recurrence was worse in many ways, for it was not just a product of human intervention which usurped the natural process; this was catastrophe with intentionality. The black blizzards were back, and the vast region now known as the "Windswepts" encompassed an area as far south as mid-Oklahoma stretching all the way up into the Canadian mid-continent.

The Windswepts of course were just a name . . . nothing really means much of anything unless you are among those experiencing the tribulation, but Parim knew the lack of contact from his brother elemental was bad because the Ourcelium and other aspects of natural connectivity were severed. The Natural Network is robust and resilient, so lapses like this do not happen unless the Coirea'cen has been severely compromised at the systemic level. *What could cause something like this? . . . the almost incomprehensible!* All Parim had the time and residual energy for was a quick well wish sent in his brother's direction. "Okaraxta, be strong my friend. No matter what manner or insidious combination of Corrupted besiege you and yours. This—all of this—is a holding action until we find our way through this dark mire. The light will find us and show us the way . . . all of us, if it be only a handful when this is done." Parim was not known for his humor. Thank goodness for the Natural Order's sake that his strengths lay in other areas more pertinent to the challenges ahead.

Then, Parim sighed with a puff of dust from his mouth crease subsequent to relinquishing his form to the approving quadra-screech of his Keeper. As his desert eagle and slab had previously been subsumed by the arid expanse, so too was Parim's manifested form. This allowed his spirit essence to return to the bosom of his 'beautiful brown.' The five-being contingent was off to rest and renew in preparation for the next engagement.

****

. . . For many battles were coming as well as heavy burdens to be borne and shared by others of the Natural Order—some of which were certain to be pivotal in deciding the ultimate fate of the North American Coirea'cen . . . and reinforcements were inbound as communicated to him by the Tree Spirit Komkom Akwini. Whether the dispersed defenders were too few to yield an outcome in favor of the Natural Order had yet to be decided, but regardless, Parim had a great expanse of biome to watch over and much to do to ensure his influence was as impactful as possible . . .

Do you hear that?
The fluttering?

. . . The Mothman is coming.

Did you enjoy *Fractured State in the Blighted Earth?*

Don't worry! Book 2 of the Blighted Earth series, *Long Leg from the Blighted Earth*, is in the works!

In the meantime, if you want to read and learn more about the Blighted Earth check out . . .

<u>A Fascinating, Eclectic Collection of Short Stories</u>
5 out of 5 stars

"Tembreull shows high promise in his first literary offering that is comprised of the products of a fertile imagination, as well as of real-life experiences. His descriptions are masterful and his stories replete with characters the reader will love."

Joseph Badal, Amazon review
Author of 18 award-winning suspense novels, Amazon and Barnes & Noble #1 Best Selling Author, and two-time winner of the Tony Hillerman Prize for Best Fiction Book of the Year
(Reviewed in the United States on December 15, 2023)

<u>A literary masterpiece</u>
5 out of 5 stars

". . . a mesmerizing journey into a hidden world beyond our conventional perception of reality. This exceptional book is a treasure trove of fictional narratives and artifacts that unveil a breathtaking cosmic tapestry."

A Look Inside: A Book Review Blog & Podcast
(Reviewed in the United States on September 30, 2023)

Glossary

Arm'nbrilt: Inani word whose closest translation to human English is "Desert Pearl." The name given to Earth by Eros, the Prospector—Calisphaer's most renowned Traveler.

absumption: Inani term; the process of extracting the energy the Inani people need to power their home world of Calisphaer and sustain their way of life in the Dark Matter Realm. This energy can only be derived from the universe's living matter which composes planets on the other side of the Great Barrier Web—the side of the light and the living, and the side on which the planet Earth also resides.

ampbot: 'Bots' deployed into the Internet by Chaos's agents, which are specifically programmed to 'amplify' and multiply the effects of the hateful and divisive messaging, rhetoric, and misinformation within the transactional flows. They constitute one of Chaos's primary enablers in leveraging the great social engineering engines of the Internet domain to manifest destructive outcomes in the Earthreal.

AOR: A military acronym which stands for "Area of Responsibility." Military units at all levels use the term to describe the slice of the battlespace to which they are assigned and in which they conduct their operations within a combat zone.

Biologicals: A term High Sentients use to describe any of Earth Mother's children whose sentience is experiencing a life in biological form, e.g., mammal, reptilian, avian, aquatic, etc.

Blue: Non-*meta'en*-specific reference to the domain of Water Elementals; encompassing any areas where bodies of water and water systems dominate, such as the ecosystems of the oceans, inland seas, wetlands, river deltas, marshes, etc.

Calisphaer: The Inani name for their home world, which is located within the Hubuv'al at the center and origination point of the universe.

Celestiality: The first sentience of the universe, and for which, She is both wellspring and womb; the source of the three building blocks of the universe, which must be present in some form for life to exist. These foundation stones of the cosmos—sentience, the enforce, and elemental matter—are the essential components of all life in all its manifested forms.

Cellulosians: General term encompassing the trees, plants, and other life forms—sentient and non-sentient—whose form is comprised of cellulose as a reinforcing material.

Centerverse: See Hubuv'al.

Coirea'cen: The Blue and the Green of our planet which together make up Earth Mother's "Living Body" as it is known in Old Tongue of the High Sentients.

Corrupted(s): General term describing sentients whose sentience has been 'corrupted' and turned to serve Chaos and enable His insidious schemes to overthrow the Natural Order. Chaos must corrupt the spirit essences of Earth's sentient beings to feed the ranks of His army, because He is unable to create sentience Himself.

Corrupted Formless: A special category of the Corrupted which includes Sentient Wind and Sentient Fire; Corrupted elemental sentience coupled to the two 'formless' foundational elements.

Crucible: The Great Weaver, Knotal-Nodum's gift to the 'First of Form.' The First, also known as the Star Children, were the ancestors of the Inani people who assisted the weaver in starting his never-ending weave of the Great Barrier Web.

Dark Matter Realm: The region of the dark side of the universe where Calisphaer is located; typically referring to the dark side within the Hubuv'al or Centerverse.

Dark Ones: Another name for the Inani people.

darklings: Any being of darkness, but most commonly a reference to 'rifters;' beings either created by or existing within rifts.

Desexets: Inani word for 'Designated Extraction Planets.' Those worlds of the living universe targeted for absumption.

Discordant: Preceded by the Great Cascade, it is Chaos's desired end state—the end of everything—on any living world; an unrecoverable state of total chaos.

Dislocation: Often referred to as a "Dislocation event;" it occurs when a transiting elemental sentience becomes trapped in the Manmade, which can include everything from human constructions of manmade materials (e.g., cities) to the Internet. The majority of elementals experiencing Dislocation perish due to severe disorientation and an inability to assimilate and reassume form in the unnatural, alien environment of the Manmade in any of its manifested forms.

Dream Walker: Shamans, medicine men, or any sentient beings possessing the supranatural ability to travel in dreams. Their spirit essence can leave their physical form and transit spheres of spiritual existence.

Earthreal (or Real): Term that describes the existential sphere encompassing the entirety of Earth's planetary biome as well as the 'physical' universe which humankind perceives as "reality."

Earth Elemental: Elemental who wields the element of earth. Their assigned meta'ens are those environments and ecosystems where landmass dominates over water. There are several subspecies of Earth Elementals, including Tree Spirits and Sand Spirits.

Epoch (of Man): High Sentients mark the major ages of Earth Mother's life by the dominant periods of the planet's apex species. The current Epoch is the Epoch of Man.

Effector Elements: The "EE" in En'Troop-EE. Effector Elements are individual operational units or teams in Chaos's army. They are mission-focused, and several different Effector Elements from multiple columns may be committed to a single line of Chaotic effort during a campaign involving multiple, parallel lines of effort.

Elementalkind: Term used to collectively describe all elemental species.

Emostrum: The spiritual spectrum of emotion; all emotions occupy a spectrum similar to radiation or light. Though there are always residual, uncommitted emotions, the only natural sources of emotion are sentient beings. However, it has been demonstrated that emotions can be amplified, manipulated, or changed through unnatural or artificial means.

endless: Another term for the Internet domain by those who exist there or operate in that sphere. The Internet is perceived as 'endless' because it does not have discernable boundaries and lacks the reference points necessary for calculating distance or assessing location when employing conventional Earthreal methods.

enforce: All energies and forces exist as a single entity at the point of their origination at the center of universe, referred to as the Hubuv'al or the Centerverse. One of three foundational 'building blocks' of the universe sourced from the Celestiality. The enforce separates into the constituents as we know them (light, gravity, etc.) once the enforce has traveled away from universal center and transitioned the Great Barrier Web to the 'living' side of the universe.

En'Troop (or En'Troop-EE): Chaos's army which is task organized to operate like a multi-spectrum insurgency whose ranks are manned by the Earth's sentient beings who have either been Corrupted or deceived into serving the Chaotic cause. Chaos's top field generals lead 'columns' which are functionally organized, e.g., Technical Column, Formless Column, etc. Their mission is to bring about an unrecoverable entropic state called the Discordant.

EOD: A US military acronym for "Explosive Ordnance Disposal."

extra-awareness: An ability or state of consciousness which is derived from acute extrospective abilities.

extrospection: A sentient being's ability to observe and examine the world beyond themselves, and more specifically, the worlds beyond their world, e.g., the spiritual realms. At one time, all humans had such attributes, but the species' collective abilities have eroded over time due to reliance on technology. These abilities can also be supernaturally amplified in certain beings, e.g., Guardian Spirits.

Feathereds: General term referring to all bird species at all levels of sentience.

Fifth Element: The element of emotion which is often overlooked with respect to the four classic elements of earth, water, fire, and wind. Chaos, though powerful, must work through the sentients of a world to achieve his aims and is considered by some to be an 'emotion elemental' or a wielder of the Fifth Element.

firestorm (or furricane): Descriptive names given to the emergence of an incredibly destructive phenomenon of extreme, hurricane-force winds paired with widespread, ravenous wildfires. Most who experience it do not realize the catastrophic convergence is the Chaos-inspired coupling of Sentient Wind and Fire.

First of Form: Earliest ancestors of the Inani. The first sentient life to assume form in the early universe.

fleshbounds: Cellulosian reference to Biologicals.

Force(s) Corrupted: Refers to Chaos's army, the En'Troop-EE, or the entire horde of Corrupted, partially Turned, and manipulated beings serving His cause.

Forestkind: Term used to collectively describe all Cellulosian species.

Free State Militia Forces (FSMF): The redesignation of the Texas military and irregular defense forces after the state seceded from the Union and declared itself an independent nation. The FSMF includes former Department of Defense military forces, Texas National Guard, and militia forces; all of which have been called up in the defense of the 'Lone Star Nation' in the face of an expected US invasion.

fúath slugair: "Hate-eater" in human tongue. A rare type of Gifted being who can detect and absorb, and thus disrupt or displace hate and other negative emotions. It is uncertain whether a being is born with this ability, or it is acquired as the result of the accidental coupling of such things as traumatic injury and supernatural sources of power. They function as something like a virus within Chaos's entropic system.

Gifted(s): This term is most often used in reference to Praeditors and Praesteans who fill specific roles within species or in service of an elemental master; they are benefactors of 'strung consciousness,' and thus, possess the accrued knowledge and experience of all the others who have previously performed their role in the service of the Natural Order. Less commonly, the term is also used to describe sentient beings gifted special powers, such as the *fúath slugair.*

Glade: The name of the 'common area' of *Kesul' Kaham*, the assigned protectorate of the Earth Elemental, Komkom Akwini; known by humankind as the Sam Houston National Forest. The Glade encompasses a clearing and the immediate natural surrounds near Lake Conroe in the national forest which is also home to the Presades of the Glade.

grayscape: A term used to describe the 'netscape' within the Internet when the proliferation of hate and hostility propagating code, algorithms, and bots have completely subsumed and corrupted the valid data and truthful information within the transactional flows. When uncorrupted, these transactional flows and knowledge structures are perceived as something akin to 'black and white.'

Great Barrier Web: Also 'Great Barrier' or 'Web.' The impermeable barrier which separates the universe into the dark side and that of the living and the light. The Web is also the unseen, energetic structure behind the universe's perpetual expansion engine which, if visible, would resemble a nautilus shell slowly spiraling outward into eternity.

Great Cascade: Chaos and His En'Troops are always seeking to initiate an unstoppable chain reaction along many destructive lines of effort (e.g., ecological collapse, environmental catastrophe, war, etc.) to drive a descent into total chaos from which a planet cannot recover (i.e., the Discordant).

Great Void: A term the Inani use when referring to the vast emptiness of space, or even the entirety of the universe. Used in the same way a human sailor might refer to landless, seemingly lifeless expanses of the open ocean.

Great Weaver: See 'Knotal-Nodum.'

Green: Generic reference to the domain of Earth Elementals in a non-*meta'en* specific sense, which encompasses any areas where landmass dominates (e.g., the ecosystems of mountains, forest, prairie, etc.). The intersection of earth and water in Earth Mother's Coirea'cen, which hosts the vast majority of life and biodiversity within the Earthly biome.

Guardian Spirit: Considered by many to occupy the highest tier in the Hierarchy of Sentients short of Earth Mother Herself. They are honored with this eminent role for having served the Natural Order through many lives culminating in distinguished service as an Earth or Water Elemental. Guardian Spirits are organized by continental landmass, oceans, and isolated seas. Their period of service spans the Epoch in which they serve, and their form is aligned with dominant sentient species of the Epoch. This allows them to exist largely unnoticed and learn the ways of the dominant species. The Guardians are called upon in times of existential threat to the

Earth Mother's Coirea'cen where they command the affected elemental forces in Her defense. Guardians can be thought of as triggering and guiding Earth Mother's "immune response" to internal threats.

Hate-eater: A slang term for *fúath slugair.*

hateout: A weather-like phenomenon which occurs in the Internet, like a whiteout or brownout on Earth, when divisive messaging and hate propagating rhetoric overcomes the sphere's inherent processes for content moderation and data integrity (mechanisms for ensuring truthful information). Within the Internet, intact virtual structures and properly functioning processes appear as 'black and white' to those who can visually perceive them, and corruptive mechanisms and destructive effects break the black and white down into gray areas where truth and knowledge are muddied by lies, misinformation, and disinformation.

hatestorm: See 'hateout.' Also an alternative term for 'hostilestorm.' A weather-like phenomenon occurring in the Internet.

Hierarchy of Sentience: In Earth Mother's world, the spirit essence or soul is immortal, and it is a gift to each of us from Her. As we progress through many lives and occupy many forms, it is expected that we live well-intentioned and purposeful lives in ascending the 'Hierarchy' of which the elementals and Guardian Spirits occupy the highest tiers.

Higher: Slang for 'High Sentient.'

High Sentient: Those sentient beings who occupy the upper tiers of the Hierarchy of Sentience and man the ranks of Earth Mother's Natural Order. The breakpoint between high and low sentients is humankind; the species can be seen as 'straddling the line,' and an effective argument can be made for considering them as either depending on the life courses chosen by individual beings.

Hivemind: The Inani people are an ancient race who possess a unified consciousness and collective intelligence. The Inani are governed by a technocracy where all citizens are assigned to Task Classes which correlate with their societal status. The level of control one Task Class exerts over others is a function of their status in the civilization hierarchy where governance is based on a system of strict rules and compliance.

hostilstorm: See 'hateout.' A weather-like phenomenon occurring in the Internet.

hovanta: A High Sentient ability unique to Spirit Guardians. When employed, the being becomes one of shadow; a ghost who blends into the surrounding environment even while on the move. This power creates the perceived effect of Guardians "appearing" in battle as if out of nowhere.

Hubuv'al: The name given to center of the universe or 'Center-verse' by the ancient sentients of the early universe, forming the 'hub' around which everything of the *All* rotates.

IED: US Military acronym which stands for "Improvised Explosive Device;" a term of modern warfare which describes the class of munitions-based weaponry employed by out-manned and outgunned insurgent/irregular forces against the armored vehicles of the combat patrols employed by a modern, high-tech invasion force.

Inani: The denizens of the world of Calisphaer in the Dark Matter Realm at the center of the universe. They are the ancestors of the 'Star Children' or the 'First of Form' who assisted Knotal-Nodum in starting his weave of the Great Barrier Web. They must cross the barrier web to locate viable sources of living matter which can be converted into the energy their civilization requires to sustain their way of life. Inani barrier traverses are only possible with the Crucible and Umbralux talisman gifted to 'the First' by Knotal-Nodum.

Innerspace: (proper noun) Another name for the Internet which acknowledges it as a domain 'within' the Earthreal or what humans would understand as their physical reality.

Innersphere: Refers to the interior of Calisphaer where the Inani people actually live. Though the Inani are a hardy, god-like race, they can only exist inside the Centerverse's or Hubuv'al's "hub," which protects them from the extreme conditions at the center of all things and around which the entire ever-expanding universe rotates.

innerverse: Another term for the Internet, which as a place, can be thought of as a microverse contained within the Earthreal's domain of existence; yet it is still entirely its own existential sphere.

intentenessence: Term from the language of the High Sentients to describe emotional changes in state which happen when emotions themselves are imparted with intentions of essence from sentient beings. Because emotions exist within their own spectrum of spiritual energy like colors in the light spectrum, hate, for example, is created by metaphysically transmuting emotional energy from a less volatile state. The emotional change in state a causal one where the causality mechanism is the imparted 'intentionality' from one or more sentient beings.

Interconnectedness of the All: (also, the 'Interconnected All' or simply 'the All') All life on Earth is inexorably connected irrespective of their place within the Hierarchy of Sentience. Every form of life has their role—predator, prey, pollinator, oxygen maker, etc.—to perform for ecosystems to thrive, prosper, and maintain the necessary biodiversity to ensure the health of the Earthly biome. Understanding this 'interconnectedness' is the key to understanding the equality of all life; this is the knowledge integral to maintaining the natural balance.

"INTs": US military slang which generically refers to 'all' the different methods and means of intelligence collection and analysis, e.g., Human Intelligence (HUMINT), Signals Intelligence (SIGINT), Measurement and Signature Intelligence (MASINT), etc.

ISR: US military acronym which stands for "Intelligence, Surveillance, and Reconnaissance." It can refer to both the military functions as well as the personnel and platforms needed to accomplish those particular mission sets.

Keeper: (or 'Keeper animal') Another name for Praesteans born of the respect and affection an elemental has for their Keeper animal. Praestean is from the Old Tongue and literally translates to "keeper of the elemental essence." Elementals and their Keepers are spiritually bound for life, and these animals are charged with ensuring the powerful elemental essence is returned to the Lifestream upon the end of ThisLife.

Kesul' Kaham: The Earth Elemental, Komkom Akwini's protectorate; his meta'en includes the entirety of what humans call the Sam Houston National Forest.

Knotal-Nodum: (also, the 'Great Weaver') An exceedingly powerful, ancient sentient energy from the early universe. With the assistance of the Inani ancestors, the Star Children,

Knotal-Nodum, who is innately compelled to serve his sole purpose, began to weave the Great Barrier Web. The impermeable barrier provides the structure for universal expansion, while also dividing it into the dark side and the side of the light and the living. The Weaver's labors are never-ending, and the universe is always expanding.

lanyafae: From the Old Tongue of the High Sentients meaning "spirit bound." It refers to two sentient beings who are bound at the spiritual level, either through a shared fate or life's purpose, e.g., a Praestean purpose-bound to his or her elemental.

Lifestream: The great spiritual river where all spirit essences of all of Earth Mother's created beings return after ThisLife's end, dwelling there temporarily until they move on to NextLife, and ideally, upward in the Hierarchy of Sentience.

LastLife: A sentient being's 'last life lived' prior to ThisLife; also referred to as PastLife(ves) when a being seeks to acknowledge previous lives in which the spirit essence experienced life as different species.

Lesser: Slang for a 'Low Sentient;' usually used in a derogatory manner.

Long-lived: A descriptor and sometimes a proper noun referring to sentient species (High Sentients, elementals, Guardian Spirits) as well as many Cellulosian species with extremely long lifespans in relative human terms.

Low Sentient: Those sentient Earth species who occupy the lower tiers of the Hierarchy of Sentience; these species typically have short lifespans and limited influence in the way of things. However, the most effective High Sentients are adept at leveraging Low Sentients in both passive and active tasks that support desired outcomes in support of the Natural Order.

machine ghost: Slang referring to a displaced elemental sentience who has survived a Dislocation event only to be trapped in the Internet or on a computer network.

malgorithims: A contraction for "malevolent algorithm," which refers to those algorithms which are introduced into the Internet from external agents or created by rogue sentience (artificial or otherwise) located within the Internet to weaponize the domain and produce Chaotic outcomes in the Earthreal.

Manmade: As a proper noun, used by the Natural Order to describe anything created or built by humankind (e.g., tools, machines, technology, and constructs) which could not have naturally occurred on their own. In general, 'anything' not of the Natural.

meta'en: Contraction of 'meta-environment;' synonymous with the term 'protectorate.' The planet's Coirea'cen is organized into elemental protectorates with Earth Elementals presiding over the Green and Water Elementals presiding over the Blue. The delineation is much cleaner in some environments (ocean, desert) and less so in ecosystems where the Blue and the Green are more balanced and interdependent (coastal forests, wetlands, any environment with large river systems).

Middleworld: The intersection of different spheres of existence for the planet Earth. This is where the Green God, Cernunnos, and the ancient Oak reside in the Grove of all Worlds at the planet's Sacred Center of the All.

MOB: An acronym which stands for "Main Operating Base." A term used by the United States military to describe a permanently manned, well protected base used to support deployed forces and possessing robust sea and/or air access. This term differentiates major strategic overseas military facilities from the smaller, less secure or temporarily manned contingency, tactical locations, e.g., forward operating bases.

MRAP: A military acronym which stands for "Mine-Resistant Ambush Protected;" a term for United States military light tactical vehicles produced as part of the 'MRAP' program that are designed specifically to withstand improvised explosive device (IED) attacks and ambushes.

Natural: Generic term referring everything of Earth Mother's world which has remained unchanged by mankind's influence and has not been assimilated into the Manmade or destroyed outright by humankind.

Natural Network: (or 'Natwork') At the strategic level, it is the collection of beings—sentients and non-sentients—cooperatively functioning as the natural world's neural network. The structure and lines of communication vary with the representative composition of the natural environment it passes through and is contained within. The Ourcelium is the backbone of the network, and the network is typically leveraged by Guardian Spirits for Command, Control and Communications (C3) in the conduct of protection operations.

Natural Order (or the Order): Earth Mother's High Sentients charged with staving off Chaos's attempts to disrupt and destroy the Earth's natural balance. Their ranks include the Gifteds and elementals led by Guardian Spirits. Sometimes humans are among their numbers.

netscape: The Internet's version of a landscape as interpreted by a sentient being's employed perceptors.

NextLife: (plural: NextLives) A being's lives 'yet to be lived.'

Nunnehi: Cherokee mythology; a race of immortal spirit people. In the Cherokee language, Nunnehi means "The People Who Live Anywhere." The Cherokee believe the Nunnehi to be supernatural beings equivalent to the fairies of European folklore.

Old Tongue: The language of the High Sentients, predating Biological life on Earth.

omnisense: Refers to how elementals and select other sentients (such as low sentient trees) perceive their world. It is best described as all of the human recognized senses—sight, touch, smell, hearing, and taste—coupled together and interpreted by the being as a single sensory amalgamation.

One-Sixers: (or Sixers) The name refers to the date of the January 6th, 2021, US Capitol Insurrection and collectively identifies the insurrectionists themselves. With the largest representation of the Sixers hailing from Texas, they formed the core of the insurgency which took over the state's security and governance apparatus and led the successful secession from the Union.

OPSEC: A US military acronym which stands for 'Operations Security;' a program encompassing all the tactics, techniques, and procedures for maintaining security of military units during mission operations.

Otherside: A reference to the opposite side (dark or light/ living) of the universe by denizens of one side. Typically, an

Inani reference when referring the "living universe" or "universe of light." Occasionally, Dream Walkers use the term for referring to the spirit world.

OtherWorld: (or Otherworld) The Middleworld where Cernunnos resides can be thought of as a metaphysical plexus for our Earthly world. There, one can access all Earth-connected existential and spiritual domains collectively referred to as the OtherWorlds. With the exception of the Underworld, the OtherWorlds generally refer to all metaphysical domains which influence and shape sentient existence in the Earthreal.

Ourcelium: The primary backbone of Earth Mother's Natural Network, underlying the full extent of Her land-based Coirea'cen. The 'Our'celium is a robust fiberworks constructed of a kind of robust mycelium which hosts a diffused sentience dedicated to chronicling the histories and knowledge of the Natural Order. Additionally, High Sentients of the Order, particularly Guardian Spirits, tap into the Ourcelium in leveraging the Natural Network, or 'Natwork,' for command, control, and communications during active defense of the Coirea'cen.

PastLife: (plural: PastLives) Singularly, refers to the last life lived, and in plural form, references all of a sentient being's previously lived lives. Most beings do not consciously remember their PastLife or previous lives, though these experiences directly contribute to the whole of who they are. Remembering Past-Lives can be both gift and curse.

Partemus: The convening amphitheater of Calisphaer's technical elite and de facto ruling class. 'Partemus' is an interchangeable term which refers to both the place and the governing body of the Inani technocracy.

perceptor(s): In all its forms (perception, perceptory, etc.), it is a term which encompasses the entirety of senses and abilities of living beings to perceive their world, including but far from limited to the human acknowledged senses of sight, hearing, touch, taste, and smell.

Praeditor: One of the two primary species of Gifteds. Praeditors are demigod-like 'apex predators' who are supernaturally endowed with the natural abilities to lead the species in large regions which can include extensive migratory ranges; thus, they are not tied to meta'ens. Praeditors are graced with 'strung consciousness;' thus, they benefit from the accumulated wisdom and experience of all those sentients who have previously served in this preeminent role. They are called upon by Guardian Spirits and elementals to rally predatory species in the defense of the Coirea'cen and constituent meta'ens, respectively.

Praestean: (also called 'Keeper' or 'Keeper Animal') One of the two primary species of Gifteds. Praesteans are chosen by, and spiritually bound to, their elemental master for the entirety of ThisLife. Once chosen, the Keeper's sentience adopts the wisdom and experience of the 'strung consciousness' of all Keepers in the line of succession before them who served elementals of their assigned meta'en. Praesteans live as long as their elemental and exist to ensure the elemental's spirit essence is returned to the Lifestream in the event of their death.

Presades: The Glade of the *Kesul' Kaham's* Elder Council of High Sentients. The 'wise' Old Growth of the Glade who have been in the forest longer than the presiding elemental, Komkom Akwini. All predominant tree species composing the Sam Houston National Forest are represented among them.

protectorate: See meta'en; an elemental's assigned meta-environment. Elementals use the terms interchangeably.

purgatorium: A combination of the terms "purgatory" and "sanitarium," describing a self-destructive state of consciousness where sentient beings are 'imprisoned' of mind. The affliction has several different causes and manifests in several different forms; each of which is unique to the individual.

Rainbow Winds: Name given to extinction-level event of several butterfly species in the Western United States when fierce windstorms descended upon the West Coast without warning. The sudden onset was an environmental catastrophe, because the massed congregations of butterflies were unable to flee and were ripped apart. All of the colored skin scales were carried aloft by the winds in a horribly beautiful, short-term weather phenomenon dubbed the 'Rainbow Winds.'

RF: Acronym for "radio frequency;" typically referencing the type of initiation system or trigger for an explosive device.

rifter: A child or being of the rift.

rift: A crease, tear, or void in the Great Barrier Web which allows beings and entities to travel from the dark side of the universe and afflict worlds of the living and the light. Like dark matter itself, they are almost impossible to detect by physical or conventional human means.

rootweb: A system of roots from one or more sources which are interconnected into a weblike structure which is less dense than a lattice. A rootweb can be either a physical or a spiritual structure or manifestation.

Rúsea'lasse: Term from the Old Tongue of the High Sentients which refers to *the anger-happiness nexus* that resides in the emotion spectrum of the Fifth Element. It is the emotional basis for life; essentially it is the 'motivation to survive.'

Sand Spirit: A subspecies of Earth Elemental who presides over desert or arid meta'ens where the water element has minimal influence.

sentient spur: A 'created' elemental construct which is a part of, yet distinct and separate from, the elemental's manifested form. It is preprogrammed to operate independently in the performance of a specific task as a kind of natural variant of a Manmade automaton.

sheath: Synonym of 'form,' referring to the body a sentient being occupies in a given life. Most often these terms are used in reference to Biologicals and the other Short-lived species but is also used in reference to elementals as well (e.g., Tree Spirits).

shmog: Lesser sentient winds where Chaos has paired the element of wind with something "less than" elemental sentience. Elementals are the only sentience powerful enough to survive both the Corruption process and the involuntary coupling with the formless elements with sanity of consciousness remaining intact. Thus, shmogs are like small children—clumsy, undisciplined, and unruly—with little control over the wind element. They have a penchant for wreaking havoc and require the strong leadership of powerful Corrupted Formless who are typically responsible for leading several shmog in a pod during the conduct of Chaotic operations.

Short-lived: Descriptor for species with short lifespans relative to High Sentients and Cellulosian species, such as humans and most other Biologicals.

statesmission: The Inani people are 'Hivemind' and do not speak, because they do not 'breathe.' The term describes a formal broadcast which typically involves one Inani Elder addressing the other Elders of the Partemus on a matter of concern or one requiring Partemus decision.

"The 63": Of the over 700 insurrectionists charged in the Capitol Riot, the '63' rioters from Texas were the highest per capita representation of any US state. The 63 formed the core of the Texas secessionist movement.

ThisLife: The life a living being is currently living, as distinguished from PastLives (or LastLife) or NextLives. These distinctions are important because the immortal spirit essence (or soul) gifted to every living being from Earth Mother progresses through many lives. This progression is sometimes referred to as the "life chain."

Treefolk: A term sentient Cellulosians use in referring to themselves collectively, singling out the tree species of their kind.

Tree Spirit: A revered subspecies of Earth Elemental, distinguished from other subspecies for having chosen to leave the fluidity of form behind and restrict their essence to a single tree sheath. For an elemental, the choice of becoming a Tree Spirit is one of true devotion to the forest born of the experience of holistic fulfillment as a tree in past lives.

Tree Tongue: The special language of trees shared by all species, including High and Low Sentients and even the non-sentient. The natural language can be learned by other species, such as humans, but it requires a devotion to acquiring the skill along with honing certain aspects of individual perception to extrospective levels.

Turned: A term used as an adjective or noun to describe humans and other living beings who have been co-opted by Chaos and knowingly serve his cause. Most often, Turned individuals serve among the "Effector Elements" of Chaos's army, the En'Troop-EE. It is important to understand that the Corruption or turning of a sentient being is a process, which is reversible up until the point the afflicted have been completely 'Turned' to the way of Chaos, placing them among His Corrupted.

Underworld: The physical and metaphysical spheres of existence which are located below the planet's surface within the Earth Herself.

USG: Acronym which stands for "United States Government."

vicissimorphosis: A spiritual degradation, mental impairment, or loss of purpose; or a combination of the three. Describes a negative or degenerative metamorphosis within an individual's consciousness of being.

Water Elemental: Elemental who wields the element of water. Their assigned meta'ens are the Earth's oceans, seas, and great lakes; also referred to as "the Blue" or the "Big Waters." Water Elementals sometimes have earth landmass in their protectorates, such as littoral regions or coastline, but water is always the dominate element in their ecosystems.

Wild: Another term for the "Natural" but more specific to the natural environment and associated ecosystems, which are either undiscovered or untouched by humankind. At the very least, the Wild is predominantly free of direct human influence so that referenced areas are still considered "pristine" wilderness.

Windswepts: Name given to the region of the North American mid-continent from the Continental Divide in the west to the eastern extremes of the Mississippi River Valley, and stretching up into southern Canada and as far south as the state of Oklahoma. Also referred to as the "Dust Bowl II," because of the regularity of brownouts and 'black blizzards' in the

Great Plains and haboobs in the desert climes. The underlying causes of the climate disaster were the extended droughts and increased heat of climate change, coupled with the effects of human industrialized agriculture, terraforming, and water mismanagement. Chaos's Sentient Winds are behind the unrelenting winds which precipitated and subsequently multiplied the effects of the environmental catastrophe.

Yvwi Usdi: Cherokee mythology; singular form of Yunwi Tsunsdi´, which literally means "little people." A race of small humanoid nature spirits. Usually invisible, they sometimes reveal themselves as miniature child-sized people. Yunwi Tsunsdi are benevolent creatures with magical powers who help humans in Cherokee stories but are believed to harshly punish those who are disrespectful or aggressive towards them.

About the Author

R.M. Tembreull is a devoted husband and proud father, a combat veteran with 26 years in the US Air Force, and an accomplished career professional in law enforcement, physical security, and antiterrorism. In his travels and endeavors, he has experienced the best and worst of humankind. He's also an avid scuba diver with a lifelong passion for experiencing the planet's natural wonders, employing his skill as an artist at every opportunity. His love of writing is only matched by his respect for nature. He has distilled the whole of himself into his literary works—the new genre of "Eco-fantasy."

9 7 9 8 8 9 1 3 2 3 5 9 9